THE GIRL WHO STOLE EVERYTHING

THE GIRL WHO STOLE EVERYTHING

a novel

Norman Ravvin

Krzysztof Majer, Elise Moser, Linda Leith, Shelley Butler and Nancy Richler helped me think and write about Poland and Vancouver.

Copyright © 2019, Norman Ravvin

All rights reserved. No part of this book may be reproduced, for any reason or by any means, without permission in writing from the publisher.

The following is a work of fiction. Many of the locations are real, although not necessarily as portrayed, but all characters and events are fictional and any resemblance to actual events or people, living or dead, is purely coincidental.

Prepared for the press by Elise Moser.
Cover photograph by Cezary Jurkiewicz, reproduced by permission.
Excerpt from "Family Home," in Unseen Hand (2009) by Adam Zagajewski on page 5 is reproduced by permission of Farrar, Straus and Giroux.
Author photo by Allen McInnis, Montreal Gazette/Postmedia.
Cover design by Debbie Geltner.
Book design by Tika eBooks.
Printed and bound in Canada.

Library and Archives Canada Cataloguing in Publication

Title: The girl who stole everything / Norman Ravvin.
Names: Ravvin, Norman, 1963- author.
Identifiers: Canadiana (print) 20190066768 | Canadiana (ebook) 20190066776 | ISBN 9781773900278 (softcover) | ISBN 9781773900285 (EPUB) | ISBN 9781773900292 (Kindle) | ISBN 9781773900308 (PDF)
Classification: LCC PS8585.A8735 G57 2019 | DDC C813/.54—dc23

The publisher gratefully acknowledges the support of the Government of Canada through the Canada Council for the Arts, the Canada Book Fund, and Livres Canada Books, and of the Government of Quebec through the Société de développement des entreprises culturelles (SODEC).

Linda Leith Éditions
Montreal
www.lindaleith.com

. . . all the nights since you left
are snarled like the yarn of an old sweater
in which wild cats have nested.
You come here like a stranger,
but this is your family home.

— Adam Zagajewski

PART ONE

Ania watches the boy run toward her. In his hands he holds a box big enough for a pair of shoes. It is the Czaykowski boy, isn't it? She grew up with his mother, and their mothers were children together in wartime. But maybe this is another child. They all look the same now, with their buzz cuts, their summer shorts and T-shirts with American slogans. The boy's reads: Madonna World Tour.

He stands in front of her, saying something about a hole he dug in the back field.

"Calmly," she tells him. "Let me see what you have."

They sit at the corner of the square, on the stoop of a house a few doors from Ania's mother's. The boy hands her the box. As she looks through its contents, he tells her his story in a high breathless voice.

The family cat, he says, died on Tuesday. His mother wanted him to take care of it, to get it out of their yard. She always said it was dirty.

"But the cat never went anywhere but the woods. It's clean in the woods, isn't it?"

"It is," Ania says. "As clean as can be."

The cat—the boy says this with the greatest seriousness—was the cleanest animal he knew. It was cleaner than most people. It cleaned itself with care and regularity. Its name should have been Mr. Clean. But it was called Jósek. An unusual name for a country cat, whose counterparts might simply be called *kot*.

"For Piłsudski? Like this square?"

"No." The boy does not think it was named for the square. Why would they name the cat after this lousy square? He's heard of Piłsudski but he forgets. Was he president? Or a soccer player?

Ania smiles. Sometimes a child's ignorance is a pleasant and freeing thing. She rests the box on her knees, and he rattles on with his story.

At first, he thought he would take the cat to the far corner of their property, over near the big willow tree. Does she know it? He points, past the rooftops, beyond the church, at the summer sky. In order to make things easy, she nods.

But then he remembers something he'd heard about the cat.

"It's a rumour. My father used to joke that the cat was Jewish."

"What can this mean?" Ania asks. "People can be Jewish. The building across the square from the church was Jewish once. Possibly it still is. But how can a cat be Jewish?"

The boy shakes his head. He never really understood. And he was afraid to ask. They'd been given their cat by the Grabowskis, after theirs had kittens.

"When Jósek died I wanted to bury him in the Jewish cemetery. But I was always told not to go to that place."

This takes Ania by surprise. She knows where the Jewish cemetery was in the village, before the war, because her parents owned land next to it. Old-timers know, because once they watched as the village's Jews made their way there along the back roads. But each year this contingent of old-timers is fewer in number. And the cemetery grounds are nothing more than an open field where gravestones once stood. Someone has been telling him ghost stories.

"It's over there," the boy says. Again, a finger to the horizon. "Where Shnigorsky keeps his cows."

Ania nods. Her mother used to point out the cemetery site

when they went to visit their property at the edge of the village. After Ania's father died, her mother had refused offers to buy the land. Some were miserly, but in one case the money would have been a windfall. It was a few years after the fall of Communism. A speculator came from Warsaw in a BMW the size of a tank. He parked in the square and marched up to their door. In his jacket pocket he carried payment in cash, as if this guaranteed compliance from yokels. Now there were rumours that a Jewish organization in Warsaw wanted to recover the cemetery land for the *gemina,* the overall Jewish community in the city. But these discussions had stalled, and her mother was glad. She followed developments in the news. Her land alongside the cemetery grounds was a wide sweep of fields to the south of the village. Ania's mother walked there to pick wildflowers and roots, which she put in teas and homemade medicines. What, she asked Ania, would Warsaw people want with our village land? Who would build, or, even stranger, *buy* a new house on the outskirts of Radzanów?

On this topic Ania knew her mother was not as up-to-date as she believed herself to be. Radzanów was an hour by car northwest of Warsaw on a good highway. Contractors were putting up modern villas for professional families who were willing to commute to the city in exchange for some peace in the countryside.

In addition to the fields on the village outskirts, her mother hangs on to another bit of property. A house on the village square that has been derelict since the war. She'd put up a few *zloty* for it when abandoned properties came available. Behind it there are stables and a brick farm building. Ania passes the house each time she visits Radzanów, alighting from the Mława bus.

She last visited her mother's fields during the Potato Festival. Everyone was at church bringing offerings to the altar. She walked by herself to the cemetery's edge and sat on a big stone on the Jewish ground and breathed in air that she felt was hers alone.

As if she were the last person in the village. When she got up to go, she felt something inside, which she couldn't describe, least of all to a child.

The boy describes how he visited the cemetery grounds at night. He snuck out of his house through the bedroom window. He carried the cat in a satchel he used for school.

"I was scared," he tells her. "I'd never gone on the Shnigorsky land, even in the daytime."

Old Shnigorsky, some eighty years old, was still tough, Ania knew, his bald head like a cannonball.

"And there was no moon that night, so it was awfully dark. Like the basement. The countryside at night was as dark as my parents' basement."

"I would be scared too," she tells him.

He nods. She understands him. He has brought his story to the right person.

He brought a shovel and a piece of paper with a prayer written on it. He had asked his mother what people said at burials. He understood a bit of what she told him, which he'd scribbled in pencil and slipped into the satchel with Jósek. Even if it was Christian stuff, he hoped that saying it in the Jewish cemetery made it all right. He set the bag near the old tree where Shnigorsky sometimes tied his favourite cow. The one with the white and black markings. Did she know that tree?

She thought she did. The crippled one, like an old man.

"Yes," the boy says. "That one. I put Jósek there. And I began to dig behind the tree, out of sight. There are a lot of stones in our ground. It was hard work. Did you know that when a shovel hits a stone in the night there is a spark of light?"

She did not know about stones and sparks.

This raises the boy's spirits. He has told her something she did not know.

"I dug," he says, "for what seemed like forever. This deep." He holds his arms wide. "Sparks popped like fireworks."

When he thought the hole was deep enough to prevent it being dug up by raccoons, he put Jósek by the edge of the hole, to say the prayer before he lowered him in. It was then that he noticed that his digging had uncovered something. Not just stones.

"This?" Ania lifts the box from her dark-stockinged knees. They look at it together. It is made of yellow wood and is very light to hold.

He nods.

"Did you show this to anyone else?"

The boy shakes his head.

Could she keep it for a few days? To look carefully at what was inside.

He nods, enthusiastic. He is anxious for someone to take his discovery off his hands.

"When would you like it back?"

The boy shrugs. Time means nothing to him. Days. Weeks. Whatever. He is going to live forever.

Ania smiles and wraps her long, manicured fingers around the box and bends forward to kiss the boy, lightly, on his forehead. A kind of christening. He must think of her as a person of impressive authority, not just a thirty-something ex-villager who has remade herself in Warsaw. Because of her link with her mother, who is a person to contend with in the village, Ania must be someone who can solve mysteries.

The kiss makes him smile and stand up tall. Off he runs, free of his weird find. It is in her hands now. And he's been kissed by *Pani* Ania, who went away to another life in Warsaw.

A Calling Card

Nadia is heading west. Jess is behind her, his jacket flapping. But as they hurtle around the bridge skirting the port, he flies past and disappears into the dark. This route was once entirely suited to commerce—trucks and trains and workers on the port elevators. But it's been retooled as part of the cycling lanes from Vancouver's east side into downtown. Nadia's heart is in her mouth. She doesn't own a bike. She prefers to feel the ground under her feet. But somehow Jess coaxed her into a nighttime ride. He has something to show her. This is what he said over the phone. And now she feels she is risking her life trying to keep up with him to find out what it is.

After a long tunnel under the convention centre—air vents that look like jet engines whir high above their heads—they stop by the water, at one of the city's remarkable seawall views. This one looks out across Coal Harbour at Stanley Park. As Nadia straddles her borrowed bike, winded, she watches little waves carry the moonlight across to the park. It is oddly quiet at the edge of the country's busiest port. But it's late, almost midnight. The lights are out in the bank of sky-high condo towers behind them. The rumour is nobody lives there. They are said to be among the favoured real estate investments for offshore money.

In the dark, she can just make out the seaport where planes and helicopters land. She sniffs and catches a hint—the idea shocks her—of the past. Not a memory of the past. The thing itself. Those long-ago days reared up before her: when she'd lived nearby, in her aimless twenties, a punk extremist for whom everything was about the here and now, the next twenty-four hours, the next—as her friends used to say—*fucking five minutes*. It was the moistness in the air, and the calm hovering over everything. There they were, those days, lingering above the water. She tries to explain how she feels to Jess. But it's pointless. He gives her a peculiar look and giggles. Giggles. It is the most discomfiting response imaginable to her effort to unburden herself there in view of the dark water. But it is exactly what she should have expected from him. What had he been to her? A would-be boyfriend? She is about to throw the bike down. Tell him he can return it. And to never call again. But before she can do this he reaches into his pocket and says, "Here."

He holds a business card. She considers not even looking at it. Pocketing it. She'll throw it away later. But he says, "There's something at my work you'll want to see. Connected with you. Nadia." He looks away as he says her name and breathes in as if to try to make up for laughing at her response to the drowsy port air. She moves into the amber glow of a streetlight to see, first one side and then the other:

It is obviously old. Its edges are furry with wear. The giveaway is the telephone number cued by a word: "Marine 3647." Did that take it as far back as the fifties? Something is lurking, but she has no idea what it could be.

Nadia feels winded. First by the bike ride, its speed and views and the familiar shock of how exhilarating the city is at night. The view of the single remaining boat gas station, throwing its ribbons of Shell yellow onto the water. Then the gloved hand of the past in her gut. What is she supposed to say?

"Come down and see," Jess says. He hops on his bike and leaves her there with the rented bike, which he'd rolled up to her at the corner of Robson and Denman, saying, "Get on, Nadia. Let's go for a ride."

She has no desire to ride it another inch. The nearest object she can lean it against is a monument, to the side of the bike path, telling passersby of Canada's rejection of a ship full of Sikhs a hundred years before. Its photo of rejected people gazes into the dark, quizzing her, a tableau of ghosts in their buttoned suit jackets and white turbans.

Cordovaland

Nadia stands on the corner of Abbott and Cordova in her sensible shoes, white joggers with the bounce of a pair of pillows. She does not care if they match her Levis and her logoless white T-shirt. She thinks of a time when she wouldn't have been caught dead in the same room with someone wearing shoes like the ones she has on. But that was a decade ago, in her aimless twenties. How, she often asked herself back then, getting herself ready to go out, can I express *just who I am*? Every person who saw her had to get it. Strangers on the bus, classmates, and friends. Why? She cannot remember. But that was her focus: her self. A totally coherent message. *This thing I am now and its particular commitments must be understood.* How little she cares about such things today, as she takes in the grit and rush of Cordova at the corner where Vancouver breaks into its west and east sides.

She walks down Abbott and marvels at how much has changed in the last few years. Wall murals. Whoever thought these streets would spawn wall murals? One is of a stenciled girl with blunt-cut yellow hair. She blows fluff from the head of a dandelion. Above it is a banner promoting "all-new concrete homes." Here come the new neighbours. Once upon a time the locals were punks like herself, social workers, down-and-outers, and cops. But the surrounding streets were open for business, just a few minutes from the old flophouses. She passes an impromptu sidewalk market offering a jumble of odds and ends, rags, radios, and jars full of nails. She passes too quickly to take it in properly. She is no longer Nadia Baltzan the Here-and-Now Girl. She is a graduate student and a walker in the city. She is just passing through.

So, why is she here, headed east?

It is the business card. She feels for it in her chest pocket. The card is the reason she is headed for RR Auctions down by the tracks. It was there that she and Jess had their final argument. He'd insisted she visit, thinking she might be interested in the weird memorabilia and the freaks who came crowding in to bid on it. What else besides "freak" could you call a grown man who pays thousands of dollars for Bonnie Parker's bloodstained stockings? That had been one of the most sensational lots, along with a jewelled compact found beside her in the death car. These had been uncovered in some long-forgotten police locker in Texarkana, with a shrunken banana and a workman's lunch thermos full of shattered glass. Jess had led her around. They'd peered into the spot-lit vitrines. Then Nadia had told him, "Never ask me to come back here, okay?" But here she is on her way back to see him there

She and Jess were seeing each other around the time she'd begun to wonder if a man, any man, including boy-men like Jess, would ever make her feel excited. She'd gone as far as taking a number in a study being done at the Pine Avenue clinic testing a new pill, a kind of female Viagra. The young doctor told her to put one pill on her tongue at the same time each evening and let it dissolve there. In addition, she was to keep a pill diary. Each day, she was supposed to note down any ideas she had about sex, or any experiences and thoughts after sex, even any conversations she might have about sex. If she did not follow up, did nothing further in the way of therapy or talk about her sex issues—this was what the doctor had called her condition—she'd still have the diary as evidence. Of what? she asked. When she took the pills she was seeing Jess, sometimes letting him stay over at her place because they'd stayed out late and he was too exhausted or high to find his way home, but her unwillingness to be intimate did not change. So her pill diary was rather monotonous: "No change." "No." "Did not feel like it." "Well, no." "Same as usual." "Oh, this can't work on me. So why take it at all?" And so on, until she stopped altogether.

As she walks she consoles herself by remembering how much she likes the neighbourhood. For a year, maybe more, she lived nearby in a falling-down walk-up with a view of the port elevators. Her undergraduate squat, a friend had dubbed it.

RR Auctions is hard by the tracks, near a monument to local history so conceptual that Nadia has no idea what it is meant to commemorate. She puts her nose to the high steel fence and looks at the trains, their containers nearly within arm's reach. High in a shifting locomotive cab, a face behind goggles seems to watch her.

At the auction house, she pushes the heavy front door open. Inside it smells like what's left of a fire. Were they selling burnt things? A new line in disaster-fetish material.

Jess sits in his office at the back, hunched before a computer screen. He lifts his head and gives Nadia a long looking-over. He cocks his head, narrows his eyes, as if he's appraising a painting. He has grown a little scruff of a beard, but it doesn't change his face. He is the same skinny, sheepish boy-man.

"I never asked how you ended up working here, Jess."

He shuts down his computer and takes a file from the corner of his desk. "That's a long story. Here. I'll show you what I was talking about." They step into the showroom, which reminds her of a livestock yard, with its high ceiling and surrounding guardrails.

Behind them, up to the rafters, she imagines customers—bidders, hangers-on, freaks—piling in to bid on Bonnie Parker's stockings.

Jess makes his way around a group of vitrines, black stands with glass-encased objects atop them, each one lit from above by a pot light.

"Who bought the stockings in the end?"

"What?"

"The Bonnie-and-Clyde bloody stockings."

"Oh. You know, I don't know if I followed that one. Ask me who bought Ma Barker's purse, perforated by a bullet hole. That I remember. And what was supposedly the fried banana sandwich Elvis would have eaten if he hadn't died in his bathroom. They had it flash-frozen and, I don't know, cryogenically locked up like Lenin in Red Square. I thought that one was a fake. That banana could have been anything. Look. Here." They stop in front of a presentation stand with a white card on it that reads: "Murder Weapon. Vancouver 1962." In the centre of the stand, lit from above, is a pop bottle. It is vintage 7 Up, with letters on an orange shield topped by a crown of bubbles. "Fresh UP!" it advises. "It likes you!" The light gives the bottle glass a halo, a glow, and the place where it is fractured from whatever use it was put to is easily seen. Leaning against the bottle is a card exactly like the one he'd given her, its "Reliable Loan" side facing out.

"The victim was named Israel Batzanoff. You always said there were no other Baltzans in the phone book. You were right about that. But I looked back in the old business directories. We've got a full set. So I figured something out that maybe you don't know." Jess takes a sheet from the file he has prepared. It looks like a kinship map prepared by an anthropologist. "Look. In 1929, a Moishe Batzanoff has a pawn and loan place on Alexander. That's way back in this neighbourhood's history. He's a pioneer. He passed the business on to his son. That's when it moved to Cordova. I took a look in the old newspapers. He placed greetings to his customers—they were ads really—at Christmastime and New Year's. Once he mentions his sons. Saul and Aaron. I checked on these two. Aaron had two sons, Israel and Joshua. Wasn't your dad's name Josh? Nadia, you never told me about this."

"About what?"

"That someone in your family was murdered in 1962. Your father's older brother."

She has no idea what he is talking about.

He hands her the file. "Here's the provenance, as we like to say around here. Everything we show here has a provenance. I made you a copy." A sticker on the file's tab reads: "For Nadia. Murder bottle."

She feels numb. She stuffs the file into her bag. Jess watches as she heads to the door. What does he think? That the murder bottle is an entrée to lunch? That it's the real pill, unlike the failed one from the Pine Avenue clinic?

A Little Town Called Vancouver

The bus ride to campus takes half an hour, but it might as well cover half a continent, as the fleabag, teardown street atmosphere of the east side falls away and everything turns into bright green prosperity. Students get on. They carry backpacks and slump down in their seats, eyeing their phones as they send off messages. She looks them over—especially the females. She is older than they, so invisible to them. The dulcimer case sits between her knees as she watches the blocks pass. They are named for trees and Napoleonic battles.

On campus she sits under a shade tree near the university library. The air carries its usual hint of ocean and the green depths of the endowment-land forest. Jess's file is open in her lap as students—backpack-laden, giggling, holding hands—pass her on all sides. Its contents have the neat, detailed look of a sheaf of evidence prepared by a trial lawyer. There is an index of documents and one for photographs. She looks first at a photo of the pop bottle, sunlight falling on her through the shifting branches. The index of newspaper headlines reads like a set list for a comedy troupe with a dark outlook:

Demolish City's Skid Row, Murder Protest Demands
Wife Feared for Broker
Skid Row Question to Mayor: 'Hey, you some kind of cop?'
Murder Reward $4,000 for Robbery, Killing on Cordova St.
Knowing Common Kettle Takes Quiz Jackpot of $57
Well, Barney Boy, We'll Pick up the Trail of That Brutosaurus Tomorrow
Two Questioned in Slaying
Sister Hunting for Brother who Disappeared in Klondike
It's Not a Skid Row, Says Albury
Laurence Welk July 17
Funeral Services Today for I. Batzanoff
Card of Condolence
A Rare Treat for All Yugoslavians: Two Exciting Films, *Viza ZLA* Plus *Riton-I-Zvuk*
A Jewish Idealist

Yugoslavian cinema. A tea kettle. She almost wants to call Jess, that lunatic, to find out why he has seeded this nonsense in with the rest of what he's given her. But the headlines take her back to her Richmond childhood. So much of it is forgotten, vanished. A featureless past no archive retains. Riverdale High, named for the nearby Fraser, though it reminded everyone of Archie and Jughead. And before that, the middle school that looked like a gigantic parking garage, and before that, what did her first school look like? She has no visual memory of it. Only the smell in the girls' washroom, a blend of toilet cleaner and car exhaust, where the older girls smoked cigarettes.

What Jess has gathered lets her see her family differently. The thing hidden might prove to be the key. Other professor fathers bought houses near the university. Maybe her father moved them to the suburbs to get as far away as possible from the neighbourhoods of his past. She'd known about an older brother, but not much beyond the fact that he died young. Questions were waved off until she quit asking.

What year would they have bought the Richmond house? Maybe her father was starting to lose it by then. His capacity for professional decorum and social niceties had failed him. In those days, professors wore tweedy coats and ties, patterned shirts and loafers. Her father's work duds consisted of a drawer full of baggy trousers, jeans, and T-shirts he found in the basement bins at the Bay. It was a merchant-marine sort of uniform—a good get-up for polishing a ship's mechanical parts, but a little rough for leading a class.

She gazes through the trees at the tower where his department is housed. His office was on the fifth floor of the Buchanan Tower, a few hundred yards away. It was there that he'd developed the crazy habit of circling the halls looking for posters devoted to causes and events he despised. She knew this because, when she showed up as an undergrad, his behaviour was still legendary: "Oh, Baltzan. That nut. He was proof you could totally lose it and keep your teaching job." Women's rights; poetry readings by people he didn't think deserved the title of poet; be-ins of all kinds. These got the tear-down treatment. He'd circle the relevant floors (the fifth, sixth, and seventh, where English and history students were a likely audience for the things he hated), find the offending posters, and, upon ripping them down, tear them into smaller and smaller bits until he held a handful of confetti, which he dropped into the nearest garbage pail.

His final years teaching were a kind of carnival. This she'd heard from a professor who'd known him and was still on staff, bucking retirement. It was a year ago that he'd pulled her aside while she waited to see another prof. She'd been sitting patiently on a window bench, looking out at the sound and the North Shore mountains.

"Excuse me for asking," he said, bending over her. "You're Josh Baltzan's daughter, aren't you?"

She nodded, ready with her usual *But-he's-been-dead-a-long-time* rejoinder.

"Are you waiting to see Sullivan, that geezer?" He pointed at her professor's door. "God, his theory's fresh, eh?" He broke out in a braying laugh.

She had not made an appointment. Dr. Sullivan was her Modern English Lit prof. His course was one of the few electives required by her music program. She had come to try an idea for an assignment on him. But she disagreed with his take on Virginia Woolf and wondered if what she wanted to propose would assure her a C. She had never thought of her professor as anything other than Dr. Sullivan. Forever afterward, as he lectured, he would be *that geezer*.

"Well, if it's okay with you, come on in."

She entered the book-lined office. Her father's old colleague introduced himself as Peter. In front of his desk stood a beat-up armchair.

"Grab a seat. Sullivan mentioned you were in his class. What brought you back to campus?"

"I was accepted in piano performance. But my interests have shifted, really, to my second instrument."

"What is it?"

"The dulcimer. If I'd pitched that as my first interest I probably wouldn't have gotten in. The university has one, the kind you play with hammers. But it's in a collection you're hardly supposed to touch. I have a regular one, like they played in the sixties on folk records." She pointed at the case at her feet.

Peter took this in. "When Sullivan said you were around, I started to think again about your father. I miss him. He used to come in and sit where you are—same chair—and talk. You know? Some people can talk. But good God, he went sideways toward the end, didn't he? All that walking. I'd see him marching up University Boulevard. The others thought he might be drinking, which was common back then. We were all boozers, really. Some handled it better than others. One time he came in here. So shook up. Saying he needed to talk. It took him a while to get it out. He'd been out to his brother's grave for the first time. I didn't know he had a brother. I asked him when his brother died. You know what he said? 1962. 1962 and he'd not bothered to visit? He said it had been impossible, but I didn't ask him what that meant. They got rid of him not too long after that. There had been a few complaints, but mostly the students thought he needed help. I imagine the leave salary they put him on put your family under pressure. I know it's forward of me to ask, but I've wondered over the years, what went wrong?"

She shook her head. She knew nothing about her father's demons. Her mother refused to talk about these things. She had no idea what to say. What she'd seen up close was the divorce. A child's view of adult disaster. The unpleasantness of her father moving out. Nadia read the spines of books over Peter's shoulder. Gertrude Stein. Ezra Pound. She knew these presented an impressive array, a solid postwar tradition. If you viewed things through these, did the world make sense? He stepped out from behind his desk and perched on its edge.

"There was one incident near the end. From what I heard, someone said something, a kind of offside remark about Jewish businessmen. Your father went crazy. They had to pull him off the guy. I had to talk the Chair out of calling the cops."

Nadia crossed her legs and tried to sit calmly. Her heart was pounding, and she'd broken out in a hot, wet sweat. Could he smell her?

"I always wondered what set him off. Nothing he said ever

suggested he was Jewish himself. Was he?"

She shook her head. He was, as far as she knew, no thing at all beyond a father and a husband who taught at the university. But what did she know? She had never been told anything to suggest that her father or anyone in her family was a Jew. What Peter had told her made her think of the first night in their house after her parents separated. She lay on her child-sized bed and thought of her mother, down the hall, alone. The headlights swung around the corner in the parking lot beside their house and lit her wall, for a second, like a lighthouse beam. It seemed to Nadia that she'd been forgotten. Like a survivor the rescue boat had missed. The suburban calm claimed her then, but she knew things were beginning anew.

Nadia returns to herself and the campus, the young people on the grass laughing. She packs the file away and walks to her practice in the music building. Her group works hard for two hours. They are an odd foursome, two skinny guys from central Canadian cities with hair in their eyes and a shy girl, an international student from Mexico who seems to be able to play any instrument she picks up. They focus on a piece with odd syncopation, which Nadia can't quite get hold of. She would like to count the beat out loud, but this would reveal her difficulty with it. The professor who directs them is not pleased. He shakes the hand of each of her colleagues as they pack up their instruments, keeping his distance from her. She is not practicing her piano, he tells her, because she is busy with her folky stuff.

There is a research project at the library that demands her attention, but she doesn't feel like going inside. She sits on the bench out front of Main Library and watches the afternoon go by. The sun is high and the air crackles in the light. It smells of broom and loam. The library's grey granite walls seem to turn white-hot.

On her walk home, she eyes the golfers on the course along University Boulevard. They look funny in their motorized carts. She'd heard stories of wild shots hitting passing cyclists, but she'd never seen anything like that happen. In front of her place, the landlord is cutting the lawn. Old Mr. Marini. He lets go of his machine to chat. She is usually agreeable—sometimes they stand out front for an hour, the afternoon breezing by. He relies on all the old-fashioned questions: Where do her parents live? Does she have a boyfriend? Why not? What does she plan to do when she's finished her degree? There's not much money to be made, is there, playing—what kind of music was it again? He means well, and he's often got some homespun philosophy to offer, along with gifts, which include his homemade wine, the colour of dark plums. Once he offered her an espresso in a tiny white cup. But she doesn't have any patience for it today. She moves quickly by, and he pushes on with his mower. The air is rich with his cuttings, the smell of grass and milkweed.

Upstairs, she sits in front of her computer. The pigeons—one of the things she hates about her place—scratch and coo and shit on the roof outside the kitchen window. She points a pop gun she found in Chinatown out the open window. One pop and they're gone for at least fifteen minutes. She is tired, but makes herself write something. She is keeping a blog, which she calls *Rommel Drives on Deep into Egypt*, after a poetry collection by the American writer, Richard Brautigan. The book was given to her in one of her undergraduate classes by a girl who tried, unsuccessfully, to seduce her with poetry. This particular classmate had given her many little poetry books, saying things like, "This is pretty weird," or, "I got this down on Pender and it made me think of you." At that point in her life, young gay women often mistook her for one of their own (which made her wonder if that's what she was, without knowing it) based on the way she wore her hair or dressed, or the downtown clubs where she liked to dance by herself—Luv-a-Fair, the Gandy Dancer—until at some point things shifted and the overtures stopped. The poetry went unread. Reading would have meant accepting the overture. But more recently, looking for inspiration on her shelves, the titles of Brautigan's poems offered starting points. The cover picture of *Rommel Drives on Deep into Egypt* serves as her blog's signature image: a young woman in a sandbox, in front of what might be a mansion in an American college town. For some reason, Nadia thinks it is Evanston, Illinois. It would be funny if visitors to her blog thought it was a photo of Nadia herself, because, unlike the Brautigan waif, she has dark hair and pale skin. When she looks in the mirror, she wonders at how mild and modest she's let herself become after years of trying to make a statement with coloured hair and circus get-ups. One of her profs once said to her, seeming to approve, that her outfit reminded him of Tom Jones. But he meant the novel and not the singer, so the reference was lost on her. Now she wants to blend in, to be able to walk, invisible, wherever she goes in the city.

She recognizes that calling a blog something as obscure as *Rommel Drives on Deep into Egypt* will not attract readers. But she doesn't care. She writes—she is sure of this—for herself. Her method is to lift a title from Brautigan's table of contents as a starting point. Sometimes she transcribes a few lines from a poem as an introduction. This method worked for a while, but she is starting to stall. She needs a new impetus. Rereading her early entries, she is a little stunned to think she wrote them and sent them out into the world. The earliest entry is the shortest.

Just an Ordinary Girl

> Just an ordinary girl, 120 pounds, poor eyesight, street-wise, born in Vancouver, a student at the University of

British Columbia, wants to play her music in many strange and satisfying places—coffee houses, street corners, railroad sidings, ancient underpasses, on buses, and under the wings of airplanes—so that anyone passing will know that there is always the possibility of trying something new.

After a month of nothing new, she posted this:

Have You Ever Had a Witch Bloom like a Highway

All the cars and trucks of my dreams. Headlights bursting out of sleep like the garbage truck, the clatter of the cans as they empty and set them down in the perpetual morning rush. I have no car of my own. I have never owned one and don't want to. Increasingly, I don't get into other people's cars. I walk. I'm getting my sea legs. The parts of the city I visit offer themselves up best when you walk them. I've read in the paper that outsiders who happen upon Hastings see the crowds milling about and get anxious. But people are on the street for two reasons: they don't have much to do on a given day, and they don't drive. If they want to get somewhere, they walk. I immerse myself in their sounds and the city's smells: cigarette smoke, freshly cut lumber, the bouquet of beer brewing, scents that are rare nowadays. I need to remind myself of this. Dad used to describe how he'd return to Vancouver from a dusty place like Calgary, get off the plane, get himself outside and breathe. It was different. The spice of the river booms; the ocean salt; the deep greenness of things.

The longest, and now, to her mind, too-revealing entry, takes its title from the Brautigan book and is called: "30 Cents, Two Transfers, Love." It says nothing of the file that Jess handed her, nor the business card, which might reveal her own connection with 36 Cordova.

I go down to Cordova. I take my instrument along. I always feel well-defended with it on my back. It offers me a reason for being. I wear it the way a creature wears its shell at the bottom of the sea. That's how some people in the city might view where I get off, at Hastings and Main, by the old Carnegie Library. It's a short walk to 36 West Cordova. I fold my jacket and put it under me on the cement stoop. I take out the dulcimer and settle myself with it. Once I begin to play I can pay better attention to what is going on around me. The cars are a distraction. The repetitive flap of tires. Trucks idling at the light, or gearing up to make the yellow. If you can put these things out of your mind, then the rest of what's going on seeps in.

I was well received today. Little groups formed, feet tapping, off-beat clapping, even a little Irish jig from a senior in a Canucks jersey.

A building is being torn down on the block. I watched as what I took to be the property developer got out of an insanely clean black car, talking on his phone. His whole act imposed itself on the street: *Fuck you all,* it seemed to say, because *here I am! So fuck you all!* He kept the phone to his head while he conferred with a construction worker who poked his head through a ruined window frame. He made to enter the site, putting one black shoe on a heap of bricks, but someone inside must have warned him off. There was a burst of shouting as he backed away, and then a great crash that sounded like a wall falling flat. Dust billowed above the street in the slanting light.

With his suit coat flapping, phone on his ear, the property guy came marching up to me. Out of some corner of his peripheral interest the sound I was making made him drop his phone arm. It hung limp as he listened to me play. In the quiet after the crash my instrument rang clear. A familiar *I know good music when I hear it* look transformed his face and he used his free hand to remove his sunglasses. He said, sounding impatient, "What's that song?"

I told him, "You wouldn't know it," which was my way of telling him I didn't want to talk.

"That's a dulcimer, right?"

I guess I was supposed to ask him how he knew this, but I did not care, and one of my new rules is *Do not ask questions you do not care about the answer to*. Well, he was not going anywhere. He began to tell me about dulcimers. His father, he said, was from rural Pennsylvania, so he was most interested in the Appalachian dulcimer. He was a collector of what he referred to as "period instruments." His prizes were a clavier of some kind, and a cello he was paying a luthier in Toronto a "fricking fortune" to restore. I did not have the energy to explain that I did not view my instrument as a "period" anything. To me, it is as contemporary an instrument as any piano or guitar or can opener, for that matter, just a thing I love to make music on. I played as loudly as I could. I shut my eyes when the song moved into a set of chord changes I like, which I repeated, over and over, as a mantra whose message was: Move on. Move on. But he did not move on. He quieted down. I opened my eyes and saw that he had closed his. His arms were crossed over his chest. The light had come around to our side of the street. He stood like this for some time.

I paused at the end of the song. He opened his eyes, took a long breath. For a moment, I felt bad for having resisted his overtures. But then he did a remarkable thing. He pulled out his wallet—a huge, elaborate, many-flapped thing, black like the car and his suit and his glasses—and drew from it a $100 bill. He folded it in half and tipped it in where my strings meet the nut. Then he straightened up and went back up the street. I almost called out to tell him to take his money back. It fluttered in the breeze. But a truck roared by, and he fell out of earshot.

I could have offered the money to one of the locals and changed her day. Like winning the Lotto but weirder. *A girl strumming an instrument she held on her knees gave me this for no reason at all.* I slipped the bill into my jeans pocket. But I had lost my urge to play. I packed up quickly, feeling cold and alien as I headed back to where I would catch the bus to the west side of town.

The Młava Bus

Ania decides not to show her mother the box. This is an instinctive decision. But it puts her in a bind. There is nowhere in the village for her to go—except back behind the tree where the boy buried Jósek—where she might take a leisurely look. She watches as the boy disappears around a bend in the road, then takes a few things from her bag. The script of the film she is helping a crew from Warsaw organize in the village square. Her camera. She sets these down and fits the box into her bag.

From the stoop where she sits, she can see her mother framed by the big front window of her home, arms crossed over her chest. Her white hair is turned in two thick braids on the crown of her head. She waits for Ania and scans the square for developments. In Radzanów, she is the unofficial captain of a rickety old ship with no destination. Evening dinner. Ship Radzanów is sailing toward a lovingly cooked dinner.

Ania's mother opens the front door. They greet each other with their customary kiss.

What, her mother asks, was she saying to the Dembrowski boy?

So, he's not the child of the woman Ania thought of first. He is the son of another girl, who was called Agniezka, now grown and married, whom Ania also grew up with and who lives in the village, like all the other Dembrowskis in memory. Her mother had tried, on her last visit, to describe some sort of swimsuit contest that took place on the riverside, which was won by this woman's eldest daughter.

Ania is no good at lies. "He was flirting with me."

"Flirting? What, you think because you're a Warsaw girl, with a government job, they all want to know you here?"

Ania shrugs. She knows her mother is intensely proud of her, and even a little scared that having risen as she has in the Polish government hierarchy—a woman from the sticks, with no aristocratic or moneyed ancestry to back her up, just her careful competence—it will all be taken away one day. Like in wartime. They run the tanks over you and you disappear into the mud.

Mother and daughter stand at the living room window and gaze out at the square. The view is not so different from the one Ania grew up with, although they are starting to tear down the old houses to make way for new buildings. Her mother lives a few doors removed from their old home, in a new villa, as the real estate agents like to call the two-storey stuccoed structures the builders from Warsaw put up to replace pre-war wooden or brick houses. What she sees is more or less her girlhood view—the square surrounded by its array of buildings in states of disrepair, the sinking wooden houses and the approach to the great white cathedral with its iron gate. She can picture her teenage self on her way to the school bus, holding a paperback open with one hand, an umbrella in the other. Raindrops hit the pages like typewriter keys on paper—plip, plip, plop. She found the book on a high shelf in the storage room behind their kitchen, where her mother kept potatoes and brooms. *The Catcher in the Rye*. The cover of her mother's Polish copy reads: *Buszujący w zbożu*. In Polish, "Bustler in the Corn." It is her first taste of contraband America, maybe her first taste of intellectual freedom. According to her father, it was all downhill from there. His sweet Ania went crazy. Who needed Manhattan in Radzanów? Only the Jews, and they were long gone. Once on the bus, she would choose a seat at the back and read one word after the next, slowly, as the bus rolled toward Mława and her girls' school. The outcome of such reading was a great revelation, a looking-glass tour, as America appeared before her eyes.

Her mother fusses noisily in the kitchen. One of her friends is due to visit. To Ania, this old woman is one of the biddies, women who have been coming to their house since she was a child, and who have maintained the same conversation for twenty years: bread is baking, rain is coming, the priest will visit, the roof is leaking, the windows need fixing, the government is lying…

Would she like some homemade tea? Homemade meant store-bought leaves mixed with her mother's gleanings from the fields near the cemetery. It might, on the model of the morning's encounter, be called Jewish tea. It is always too strong, like some sort of bewitched drink.

"No, Mama. I'm fine."

When, her mother wonders over the sound of the kettle, must she be back in Warsaw?

Not until late tomorrow morning. If she gets the early Mława bus she can be in the city for her first meeting, after lunch, with the ministers overseeing plans to archive the last of the lustration files. The review of Communist-era security files was finally winding up.

"Then," her mother says, "I will make something nice for dinner. I must go pick some things in the garden. Maybe from the field, too."

Ania eyes her bag, which sits on a chair by the front door. It bulges, full as it is with the boy's box. "I have to go out, Mama. I'll be back for dinner. Is six okay?"

The Mława bus schedule never changes. But that has nothing to do with when the bus will be in the square. Sometimes it is half an hour late. Sometimes it doesn't appear at all, and travellers wait for whatever might come. But today it is idling, ready to go. She gets on with a few others, women her mother's age heading to the shops around Mława's main square. She puts her bag beside her on an empty seat and opens the window. They are on their way.

The countryside rushes by in its pine-forest freshness. Trucks and horse carts wait at unmarked intersections. Roadside shrines mark crossroads festooned in summer ribbons and fake flowers to ward off the devil. Who, she wonders, puts these where they stand? She will have to ask her mother.

The bus runs along a winding street of villas, not unlike her mother's, with a few remaining hundred-year-old wooden houses. It turns into Mława's main square, with its old town hall and clock tower. A crowd flows into the church. Maybe an afternoon wedding. Did they do such things here? Might the mother and father of the boy with the box have held just such a celebration? Having lived in Warsaw for five years, she is out of touch.

The Mława civic museum is not far from the city's central park. Out front, a granite monument commemorates Polish partisans. Someone has put plastic flowers beside it. Inside: nobody. She takes in the bare white walls of the Soviet-era building and a battered desk on crooked legs. On the desk sits one of those silver bells you hit with the palm of your hand. These were once ubiquitous and can now be found only in such bureaucratic outposts. She'd like one for her office, just for a joke. Ania touches the bell with her index finger to see what will happen.

The archivist comes out of the back room. She thinks she remembers him from school visits, with his tightly buttoned wool vest, smelling vaguely of cigarettes. At least, she thinks, she remembers his type. Unsmiling, bone-thin, stiff-backed, suspicious-eyed. An asshole, her father would have said; they belong in those jobs, which are like holes in the wall where an animal shreds paper for its bed. In his own embittered way her father may have been right. Why did these types end up as gatekeepers? Because saying no pleases them? It may be that to get past this gatekeeper she will have to pull her Warsaw rank. Act tougher and even more tight-lipped. And if that didn't work? She knew not what.

But he recognizes her immediately. *Pani* Ania. From Radzanów. Now of Warsaw. He ducks his head, a kind of abbreviated bow. He has seen her on television explaining ministry screw-ups. She looks, he adds, with his eyes down, good on TV. Always in black, a good colour for television.

Well, an opening. Some soft spot remained in the Soviet personality.

And, he adds, he knows her mother.

How?

His parents were born in Radzanów. Their property was behind the church. And his father managed to grab a bit more after the war. It's a ruin now. There is a barn full of cats and a cistern where badgers like to improvise a burrow. But he cannot bring himself to sell, so he passes through every now and then to make sure no one is up to anything. Once, he says, he caught kids using the barn as their secret hangout. In the hayloft they'd rigged up speakers and DJ equipment, coloured lights, and they invited their friends on Saturday nights like it was their own place. He ran them off with a flashlight and a blowhorn he borrowed from the Sanitation Department. When he passes through the main square in the village he often finds Ania's mother on her stoop. They talk things over. The old times. Her daughter's success in the civil service. The government of the day. Normal times. How long they might last.

Ania does not sense any irony in the way he says these things.

He is being cordial. He is on her side because he admires her mother. So this is what her mother does when Ania is in Warsaw. She stands on her stoop, arms over her chest, playing unofficial mayor, talking to her would-be constituents, charming them.

She asks the archivist his name.

"I am Ryszard Jankowski, at your service." They shake hands, then Ania places the box on the archivist's desk. She has heard, she tells him, that he has expertise in pre-war and wartime history.

It's true. His specialty is the Mława front, the three-week effort, not so far off in the countryside, in bunkers and hilltops, where the Polish army fought the invading Germans.

This is sacred history for those in the Polish history game, for anyone with a father who was in the army in the war, and anyone who remembers the devastation of the occupation. But she has not come to talk about this hallowed stuff. Certainly, they studied it in school. She'd hidden her Salinger inside her history book back then, when she walked home in the rain, under her old umbrella, and tried to understand why Phoebe and Holden could not agree at the book's end. She tried to envision Central Park and forget, forget, forget the Mława front.

"May I open it?"

"Please. I hope you have time to look at what's inside. I would like your opinion on it."

Jankowski nods, distracted now by what he is looking at. Ania thinks she can see his nose react, like a cat's, to the smell of the open box. He gingerly removes its contents and lays them on his desk. In a transparent envelope, there are four postage stamps—orange, red, robin's egg blue, and green. A black-and-white photograph in the style of pre-war photo studios. A hand-drawn map on curling onion-skin paper. And a card, four by six inches, with writing on one side in a wandering, dark script. Its flip side is blank. Ryszard Jankowski arranges these things on his desk, with the stamps first in line for consideration. He opens a desk drawer, removes a tiny set of tweezers, and carefully lifts one stamp nearer to the lamp on the desk, which he switches on.

"What are they?" Ania leans in to see.

"What do you think they are?"

"Postage stamps."

"You are right. No perforations. You cut them from the sheet with scissors. Or they planned to perforate them and someone requisitioned the machine for some more pressing job, like food coupons. Can you see here?" He inclines his head toward the stamp. "Can you see the languages? You have Ukrainian. You have Polish. German, the nightmare language. And?"

Ania needs her glasses. "Hebrew?"

"Close. Yiddish. See here: *Stadpost Luboml*. You might know. This place was in Poland before the war. Now it's in the Ukraine. Let's look."

He disappears into the back room and returns with a book. Ania watches as he flips through it.

"Here. When the Germans occupied it there were four thousand Jews. The local authorities produced this set of stamps during the occupation. But they were never issued. So, do not let anyone tell you"—Jankowski looks up at her—"that there never was a Yiddish postage stamp. If they tell you this, you must tell them, if you'll forgive me, that they are full of shit."

"It's okay," Ania tells him. "You likely know my mother's two favourite words."

Jankowski thinks for a moment. "*Końskie gówno Końskie gówno!*" They shout out loud together, like school kids. *Horse shit!*

"It says here," he continues, "maybe fifty of the city's four thousand Jews survived the war. They are called *Lbivners*. Many sheets of these semi-official stamps went missing during the war. There is a legend about them being used in underground activity by a smuggling network." He sets the reference book aside and lays the stamp, using the tweezers like a surgical instrument, back on the desk.

"Now. This."

The photograph. The four figures in it are unsmiling. They wear their best clothes. They are teenagers. One is older, or at least taller, with a more mature style of dress. He has on what looks like a tweed jacket, a necktie, and no cap on his head. The other three are obviously Polish children. She has seen enough old photographs in family albums. The girl's light hair; the boy's knee pants. The old-fashioned caps and big-collared shirts.

"Do you recognize this place?" Jankowski asks her. He aims a finger at the photograph's background.

She does not, though there is something about the image that strikes her as familiar. The girl, weirdly, reminds her of herself. When Ania was six or seven she had the same light hair. It was very prized hair, prized in ways both dark and wonderful.

"Look again. It's not far from here. Close to the village."

"Oh! It's the old bridge, isn't it? The one they took down, that crossed the Wkra."

"Correct. This boat. The one the boys are in? People before the war, Jews and non-Jews both, used them for fishing. A skiff? We called them skiffs. You couldn't sink one if you tried. So, they let the kids take them out alone. And the flat bottom was good in the river. These kids, I don't have a clue. They're just playing. Or someone chose this setting for the photo."

Jankowski contemplates the faces in the photo. "This one"— he places his fingernail beside the taller boy, with no cap—"looks Jewish to me."

Ania frowns. "You can't say that with confidence."

"Well, not in a court. Not to a newspaper reporter. Not to the police. But to you, *Pani* Ania, I can say it with confidence. Jewish.

And, I would even go further. Not from around here. He puts the photo down and picks up the card with its handwritten message. "This I must photocopy and look over. If you'll allow me?"

Ania tells him to go ahead. She watches as Jankowski photocopies both sides of the card, the one with writing on it and the one that is blank. The phone rings, and he picks it up.

"*Dzień dobry*. Yes. Yes. Can you hold for a moment?"

Ania places the objects back in the box. The map, the stamps, the photo, and the postcard.

"It is very powerful," he tells her, the phone pressed to his vest. "What you have found is an Archive of the Jews." He returns to his caller as if she has evaporated. On the phone, his gatekeeper soul returns. "No," he tells whoever has called. "No. No." And once more, "*No.*"

She returns to Mława's main square, holding the box before her as the boy did when he ran toward her. The clock tower atop the city hall tells her there is one last bus back to the village. Her mother will be cooking a wonderful meal from secret recipes borne with great love out of the past.

The Clandestine Book Room

Nadia stands across from 36 Cordova. The whole block, from what she can see, carries this address, though she knows the pawn business was tucked into the westernmost corner of the large redbrick building. That corner is now a blasted, dark storefront in the middle of the block. Rather than cross over, she turns and meanders along the neighbouring streets, down Carrall, along Alexander, up Main, trying to imagine the insides of the old SRO hotels—tall and narrow, rooms piled on top of each other. Years before when she'd done AIDS hospice work, she'd sometimes visited her clients in rooms like these, and, though she'd never gotten used to the squalor, the smell, the edgy front-door minders, she had become an appreciated regular visitor. An outsider with something useful to offer. Now: rags and towels and aluminum foil over windows. Husks of what had been substantial buildings, some with front doors boarded up. Signs in place for businesses long gone. The laughably inappropriate names of the places that exchanged welfare cheques for single rooms: Regal Plaza, Wonder Hotel (Rooms for Rent), Persepolis Motel. The once beloved Only Sea Foods restaurant, its windows papered over. Anchor of Hope Community Church.

Eventually she circles back to the big building at 36 Cordova. The top two floors, under arched windows, look lived in, but the fluorescents visible through tied-back curtains give the third floor the look of a sweatshop. She wonders what might be manufactured up there. The ground floor is dark, its windows papered over. A metal fence guards the front of the building. A small sign has been placed on the papered glass. She checks for cars and crosses over. COMING SOON, the sign says, with no further explanation.

Her instrument hangs on her back in its soft case. She has come to settle down on the building's front stoop; her second visit. She wonders if this gives her the status of a regular busker on Cordova. She can impersonate a busker, because she cannot be a real one. She's not at it for the money. The music fellowship she received at UBC is a fat one, funded by a forestry company. She feels guilty keeping all that cash in the bank. Maybe she should hand out fives and tens to the hard-up characters willing to stop and listen to her play. Turn the whole busker phenomenon on its head.

She folds her jacket and sets it on the stoop. Using the case as a kind of backrest, she sets the dulcimer on her lap. She plays quietly at first, almost to herself. But gradually, as usually happens, the music overtakes her. Passersby look her over. A man in a bulky winter jacket stands for a while, tapping his foot. He offers a nod before he walks up the street. While she plays she forgets about the pop bottle and the spring of 1962. It is summer now on Cordova, cars idling at the light at Carrall.

No one throws coins or even single cigarettes.

When Nadia begins to feel stiff in her backside she stands to stretch and puts the instrument back in its case. She is due on campus for a group practice. As she turns to go, she notices a light come on behind the papered glass above where she'd sat to play. Someone is inside. She stands with her nose against the window, trying to see who might be there. She feels a bite of fear in her gut. This is where the pop bottle entered history and began its ascendancy, its transformation from being just a handful of molded glass to a piece worth displaying under lights. And, too, it's where something new and strange came her family's way. A story she'd been denied.

The building's front door is barred by a roughly cut rectangle of plywood nailed over the door frame, with metal grating over that.

Maybe there is a back entrance.

The alleyways in this part of town are notorious. But in daylight, what could possibly be going on? She circles the block and walks behind the buildings that face Cordova. She isn't sure how to recognize "her" building, so she walks back out front and makes what seems like a reliable count of storefronts. This way she decides that number 36 is the fifth discrete structure west of Carrall.

She heads back down the alley and counts four separate structures leading to what she thinks must be number 36. She is stunned to see, through an open back door, a man bent over a large porcelain sink. The noise of whatever it is he is doing sounds in the alley. Water rushes from a tap and steam rises around him. He is washing things—jars and glassware—which he lays out on a towel on the countertop beside the sink. With his back to her and the noise of the water, he is unaware of being watched. The idea crosses her mind: her man, the proprietor of Reliable Loan, circa 1962, might have stood at the same spot, his back to the alleyway. She wishes that day could be conjured so it would reappear, the way a magician's trick fills a black and empty space with a big bouquet of flowers.

Calm down, she tells herself.

She watches the man's back as he moves between sink and

countertop. She nearly holds her breath, standing there long enough to recognize that the beauty of this alley is its colours. The rich red and ochre bricks on the buildings' backsides. The dark grey pavement, criss-crossed with tar where gaps have been filled. The nut-brown of the telephone poles, and the dingy blue and yellow dumpsters. She takes a tentative step toward the open screen door just as the man turns to come outside, holding a chair with three legs. Surprised, he stumbles, puts a foot down wrong on the back step and nearly falls.

"Sorry. Sorry." He repeats the word as he rights himself and sets the chair on the pavement, still apologizing. It topples over on its bad leg and rests on its side.

To her surprise, she knows his face. But where from?

He takes a rag from his back pocket and wipes his hands on it. He is almost a foot taller than she, with a tall man's thin-shouldered stoop, brought on by years of bending to talk to average-sized people. His hair is light, swept back, and his ears stick out. There is something soft in the expression on his face, and she wonders if this is forced or natural. You never know when you first meet someone. Are they playing it straight or are they acting to hide who they really are?

He takes his glasses from his shirt pocket and puts them on. It is the university, she realizes, now that he has the glasses on his nose. He is one of her regular sightings. If you spend enough time on campus you have hundreds like him, people you see routinely at the Student Union Building buying a coffee, at the pool or the library, or just crossing from one building to another. Some you nod at, some you avoid making eye contact with, some you hardly think about. She saw him come out of a building near where she practiced in the little portholed room. But they had never acknowledged each other.

"I've seen you," she says, "around Buchanan."

He looks at her, embarrassed, not recognizing her.

He holds out his hand and says his name, but she forgets it as soon as it is out of his mouth. This is one of her worst habits. She lets people's names go by with hardly a thought.

He takes off his glasses and wipes them clean with a rag.

"You're opening something here?"

"I am. It's still taking shape."

"What will it be?"

"Well, I'm working on that. A coffee house. Remember those?"

She is too young to remember coffee houses, but she has read about them. "Could I see?"

"There's not much to see yet. But, okay."

He leads her in through the alley door. It is cool and dark inside. They pass through the back room with the sink, and then some sort of office, into the main space out front. The papered-over windows are dark, but for a thin frame of light at their edges. Chairs and tables are piled neatly to one side.

"It's kind of like a boat," she says.

"You mean the wood."

She sniffs. "Smells like an old boat. Oil and wood. What made you choose this place?"

He looks at her again in his soft-hearted way, as if she is a child he's appraising. Is it the way his eyes are enlarged by his glass lenses that makes her think this?

He shrugs. "It's a long story."

They take down a couple of chairs and she lays the dulcimer in its case on the floor. He peels a sheet of the brown paper from the windows, which lets the sunlight in, angled across the room in bars.

The story he tells is a weird revelation. Having gotten used to seeing him at a distance under the shade trees near Main Library, sometimes talking to what she took to be a student, looking as he did—professorial, even conventionally so—the reality of what happened to him over the past year came as a shock. You might see someone a hundred times in your life and never find out what their story was, but here he is, his hands hanging off the ends of his knees, telling his.

His name is Simon Hanover. His academic career, as it turned out, is nearly as offbeat as hers. He is proud of the fact that he didn't get a Ph.D. "No important letters after my name," he says, smiling. He had nearly finished, but he'd found it impossible to complete his thesis. Wallace Stevens's relationship to music. It had turned into some sort of obsessive, sure-to-fail project, with no end in sight. Books piled up on the floor at home; the carrel he was assigned in Main Library filled with new critical approaches, largely unread. On yellow legal pads he tried to develop one map after another of his research goals. The department had offered him classes to teach—and he had taken them, for six years, becoming a dedicated and appreciated part-time teacher who lacked the official designation, the degree, that the university all of a sudden insisted its instructors have. It was a mark of the institution's prestige; its brand. Universities were burnishing their brands. They were hiring PR companies, coming up with logos and slick slogans and ways of distinguishing themselves from the competition. Since his lack of a Ph.D. sullied the brand, he'd received a letter from his department head, a perfectly sensible character who'd always treated him with respect and patient interest, even as his research had dragged on, incomplete and unformed, explaining why he could not be on staff in the coming fall. But he shouldn't take this personally, since his removal was caused by a larger housecleaning. He should think of this as an inevitable change, one they'd been lucky to stave off as long as they had.

"As I packed up my office I thought of that great strange Dylan song, 'Changing of the Guards.' Do you know it?"

She did. Eight or ten or twenty-five impossible-to-remember verses. She had tried it on the dulcimer, to no great effect.

"The lyric made sense to me for the first time. 'Gentlemen, I don't need your organization. I've shined your shoes and marked your cards. I've moved your mountains. But Eden is burning.'"

He looks down at her music case. "That's too small to be a guitar."

"It is," she says, "a dulcimer."

"How did you learn to play that?"

"When my father moved out, he left a lot behind. My mother paid me and a friend with a truck to take things to the dump. Clothes, books. I kept a few of his things. The dulcimer was in a box I found hidden away in the basement." She puts her toe on the case. "There were other things that looked like they belonged to a different era, even a different person. Wooden shoe trees. Silk ties. A man's wallet with nothing in it. I kept the dulcimer in my closet a long time. One day I tried it and I just fell for it."

"I wish I'd known we had a dulcimer player so close by on campus while I was teaching them *Dr. Zhivago*."

"Are there dulcimers in *Dr. Zhivago*?"

"Well, there should be. Certainly there are in Mickiewicz. The Poles have their own version, but you know all that. I rarely had the opportunity to fill them in on such things. Sometimes it was straight composition. You know, comma splices. Sentence fragments. Can you imagine how little young people care about writing in fragments? They might as well just throw out the textbooks on that stuff. Just a sec." He goes into the back room and returns with a bottle of Perrier and two glasses. He pours them each a drink.

"So, what are you doing up there? At the university."

As she offers an accounting of herself she expresses things she hadn't herself realized, as if she is unlocking an unconsidered period in her life by talking about it.

"I applied, not really expecting to get in. My undergraduate record, or whatever you'd call it, was pretty weak. I hardly went to class. Back then I viewed a boring lecturer as entirely beneath me. But when the music department wrote I went in for an audition. I could tell that it went well. They wrote a few months later to say they wanted me. As graduate students—you know—we're asked to do all sorts of strange things." She marked papers on subjects she had absolutely no knowledge of. She photocopied whole books so professors could stow them on their office shelves. She attended union meetings where the spokesperson for the university's teaching assistants used a language of revolutionary Marxism so outdated and embarrassing that she didn't know if she should laugh or scream. "It would be better," she says, "to be represented by a squirrel or a bird. I could get behind that. But these kinds of mindless people? It's just crazy."

Because hers was a performance program, much of her time was spent practicing, sometimes in a small white room with a tiny porthole in the door, sometimes onstage at the performance hall across from the music building where the empty seats stretched for what looked, in the darkened hall, like miles. She played piano with a little group of twenty-something musicians who came from all over the globe—Korea, Russia, Mexico. They practised with great seriousness. Then she spent an hour, an hour and a half at most, at the piano before switching to the dulcimer, which was the machine for making sounds she was truly in love with.

She finds it more difficult to explain the academic side of what she is doing. No one in the music department knew enough about Eastern European music to okay what she wanted to research, which was the culture surrounding the tsimbl or cimbalom or cymbalon, different versions of the dulcimer played by Roma and Jews and Poles and Romanians. She found, soon enough, that most of the relevant material was in languages she couldn't read, that there was almost no real accounting of Roma and Jewish music from before the nineteenth century. The musicians had walked the earth, largely undocumented. It had all disappeared into the realm of myth and ethnic romance, obliterated by war. She had sought out a few professors in Slavic Studies who at least understood the history surrounding the music she was learning. A few of them seemed pleased to find a student with her enthusiasms.

"Can you write a paper," she wonders aloud, "on a subject that is almost entirely lost in time? I feel like I'm making it up. And I have no interest at all in the world music that claims to take its inspiration from the old stuff."

"Yah," he says. "I hate that stuff too."

"The strongest feeling I have," she admits, "is that I'm on my own with what I'm interested in. But I can accept that. I'm working through musicology and popular culture studies and trying to understand the Eastern European borderlands, the marshes and villages along the Vistula." She hesitates, deciding whether it is wise to say what comes into her mind next. "But it all gets lost as soon as I shut what I've read. The only thing that stays fresh is the music itself. Whenever I can I listen to the few things available that include late-nineteenth-century forms of the music. They're usually transferred from wax cylinders, and they sound like they were performed in a well, or far away in a field with the wind blowing half the song away. I like the challenge of getting something out of it."

Why, he wants to know, did she choose his stoop to sit down on?

What should she say? That she is seeking a bright morning in April, 1962? That the newspapers at the university library were helpful to a point? They gave her the weather, which was fine on the morning of her father's brother's last day in his shop. But she only shrugs.

He lifts his hands off his knees.

"Listen, there's something else I'm doing. Can I show you?"

"Okay."

"You can leave your instrument here."

She shakes her head and slides the strap on the case over her shoulder.

They exit the way they came in, into the alleyway, and walk around to Cordova. He unlocks the metal grate out front and opens a section of the plywood cover that she now sees is on hinges. He switches on the light that hangs in the entranceway. It's an unrenovated space, left over from an earlier flophouse existence, but tidied up. She follows him up a steep set of stairs to a landing, and then around a corner into a room with a bay window overlooking the street. After the papered-over darkness below, this room is filled with light. Books on shelves reach as high as the ceiling on each wall.

"So," he says, "this is it."

"What is it?" She sniffs. "Smells like a lending library. Like the one I went to with my mother when I was a kid. What's a library doing here? In Cordovaland."

"Here, sit down. This is the comfortable chair."

She settles into an armchair near the front window. Below, she can see the street in shadow.

"I know this sounds weird, but close your eyes."

She sighs and shuts her eyes. The room is quiet, but for the sound of him moving off. With one eye cracked open, she watches him take a book from midway up one wall.

"Here. Hold out your hands. Tell me what this is."

"It's a book."

"Tell me more."

"A hardcover, with a dust jacket. Can I open my eyes now?"

"Wait. First, describe it."

"The book?"

"Yes."

She handles the thing, turns it over, nearly drops it as she places it flat on her palm. She opens the cover and runs her fingers over the title page. She flutters the edges of the pages with her thumb and removes the dust cover to take the measure of the inside boards. There were many like it in her home when she was a girl. She guessed some were extras, doubles, things her father had received as gifts or review copies. A few of her own childhood books had dust covers like the one she held. The one that haunted her still was called *The Magic Key*. It was serious and scary, and she'd understood nothing inside its cover, which showed an etching of a cottage in the woods and, if she remembered correctly, crows.

"I can't describe it."

"Why?"

"I just can't. It would take too long." She opens her eyes and holds the book out for him to take. He puts it back in its place, which is high enough on the shelves that he must raise himself on his toes.

"I call this the Clandestine Book Room."

Here is a word she has never heard a person use: *clandestine*. What, she wonders, can it mean?

"Downstairs I'll be a coffee-house impresario, open-mic manager, all-purpose host. Up here," he explains, "I'm a clandestine bookseller. It's not a straightforward shop. I don't advertise. I only take cash. I will trade. If someone I know wants to browse I open up for them. A few groups in town rent it from me for evening talks or literary social nights. They're throwbacks, but very savvy, and literary talk excites them. In those instances, I'm the caterer and I clean up the next morning. I think of them as sweet young kids. I'm their Andy Warhol. A quirky older guy who shares their passion."

She would like to ask him his age, but she misses her chance. Is he her age, or a few years older?

Most of the books, he says, came via two collections he inherited—from his father, and a cousin who was a kind of godfather to him. His father collected books for many years. He'd created a valuable library. But one day he decided he was finished with this kind of collecting and moved on to other things. If Simon hadn't taken the collection it would have been broken up—the most valuable things sold off to private collectors and libraries. So when his father said, *You take it all. You're already kind of in the business with the university job*, he'd done just that. He explains at length how books make him feel. She feels as if she is back in her musicology class, being lectured at in good faith about things she cannot really retain. Then he tells her how certain people who came up to this clandestine place opened up as they took in their surroundings.

"You see real excitement in their eyes," he says. "A kind of opening-up-of-King-Tut's-Tomb look. There's a good deal of stroking. No one strokes paperbacks. Those get shot back onto the shelf. But hardbacks receive a lot of loving. Sometimes the dust cover comes off to see what's underneath it, and I see them glance over to check if this is okay."

She glances at her watch. She has an afternoon practice on campus.

He should, he says, get back to work. Simon ushers her down the stairs, walking before her with an arm out as if he half expects her tumble down. They step out onto the sidewalk.

"When I open up you should come and play. What do you

think? No one else will bring a dulcimer. You'll be unique."

"Maybe. I'll see." She reaches into her bag and pulls out the book of poems she's been reading, a gift from her professor. It is full of wistful smoky Krakow streets, childhood piano lessons, the tragedy of a father who has forgotten who he is.

"I think your book room might be missing this."

He checks the author's name. "Zagajewski. Z. You're right. That goes right at the end. I've been looking for a good ending."

He holds his hand out for her to shake.

As she makes her way up the sidewalk, she feels his eyes on her back. The dulcimer beats its low inadvertent music inside its case as it bumps on her hip. She turns to look over her shoulder but he is gone, the front of the building shuttered and dark.

Free Man

The dulcimer girl is gone and there is work to do. A lot of what he'd planned was completed. He'd dealt with the dampness by removing old plaster, right down to the wood laths. He polished light fixtures and got down on his knees with steel wool and turpentine to clean the grit off the wood floor. This made him feel like a neighbourhood ghost, a ferry worker, the kind of tough kid who made his way up from table boy to captain on the Union Steamship Lines, guiding boatloads of weekenders out to Bowen Island for shoreline views.

He worries about the sound system. The mic on its stand is positioned on a little riser where a few musicians—three at most—can play. He steps up to the mic, turns it on, and speaks into the cold metal: "Test. Test. One, two, three." He can't tell if the sound is rich enough, if it is real, as a musician friend would say. *Make sure the sound is real, Simon. Otherwise, it's pointless.* He figured an old building on Cordova would have the acoustics of a garage, but this is not so. If he could get that dulcimer girl back she could do a test run. He would ask her to sit on an old chair and play a song of the Carpathians.

He pulled the paper from the front windows and removed the metal grating. He brushed the steps clean with an industrial product he found at Army and Navy. They look good now, like steps you might want to walk up. He chose the name for his new place when he uncovered what was left of a sign reading "Second Hand Shop" behind panelling nailed above the door. As he scraped and scrubbed, he'd uncovered the hand-painted script; gold letters trimmed in red appeared. This way, he'd gained a kind of second-hand name for his place. The Shop.

★

It became clear to him once he opened that he had created neither a club nor a café. And though he did not have a theatre in mind at all, what he'd made turned out to be a kind of theatre of the street for the downtown crowd and anyone willing to travel from the west side.

He opens in the late afternoon, from Wednesday through Saturday, with no regular closing time. On Sundays, the literary groupies rent it and hold their intellectual soirées. He has not bothered with a liquor license. The idea of applying for a piece of paper to put in a frame on his wall depresses him. He doesn't want to go to the courthouse or city hall to get such a thing. No one has come to inspect his credentials. Apparently, the Shop exists in some invisible crack between the forgotten side of town and everything else. It is a prohibition-free zone.

He thinks of what goes on on his makeshift stage as a Theatre of Misery, and, at other times, as a Theatre of Clowns. Some of the poetry read on it is so terrible, so scattershot and earnestly delivered, it drives him behind the back curtain where he keeps the cake and bottles of inexpensive rum. He serves hot chocolate in mugs. For an extra dollar he adds a shot of whisky or rum. He found a good carrot cake at a grocery outlet on West Sixteenth and serves that at a markup. The people who come in want, first off, not these modest offerings, but the little stage at the back with its silver microphone, which he bought from one of the surviving second-hand shops in the area. He plugs it into a makeshift PA system made up of a battered receiver and amp and four big stereo speakers that hang near the ceiling. Into this the boldest, or most desperate, or craziest among his clientele read poetry, play harmonica, recount weird stories, and sometimes make a misery of themselves and must be asked to go, which they usually do without a fuss because they want to be able to come back and try again sometime. One guy apologized—he looked like he might cry—after a spit-flying outburst, and as Simon stood on the sidewalk out front saying it was okay, he had the professorial urge to tell him to put his troubles into some more concrete form. But he gave the guy a break and simply said good night. He told him he could come back and try again but hoped he wouldn't. Once, the dulcimer girl appeared. She wore black lace-up boots and a coat with the collar turned up. She sat and listened with her instrument between her knees but did not put herself on the list to perform. She disappeared before he could make it over to talk to her. A newcomer took her seat beside two chess-playing regulars. So, he thought, she can haunt this place.

Early on, after refusing to put himself on the open-mic list, a local light, the novelist Kris Walther, took the stage and metaphorically shot up the place. Standing before the mic he spewed what he took to be his proof of ownership of the neighbourhood, repeatedly calling it, in the contemporary terms of choice, the Downtown Eastside—sometimes rendered as the "Downtown fuckin' Eastside." He told the meagre audience that he knew the "real Downtown fuckin' Eastside," and that whatever was being pronounced from the stage at this place had better take *that* into account, which, he advised, must acknowledge what a junkie's concave chest felt like to the touch, what a binner was, and how hard a speedball hit when it came on, because these were the unchangeable truths of the "DOWNTOWN FUCKIN' EAST-SIDE. And you guys are lucky I don't whip my dick out and piss all over ya!" He gave a little semi-Nazi-footballer's salute, jumped off the stage, and exited the front door onto Cordova.

Like the Silver in a Pawnbroker's

Simon runs across Nadia's blog by chance. It is absurdly named: *Rommel Drives on Deep into Egypt*. He is not a blog reader, has stumbled into one or two by mistake, rushing away as if he'd been lured to a porn site or invited to hand over his banking details.

How, he'd sat down at the computer to find out, should he price a relatively clean copy of a paperback edition of Richard Brautigan's poetry book *Rommel Drives on Deep into Egypt*? When it was published in 1970, it cost $2.35 in Canada. He has two copies on his shelf, since someone traded them for a Margaret Atwood hardcover he'd been trying to get rid of for ages. When that Atwood book left it was like the sun had come out on Cordova Street.

He sits at the desk in his apartment overlooking the park on Comox. At midday the daycares bring their three- and four-year-olds there, hitched together with rope and wearing their identities on little red and yellow bibs. Now no one is visible in the park's green corners. The dog run is an empty expanse of sand. The community garden is an overgrown and solitary place, crowned by a six-foot-tall sunflower, its head turned up at him. His strip of the West End is called Mole Hill, referring to the block of Comox below Bute, which has attained special status through a housing co-op that beautified the wooden houses south of his building.

But why "Mole," and why "Hill"? Who knew? Comox Street by the park was as flat as a wood plank.

On his computer screen the list of copies of Brautigan's work is a digital-age tour of used book offerings in Austin, Texas; Saint Thomas, Ontario; Moose Jaw, Saskatchewan. He'd driven though Moose Jaw once, without even stopping for gas. It was funny to think of Brautigan sitting there on someone's shelf.

Because her blog bears the name of the Brautigan book it pops up alongside the offers for sale. He gazes at its signature image—a young woman smiling vaguely about something, settled in the middle of a sandbox—then at the cover of the book on his desk. He does not really know what makes a "good" blog. Why does he even wonder if hers is "good"? The blog presents itself in white lettering on a black background, punctuated here and there by a photograph, a recipe, an excerpt from something she is reading. There are a few sound files she has recorded and uploaded, of birds scratching on the roof outside her kitchen window, of the sound of people talking, backed by car noise, identified as "Main and Hastings Folk." He tries the birds a few times. They sound almost human in their intermittent chatter. The "Folk" on the corner, recorded not far from his place on Cordova, do not interest him. He can hear them live on any given day as he walks home from work.

His first thought, as he scrolls through the site, reflects his age and the tendencies of his generation, having grown up in an analog universe. What right has he to find out about her this way? Apparently every right, since that is the signature weirdness of blog culture. It promotes private revelation in public, and is a bit like flashing, the old compulsion that no one would promote, which must now be almost completely replaced by people's willingness to reveal themselves in an ongoing, unstoppable way on the Internet.

He looks at the table of contents in the Brautigan collection and sees that she organizes her entries by way of poem titles borrowed from the book, choosing the crankiest and the most lyrical. "Nice Ass" was one she might well have avoided, but off she ran with it, dumping the question mark and making it her own.

> Nice ass. What a stupid remark. It had its day but now is dead, like Rommel, who went crazy on meth as his plans came apart. Egypt is in the news again. I went to a talk given at UBC by a photographer who just returned from Cairo. He took photographs from his hotel window of Tahrir Square. Then he walked among the protestors and soccer hooligans who back the military. But he left too soon, thinking things had stalled, and missed the dictator's fall. The tanks are still in the streets, but someone else owns them now. How's your ass.

Her blogging voice does not resemble what came out of her mouth when they spoke at the Shop. She seemed diffident then, a bit humourless, though full of patient interest. He recalled her unwillingness to describe the book he'd handed her. What had motivated that? In her blog entries, she paints things in ironic colours, riffing. It's a shock to read them. But he is in for further surprise, as he works his way through her twenty-five or so entries, with their potpourri of scrapbooky images. When the Swiss poet Tranströmer won the Nobel Prize—who, he wonders, is this guy, now famous and rich in his mountain house?—she set down four lines of his:

> The only thing I want to say
> glitters out of reach
> like the silver
> in a pawnbroker's.

From here, she shifts to a description of the streets surrounding his address at 36 Cordova. Filling the screen is a photograph of his block of Cordova, his side of the street, with a title attached: "A 48-Year-Old Burglar from San Diego." He checks Brautigan, and sure enough there is an entry in the table of contents with that title, but no poem, just a blank page. Was this a publisher's mistake or a strategy for radicalizing poetry? Titles without poems, to see if anyone noticed.

Her response to this puzzle is the photo, something to illustrate the title with no poem attached. It is an archival photo, tinted a light greenish shade with age, of his Vancouver block. Based on the cars in view, it must date from the early sixties. It might be a newspaper image, but it is more likely one of those photographic records that cities once made to account for how the infrastructure was fairing, to keep track of light standards, signage, the state of curbstones. It shows the entire south side of the block of Cordova above Carrall, sightlines disappearing toward the west. This was a dividing line, in fact, between east and west, that went back to the city's earliest years. His front window is obscured in the middle distance, but the neon sign reading Hildon Hotel marks the midpoint of the block where he has set himself up, and where the Hildon remains in sad, uninterrupted decline. The photographer's focal point is the Army and Navy building. In the near distance is the Rainier Hotel with its now-vanished Rainier Grocery at street level. A big red "Drink Coca-Cola" disc is the only flash of colour on the otherwise washed-out street. Two of the three men in view wear fedoras. One of these crosses Cordova in an aluminum-frame wheelchair. Above it all hovers the Woodward's "W" on its steelwork support tower. It shocks him. The whole scene so long before he encountered it, yet so much of it still the same sad street. Walking alongside the front of the Army and Navy is a young mother with a Jackie O hairdo.

Maybe this dates the photo—pre-1963, when the husband of the woman who modeled the hairdo was killed in the back seat of an open Lincoln. The woman holds her child's hand. The child is the only wholesome thing in view (unless the big red "W" fits that description, and maybe it does). Most everything else is shot through with noir, a washed-out street of failure and dissolution.

He uses the zoom feature on his software to try to bring up his own storefront, but all that comes plainly into view is the word "LOAN" on a sign over the sidewalk. The cars on the near-empty roadway are fat two-tone coupes.

Beneath the photo, he finds a description of himself. She has written up their meeting under the title "I Am Summoned by a Door." She describes his stoop, "the softness in his face," and then his account of why he is busying himself behind a derelict storefront. In her version, he is a local character, one of the oddball things going on along Cordova amidst the change and new development. It seems that she has not mentioned the Book Room.

Simon gets up from his chair and walks to the window. He looks down at the park, the lights in apartment blocks coming on behind it, the southern sky turned crimson and navy with dusk. His city. He thinks this, and experiences an urge, common of late, which quietly whispers the words, *Leave. It's time to leave.* He does not know where this urge comes from. Two men cross the park toward Nelson, one coming from the west, the other from the east. Each is arrested by something—the westerly walker by the sunflower, and the easterly by the lavender near the centre of the park. It's like a dance the way they each pause to look, one to put his fingers in the lavender. Simon pulls on his shoes and jacket. Gets his keys to go for an evening walk down to English Bay.

He reviews what he can remember of his conversation with the dulcimer girl as he walks down Davie toward the water. Did he say too much? What was she doing in the back alley behind

Cordova? The fact that they'd seen each other on campus—or at least she him, for he had no memory of her walking there with her instrument on her back—had caused him to drop his guard. They were members of the same guild of scholar-dreamers, though she'd just returned to the campus and he'd been asked, however nicely, to leave. Was it pretentious of him to quote Dylan to her?

He sits for a while on his favourite bench overlooking the water. It has a memorial plaque fastened to its back, which reads, "For our father. In our hearts forever. The Ming Family." It is dark now, and voices come off the seawall behind him, quietly disappearing as the walkers turn the bend toward Stanley Park. The slick sound of bike tires punctuates the quiet.

He heads home to read what she's written about him. In the lobby of his building, a great mound of uncollected mail sits on a leather bench. Above it, a bulletin board displays a warning about the threat of bedbugs. Off to the side of the lobby is the building's makeshift lending library. One of the tenants set it up in a cast-off bookshelf, which is full of *Readers Digest Condensed* hardbacks, old copies of *Self* and *Elle*, and paperbacks. He keeps an eye out for books inscribed, in neat penmanship, with the name Emily Hopkins. These books show up from time to time, and he takes each one, as if he is getting to know a stranger by way of the books she's read. Today, it's Ray Bradbury's *Something Wicked This Way Comes*, in what looks like an unread paperback edition. He calls the elevator. As he ascends, he gazes at the mirror on the elevator door. His skin is pale, grey. Too much time spent inside, he thinks, and vows that his next seawall walk will be in sunlight. He'll walk the full six-mile route with his gaze firmly on the horizon line. He'll look out for cormorants, seals, herons, all the great surprises of the park.

Once inside his place, he leaves the lights off and sits in front of the glowing computer screen. The city's necklace of lights rises in the darkened southwest.

The blog tells his story in remarkable detail. Apparently, she has one of those old-fashioned journalistic memories. Was it true about Dickens, that he'd walked the streets of London's underworld scribbling things in a notebook he kept hidden in his pants? And Joseph Mitchell, who'd gone down to the Fulton Fish Market to talk for hours about oysters and the harbour life, then come home and put it all down on paper. She has no hesitation about adding colour and detail where needed. She begins with a preamble about being "back on Cordova," with its "dropped-off-the-edge-of-the-world feel." And then there he is, in an open alley doorway.

There is a long digression regarding old-style outfitters' buy-and-sell shops. But parts of what she's written are fanciful. He has never been "sized up" by a prostitute. Sometimes, it was true, he was hit up for a handout, but that was as far as things went. The girls had seen him enough to know he wasn't coming around for afternoon sex. She presented a concrete picture of a character not quite himself, someone with more defined edges. It helped him see himself more clearly: if this was who she imagined him to be, maybe he ought to try harder to accomplish what the hell it was he'd supposedly set out to do.

She left herself out of it all. Though she was at the centre of most of the rest of the entries, she neglected to describe herself visiting his shop.

He is tempted to write to tell her that when he imagined hearing her play her dulcimer in his place, he'd understood what he was doing on Cordova in a new way. What he was creating became clear. The books upstairs were a hobby, leftovers from his work life and his father's collecting bug. But what was taking shape on the main floor was his real job. He was a working man now, like the loggers and dock workers and ferry boat guys who'd lived in the area for decades and then vanished. Regardless of her additions, the picture she drew of him—his back to the alley, shirtsleeves rolled up, washing glasses and plates, getting rid of a three-legged chair—was the real thing.

Stalin's Gift to the Ruined City

Ania gets off the train on Warsaw's Soviet-era underground tracks. They have been revamping things. There is an elevator now, and a proper set of shops. But something still reminds her of her childhood world of Russian-style squalor. She wheels her bag to the stairs and lifts it just high enough to lug it up to street level. She pulls it along the busy sidewalk to the ministry office, which is in the centre of the city. The trams roll by full, old folks and teenagers staring through the windows. She moves quickly through the sidewalk crowds. At her building the security guard—another born gatekeeper—insists, as always, on seeing her identification card. He runs it through the reader modeled on those used in airport passport booths and hands it back to her. She hears the cheery "okay" beep, which means she is, surprise surprise, still on staff and free, as the gatekeeper surely knows, to enter the building. Then her bag. He must have a thing for women's bags. Why else would he reenact this nonsense day after day? So he can put his hand on her scarf, her toiletry case, her copy of Edith Wharton's *Age of Innocence*. Once, he gazed hard at the copy of her mother's old Salinger book, as if it might offer up some revealing secret. Creepy. An asshole. Her father, so wrong about so many things (about almost everything, really), was right about the soulless gatekeepers.

She rides the elevator to her floor. Outside her office there sits an unfamiliar man. He wears some sort of casual tourist outfit, his face expectant. She remembers that a colleague had asked if she'd tour a visiting scholar around downtown Warsaw.

Ania does her best to cover her surprise at her own forgetfulness. This is the sort of thing that never happened to her until she embarked on her regular visits to see her mother. Lately, there was even more business and distraction as she served as the local liaison for the film shoot in the village square.

Her visitor is Dr. David Morgan from the University of Toledo. She invites him to sit in one of the lavish leather armchairs before her neatly organized desk. What sort of pat-down did he receive, she asks him, as he declared himself downstairs?

The guard treated him with some suspicion, he admits, until he spoke Polish, which seemed to help. His research is on wartime Warsaw, and his Polish is not bad. This is his first visit to learn first-hand about the city, its remaining Jews, the revival of interest in Poland's Jewish past.

"Well," she tells him, "I'm no expert on this. My expertise is quite specialized. More political than cultural. You should interview my mother. She's an expert on the things you are interested in." But when she sees he is about to take her up on this, she adds, "She lives far away. In the Stone Age. So you are stuck with me. Would you care," she asks, "to take a tour of the surrounding neighbourhood with me?"

Dr. Morgan is game. This is exactly what he wants, so they walk out together, heading toward the streets overshadowed by the grandly kitschy Palace of Culture and Science, the most grotesque monument in Europe to the cynicism and brute strength of Stalinism. Now in its vicinity, there are a Holiday Inn and a substantial shopping mall designed by Daniel Libeskind. When she points this out, David Morgan exclaims, "Ah, so that's what he's been up to." On Złota Street, the professor is pleased by something he sees.

"Here we say *Zwota*," Ania tells him. "Does it ring a bell?"

"It was inside the ghetto. The Jewish ghetto."

This latter phrase surprises her. Does he think Poles do not know what "the ghetto" refers to?

"In his diary, Emanuel Ringelblum mentions it many times. In one case, a Nazi functionary slaps him on Złota Street. It was a transformative experience, like when Sigmund Freud, walking with his father, was told by a policeman to get off the sidewalk."

Ania realizes that she must shift her points of reference when she talks to people like this. The past is the present. What is the movie title that sums it all up? *Back to the Future*, she reminds herself, as a red and yellow tram runs past them down the centre of the boulevard like a toy train.

They slip into a quiet neighbourhood and into the shadow of a large grey church. In postwar photos of Warsaw, it is one of the few structures standing. On Prozna Street, the sidewalk is covered by scaffolding that rings a block of derelict brick tenements. In a darkened window, an architect's model sits on a table. One storefront, a lone island of light, has been renovated to house a shop.

They enter. Inside, the proprietress has created a clean, well-lit space for the glass she makes, and for wooden lamps, which are the work of her son. She explains that the building belonged to a Jewish man before the war. He was killed and left no family. The city has owned it since the war, but she cannot explain why nothing was done with it for so many years. She points across the road at the matching tenements on the other side of the street. They were bought fifteen years ago by an American philanthropist for one *zloty*, with the promise to restore the block to the way it looked before the war. A kind of recovery project. Why he never carried through with this, she doesn't know. She has heard that an Austrian company has bought the buildings and will develop a luxury hotel, which will be good for her shop.

Ania leads the way around back into what is a familiar Warsaw courtyard, the building five stories high on three sides with an entranceway in the rear. The cobblestones in the courtyard are new, but everything else is of pre-war vintage. Ania points out the detritus of past lives: walls painted a sickly institutional green; a sheaf of brown packing paper against a window; the wing of a fan; the wrought-iron balconies. At ground level the only activity is provided by a trio of cats. The animals descend one by one into a window well. Efforts to seal it up with grates, upturned paving stones, cinder blocks, and plywood have not succeeded in preventing these basement dwellers from making this place their home.

To everything she points out, her visitor nearly shouts, *Amazing. Incredible. Unbelievable.* She wants to ask what, exactly, is amazing and incredible about these decrepit things? But she is not sure she wants to hear the answer.

"This is all very Polish," Ania says. "Old Polish things. Warsaw, from what I'm told, was a very different, lovely place before it was destroyed. But these things have nothing really to do with the New Poland. What we're looking at will be swept aside in the next few years. You and I are among the last who—pardon me for saying it this way—give a shit. If you visited my mother—which you can't—she would ask you, with her hands on her hips, in her country Polish, 'Who do you think, young man, cares about all this?'"

David Morgan considers this as he gazes up at the war-era tenement windows. Has she caught him wondering how the two of them might levitate up and through one of those windows to see what remains inside?

"I must get back to the office, Dr. Morgan." She offers her hand to shake. "I'm glad we met. We've seen a fair bit in a short time. Maybe it has changed your view of things."

Her visitor nods and thanks her for her time. With her hands in her jacket pockets she turns the toe of one shoe outward and points it back the way they came.

The Green, Green West

It is in the deep summer, with the beaches full, that Simon's mother seems to forget who she is. She goes out for a walk without her keys, then calls him from a payphone to come and let her into her house, even though a neighbour has a spare set. She reads novels late into the night, and, when she tires of that, watches the endless idiocy on American cable news. Fox fills her with another country's fears, which she accepts as her own. Then she is too exhausted to get to a doctor's appointment in the morning. Still, she is as purposeful as ever about keeping things in order in her kitchen. Simon has offered to find someone to help around the house, which is a big, old two-storey family home, with a steep set of stairs to the second floor and another, even steeper, to the basement. Nobody uses the upstairs now, but the washer and dryer are in the basement.

His mother won't consider hiring a stranger, so Simon visits often to keep an eye on things. When he does, he feels an odd combination of comfort and estrangement—almost an out-of-body experience—as he makes his way up the hill to the house where he grew up, as if he's both himself, as he is now, and the kid he once was. When he approaches at night, the lights in nearby houses are out. On the main floor of his mother's house they are all on. The yard is a jumble of overgrown trees. Branches heavy with leaves obscure the driveway where a neighbour parks a microbus with two rear flat tires. In order to have the spot, the bus owner is on standby for house repairs. Last autumn's leaves are on the ground, oak and chestnut crunching beneath Simon's shoes. The cement walkway is cracked. Roof tiles are nailed in a line on the wooden stairs. Who, he wonders, came up with that repair method? Maybe the microbus guy. On the porch, a kitchen chair stands with a bag of newspapers on its seat. He checks the date: six months past. He looks in through the glass in the front door, past the old couch and coffee table, at the old wooden piano against the far wall. There he'd practiced, as a kid, his hapless, rhythmless road to musical nowhere, regardless of his teacher's care with each new piece.

He presses the bell. It rings with a familiar half-broken quack, like a joke bell in a *Tom and Jerry* cartoon. He sees her coming from the back kitchen. A mug in one hand, her glasses around her neck on a chain. She opens the door and gives him a hug.

"It's a nice night," his mother says. "Let's sit out back." So, they go there. On the table on her porch, water—is it rainwater?—fills two pottery bowls. She asks the same questions each time he comes.

What is he doing for work?

Has he spoken to his father?

Where is he living?

The last question is the easy one to answer. He's been in the same studio apartment on Bute for more than four years. When he first moved in, he took her to see it, thinking it would give her something solid to hold in her mind. She could come by whenever she liked. He gave her a bus map on which he'd marked the route from her side of town, which required just one transfer at Smythe. They could eat dinner together, or watch from his window as the sky changed colours at sunset. He told her how reliably magnificent this was, on any day that wasn't completely overcast. But, naturally, the place hit her wrong. It was too small. The building was old. The one time she came a neighbour was out front smoking a fragrant cigarette; another had his saxophone on his knee and was making believe he could play it. The elevator smelled (as did the hallways) of cat spray and the new ethnic variety of Canadian cooking. It was city life distilled into a blend she didn't want her son to mix with.

And what was he doing for work? This theme had increased in anxious volume since the university let him go. Told him to hit the road. No doubt, she worried that he would soon be destitute. What, she wanted to know, was he doing to ward off disaster? Did he have a plan? His answer to this had shifted in the past months, in light of his project on Cordova Street. But this development made things seem worse to her. She hadn't been to Cordova Street in forty years. Wasn't it where hobos went for a drink and a flop? And a coffee house was something they had in pre-Soviet Russia, where revolutionaries discussed upending the empire. Was it not? Open stage, as far as she knew, was where people with no talent offered their work for free because nobody in their right mind would pay for it. How is he paying the rent down there? Who does he bring with him when he opens and closes? Does he read the newspapers to educate himself about the type of people who inhabit the beaten-down blocks of Hastings Street? Does he have some sort of death wish?

Their repetitive conversations are a workout. The death wish question makes him laugh. His laughter makes his mother even crazier with worry, because to her, laughter in the face of indiscriminate danger only confirms a total lack of common sense. *How, how, how* had they produced a child with such offbeat goals and hardly a plan? "They" meant herself and his father, whom she does not refer to by name, has hardly ever done since their divorce two decades before, when he walked out, sicced the meanest lawyer in the city on her—a lawyer whose effect on a room was like that of a tornado—leaving her with the house and not one penny more. To stave off disaster, she'd offered basement rooms for rent to put what they brought in together with what came from her government pension. With that she gets by, living frugally on some of the most valuable real estate in the country.

She unwraps her hands from the coffee mug and sets it down by the bowls brimming with rain.

When, he wonders, did it last rain? It seems like months since the last sighting of clouds in the west. Now and again a big crown of clouds sits atop the coastal mountains, but it never does roll down the western slope. What she has on her tabletop is *old water*.

"There is nothing I can do to help," she tells him, as if this is pressing news.

"Mom. I don't come up here for a handout. Dinner maybe."

She nods. But it was clear that out of this subject welled more guilt, more regret that their family life was a failure, leading to the final and most awkward question, about his father.

Has he heard from him?

"Not in a while."

"How long?"

"Oh. I don't know. He called a few weeks back. That was the first time in a couple months."

"Did you see him?"

"Mom. He was calling, I think, from Newport Beach. He just wanted to talk."

"About?"

"You know. The usual big plans. Some property he's developing near Coal Harbour. And he's feeling younger than ever, because of whatever new enthusiasm he's dedicating himself to. A new girlfriend. Pilates. He mentioned an invitation to a wedding in Queens."

"Queens. New York."

"A cousin is getting married. He hadn't planned to go but he heard from an old friend. Somebody he's known since before the war."

"In Queens? Your father was a child in Poland. Then Vancouver."

"He knew this guy when they were children."

"In Poland?"

"That's what he said."

She looks amazed. What is it she thinks in response to this? Whatever it is, she changes the subject. To raccoons. Raccoons are making a nest under her back deck. Would he go down and see?

He would. He is good at this sort of thing. He goes inside and gets the flashlight from the drawer where it sat when he was a child. He checks to see if the batteries are okay, and they are. Simon takes the steps down to his childhood backyard and looks up at the navy sky diamond-pinpricked with stars. He hears his mother shut the sliding back door as if to ensure no raccoons can follow her inside.

He sees nothing in the flashlight's funnel of light except a coiled hose. He backs out from under the deck and steps into the alley behind the house. Up it, a quick and demanding bike ride away, was the university. This is the closest he's been since he emptied his office and drove away, his mind such a frozen blank it was a miracle he didn't crash the car as he went. It had been one of those late long summers that Vancouver sees every decade or so. A month-long orgy of ear-popping dryness, an almost too-lovely kind of beach weather. Kits and Third Beach in Stanley Park were packed. The maple leaves had turned, caught fire, and filled the air with crimson and gold. How it broke his heart now to think of it. It made him think, too, of his childhood in the house where his parents' marriage had fallen apart, where he and his sister had grown into two remarkably different kinds of people and gone off to their separate lives, leaving their mother alone, surrounded by her own flaming trees. Eden was burning up here, no doubt about that.

He'd packed the books in his office in boxes he cadged from the liquor store on Fourth. He threw out file cabinets full of students' essays. For what laughable reason had he saved years of essays by students who had not even cared to pick them up? Some pseudo-legal expectation that if one had returned, two years after the fact, and found his B essay shredded, he might launch some sort of bizarre appeal. It surely didn't matter in the end. Everything in the file drawers was trash. He drove away from campus, the little borrowed blue Beetle packed with lamps and staplers and shelving, the windows rolled down to increase the bulk he could carry. He'd borrowed the car from a friend, and managed to graze the paint on a parking stanchion when he pulled up close to the building that housed his office.

It took him almost a year to figure out what was next. He had some money in the bank, and he knew, in the worst-case scenario, he could count on a loan from his father. He spent the ensuing year alone. He maintained his customary weekend visits to his mother's house. He took her to the Safeway, cut the lawn and bagged the greens for composting. Gradually, as the months passed, he felt his spirits lift, his sense of defeat forgotten. He passed long coffee-drinking afternoons at the kitchen table of one of his neighbours. His apartment in the West End was on a street that included a few of the old rooming houses and low-rise apartment blocks. The people who lived in these buildings were around a lot. He devoted a great deal of time to daily walks. He walked out of the city's more prosperous and pretty precincts and aimed himself at the failed old side of the downtown, which included Chinatown and the once-central business strip along Hastings, Pender, and Cordova.

His walks led to a new hobby. He stopped in pawnshops along the way. Their windows were hung with thousands of things on offer at little cost. One place specialized in boots and belts and suede jackets, workingman's gear of a long-ago era, now the get-up of downtown artists and students. Tennis racquets and guitars were mixed in with the rest. Another place he liked to visit specialized in wristwatches and a dizzying array of hand tools. In the outfitter's place, he bought a few pieces of clothing he liked, with the wet autumn in mind. It was then that his father called to tell him he was planning on getting rid of his books. Did Simon want them? He could keep or sell the collection, it was up to him.

Not so long after this, Simon was surprised to find one of his favourite second-hand stores closed. The sight of the locked door, the papered-over window, set his heart pounding. In the weeks that followed, he walked by to see what state of transformation the place was in. Movers emptied it out. A FOR RENT sign appeared. The idea crossed his mind that he might start something in the main-floor space. A new thing. But what? He put two quarters in the phone booth around the corner. It was a prop out of *Blade Runner,* broken and bent and graffitied with people's disdain for dying technology. He asked the agent what the rent was at 36 Cordova. It turned out to be cheap, month-to-month, and the lease included an upstairs floor in the building. There must have been a plan to tear the place down and the owner was buying time, hoping to cover the property taxes.

The businesses he'd come to like in the area were marginal places, side-thoughts in the neighbourhood's overall seediness and incompleteness: a coffee and jazz spot, a kind of throwback to some earlier forgotten bohemia; a gallery where the owner hung her friends' weird art, some of which was fashioned from hair, bees' wax, candle wax, from great mountains of collected cast-off objects. In one show the gallery's wood floor was entirely covered in sunflower seeds. What sort of sure-to-fail side dream might he pioneer, for a season or two, before it foundered and he, like the outfitter, was swept clean from the scene? As he figured this out he realized that he felt, for the first time in ages, like a free man.

The lights in his mother's house are out. How long has he stood out back in the yard? He places the flashlight on the edge of the back deck and turns down the alley. He will walk all the way home.

Abbott & Cordova

Simon finds himself visiting Nadia's blog against his better instincts. He tries to keep it to once a day. He has read about the time-wasters, the people addicted to repeated visits to social media sites, posting their latest meal or some funny thing written on the back of a bathroom door, until their minds are salads of harebrained two-second thoughts. Often, she does not add anything new for weeks, so he rereads old posts. He is embarrassed, always, when he rereads the entry that describes him. He has probably read it ten times.

Finally, something new appears. She has been back to his side of town, though not to his place. This disappoints him. He would like to make up for whatever he might have said that was odd or off-putting when she visited his Clandestine Book Room. It may be that showing it to her was an unfixable mistake. A sign of an idiosyncratic personality best avoided. Could his interest, fascination—whatever it is—with what she writes have anything to do with romantic ideas? If so, that will be news to him. He's alone and likes to be. The West End is full of loners like himself, which is one of the reasons he chooses to live where he does. He likes going home to make dinner for himself. When he heads over to the Shop, he leaves time to walk out of his way, to look in store windows and take in the vistas offered by West End streets. Sometimes he sees a neighbour, and they stop somewhere for a coffee and a slow, meandering talk. It's a West End kind of talk, he's decided, as if his big downtown neighbourhood is an isolated village in some far-flung landscape. We talk our own talk here, he tells himself. And it is when he thinks this that he feels he must never leave the city, not even the very street where he lives now. If he lives another sixty years—is that much available to him, like a couple of his long-living ancestors?—he must spend each season of those years between his corner of the West End and wherever he is headed. He feels, for the moment, like he's found his life, the life he was meant to lead before he managed to lose his way.

Nadia writes, under the title "Up Against the Ivory Tower."

This might read like an editorial (which it's not, I promise) but here is what struck me today: have you been down to the Woodward's stuff, the fake Aztec tower, the old store refurbished for TD Bank clients, the posters showing faces of locals, insisting on the new development's diversity? D-I-V-E-R-S-I-T-Y. I finally took a look at the gigantic art installation there, inside, by the pharmacy. Its name is *Abbott & Cordova, 7 August 1971*. Technically, it is spectacular. The glowing digital squares that make up the big picture. It is a beautiful, mesmerizing alternative to those Jumbotrons in sports stadiums. It's true that the east side has little public art, and most of the public undertakings are related to addiction, community networking, and housing, and on and on as if the people here have no brains, no hearts, and are creatures whose needs stop at clothing, housing, food, and social services. Well, we all need a little art sometime, so *Abbott & Cordova* is what the neighbourhood got.

There is some carping about how much it cost. Over a

million dollars. This could have been spent on more practical things (so says an aggravated, holier-than-thou skateboard spray-painter who got the ear of the community organizers and is now their local saint).

I think it's okay if it takes $1 million to make a thing as large and incredibly detailed and unusual as *Abbott & Cordova, 7 August 1971*. That is what art is about. Sometimes it's paper and scissors. And sometimes art is $1 million on the wall very high above the courtyard of some dark and towering buildings.

Abbott & Cordova, 7 August 1971 is a picture of a street corner not far from where the installation itself hangs. Its subject is the faraway edge of a disturbance, a riot, a fiasco that pitted hippies against cops. It pictures long-haired girls, running teenage boys, helmeted cops on horseback, and it points back to a nearly forgotten time in the city's past. I know who was wrong and who was right back then. I wonder if the artist meant to tell a morality tale. In shimmering blues and reds and greys he lets us know: cops bad, hippies okay. You can look at the mural and know whose side you're on. Not the dumbly assertive, neatly uniformed, pointlessly aggressive cops. You are a hippie for the couple minutes you gaze up at a long-haired guy being shoved into a police van. You are surely not one of the middle-class types who stand on the fringes, in neat suits and colourful dresses, waiting for the light to change, for this whole demonstration situation to blow through, so they can get on to whatever it was they came to do on the early 1970s streets of the city's east side. No. You cannot be one of these average types without feeling stupid. And you can't be one of the cops without feeling like you've sold your soul.

So it's worth asking, who is this picture for? The students attending courses at the new downtown university campus? If they bother to look. The owners of the pricey condos in the sky above the mural? Maybe. Does public art raise real estate values? But how often do they care to stop in for a peek at the courtyard where it hangs? I stood there once. I was the average-sized girl, dark hair and eyes, in jeans and a T-shirt, thinking. I was thinking about Carrall and Cordova, April 1962. Bright morning blue. The way things turn against you. And that's it. You're finished.

★

Simon goes back to the top to reread Nadia's post. How much he has learned, in a few paragraphs, about the neighbourhood he's taken as his own. He will have to visit this art installation. He hasn't bothered to go over in the time he's been working downtown. But now he has a reason. To check her words against the million-dollar thing high up in the air.

He thinks: that dulcimer girl, she has the strangest Tinker Bell effect on me. Just her words on a screen offer that sudden shift in temperature, a change of mind.

Something This Way Comes

Simon is busy doing nothing, musing over what she's written about Abbott and Cordova. There is work to do down at the Shop. A business is a twenty-four-hour-a-day responsibility, as he reads in the business section of the newspaper. After this, the article lists ten or fifteen things he already knows, having run his place for some eight months. He shoots the newspaper into the recycling box.

The lobby buzzer rings. He presses the button for the intercom.

"Yes?"

"Son?"

"Who?"

"Simon."

"Dad?" He nearly reels. His father has never visited him at this address. He rarely calls. Dead air follows. Maybe if he says nothing his father's voice will turn into someone else's. Another person altogether will be down there in the cat-smelling lobby.

"Simon. Can I come up?"

"Dad. Why are you here?"

"I need to talk." His father's voice lacks its usual timbre, as if he's fogged by flu. Simon hears something that sounds like a sob.

He holds the button that unlocks the front door and steps into the hallway. When the elevator clatters to its place on his floor, there is a moment after the door has opened when no one appears. Has his father changed his mind and headed for the street? He steps toward the elevator and his father turns the corner. Rushing forward, his father takes hold of him and holds on tight, sobbing.

"Dad?"

"Oh, Simon."

"What's happened?" He thinks of his mother. Or is it the latest failed romance? In the past, his father's would-be partners came and went without any emotional ups or downs. Is it an earthquake? Has a disaster in some far-off country taken out some big investment plan?

"It's Ray Bradbury."

"Who?"

"Ray Bradbury's dead." His father stands nose to nose with him, resting his hands on Simon's shoulders. It's a kind of Godfather pose, expressing love and total authority at the same time.

"Ray Bradbury. He summed up my youth."

"Dad. Your youth wasn't spent on Mars."

This breaks the spell. His father marches into his apartment and Simon follows, as if he is the visitor and his father the owner of all that he sees. For a moment they stand, one behind the other, before the remarkable view. The park below. The downtown high-rises and the streets approaching the Cambie Street Bridge. The bridge's amber lights glow in a soft procession across to False Creek, where the roadway lifts again toward the wedding-cake silhouette of city hall. His father turns his attention to the apartment, which, though it may have a million-dollar view, is inescapably odd in its Art Deco compactness. The bed, not quite a Murphy bed but something stranger from the forties, slides out of the wall like a huge drawer. Sleeping in it makes Simon think of lying in a coffin. Once he dreamed someone snuck into his place at night and shoved the drawer-bed back into the wall with him under the covers. On either side of the bed, up a couple of narrow linoleum-covered steps, are strange cubbies, like a ship's cabins. One is the kitchen, the other a bathroom suited in size to a child. He's lived here alone now for four years, devoted to the view and reasonable rent.

His hands on his hips, his big head surveying the place, his father nearly yells, "How in hell do you live in a shithole like this?" And then he's off, marching about, poking into the kitchen and bathroom. Simon's father manages a half-hearted effort to drag out the drawer bed, but it resists him, and he leaves it jammed partway open.

"Dad. Honestly. I don't remember a thing about Ray Bradbury. I might've read him in junior high. What's his big one called? *Dandelion Wine*?"

His father opens one cupboard after another, takes down a glass and fills it with tap water. He drinks and sets the glass in the sink, then reaches into his breast pocket for a page of newsprint, which he unfolds carefully.

"Listen. From the *New York Times*. They've got obituaries that read like novels. This is what Bradbury said about his boyhood in Waukegan, Illinois. *Waukegan*. Don't you like the sound of that? 'It was one frenzy after one elation after one enthusiasm after one hysteria after another. You rarely have such fevers later in life that fill your entire day with emotion.' And here, but it's too long to read. I'll leave it for you. It's this wonderful description of how, when he steps out the front door of his family house into the early morning, it feels as though it's him setting everything in action. Here. 'He gave the town a last snap of his fingers. Doors slammed open; people stepped out. Summer 1928 began.'" His father looks up from the paper in his hand. "That's exactly, exactly how those years felt to me. When I was six or seven. Listen. I told you about my travel plans. The wedding. I'm going because it's a chance to see an old friend who happens to be close with the groom's parents. We're all, in a way, connected."

"You mean from Poland."

"Yes, but it's who we were that counts, not where we're from. Something in me wants to see him again. Old Mike. And I'm a free man. You know Christie?"

"The investment manager. I never met her, you told me—"

"She moved on. Holy shit, am I relieved. She was possibly—now I know these things are difficult to measure—the most expensive girl I was ever with. What was her salary? Over two hundred thousand a year. And do you think she ever picked up a restaurant cheque?"

"I'm a cheap date, I guess."

His father considers this. "You are, but that's just a coincidence. You are good company, too. I thought of asking because you always wanted to know where our family came from."

"Remember what you used to say, Dad? 'I come from Prior Street,' from 'Abbott and Cordova.' Because that's where you got started." He was a child again, asking the same questions that had never been answered.

"Well, that's it. That's where I got started. What, maybe a year with the chickens for koshering house to house. I forget what made me look downtown. Some of the guys I delivered chickens to had shops along Hastings and Cordova. Usually rented, and the odd guy would tell me how the rent was going up. Back then a $10 hike could kill a guy. So, it was clear to me that owning was the avenue to independence. Jesus, I got some of 'em for a few thousand dollars. Clear title. Like I owned my own little corner of the world. In those days you could always eyeball a tenant, the taxes were nothing. The city never bothered you about anything.

I don't know what the city was busying itself with back then. Harassing the Japanese? There was good business to be done down there."

"There still is, in its way."

"I want to talk to you about what you've started. I'm gonna come down some time and see. Anyway. I wouldn't be surprised if I owned the building you're in at one time. What's the address?"

"36 Cordova."

His father thinks, trying to visualize the block.

"Sounds familiar. Anyway, what do you say to Queens? You and me. Like when you were small and we went out to the beach and walked and talked. Remember? Like a normal family. Wait. Let me read you one more thing that got me. Honestly, Bradbury dying. It just drowned me in a wash of memories. Now that you mention Cordova, there was a place down there—what was its name? Salvage or Salvation Association. Something like that. I'd come down, collect the rents and grab a few paperbacks. Some, I'll admit, were a little smutty. Or they made the covers smutty and what was inside just made no sense. *Mandingo*? Remember that one? Do they ever teach that in university?"

"Dad, that's horrible soft-core garbage."

"But they're teaching the soft-core garbage now. I know. I check the course listings in the fall for the downtown courses. I will find you a course with just that title: 'Horrible Soft-Core Garbage 101.' Am I right or am I right?"

"Well, you're not far off."

"Twenty-five cents apiece. For *Mandingo*, and whatever else was there. You read 'em and you tossed 'em or you threw 'em in a box in the basement. Or the guy would trade you. No user's manual required. That's when I rediscovered science fiction. A huge blast of memory came out of that, of when I was a green kid here in this city, reading the pulps to try to figure out what it meant to talk like a guy off the street. You know, into the sixties, the writers were still coming up with how the space age would look. Some of it ended up happening. We'd all move to Mars, or no more cars. Jet packs and freeze-dried doo-doo for dinner, like the astronauts. Bradbury's books were a little different. They had a sweetness to them that the others lacked. Listen." His father gazes at the news clipping. "Here it is. He told an interviewer, 'All my life I've been running through the fields and picking up bright objects. I turn it over and say, Hey, there's a story.'"

As his father reads this, a tear moves in a straight line down one cheek. No sobbing or gesticulating. Just the silent tear pointing somewhere deep and hidden. It's the tear that causes Simon, against his better instincts, to agree. He'll go along to Queens to see what's on offer.

The Eighteen

Ryszard Jankowski sets foot in Piłsudski Square, hands in the pockets of his day-off jeans, tan pork pie hat perched on the crown of his head. The movie people rush around him. He scans the crowd and catches the eye of the young production manager who visited him at the archive. She said her name was Charlotte, but he should call her Charlie. She is American, with Polish-born parents. There was something, too, about a grandmother living near Krakow. She speaks passable Polish, enough to read a Polish-language newspaper and understand the gist. But they came to know each other in English, which Jankowski handles with precise formality. During university he took a year abroad with the idea that he might become a teacher of languages. But nothing came of this. He lived in a little room in a London tenement, then brought his newfound skills—useful to spies and underground agitators—back to his hometown, Mława.

At the archive, Charlie had asked to see anything he had regarding pre-war ownership around the square: who owned which properties; what sort of businesses had been in place up until the occupation? And then she asked if he had contacts with the present owners, anyone who might be willing to rent their property as a location for the film she was producing? She was hoping to find an authentic, well-preserved prewar interior. He was habitual in his response to such queries—some were potentially very dangerous questions—so at first he had said no to everything, without hesitation. He had no information of this kind at all. But when he realized it was for a movie project, which would put the area on national television; that the people working on it were from Warsaw and had support from the city's cultural grants office; that it would bring money into the village and its surrounding area; and that nobody was in danger of having their property claimed by the children of murdered Jews, he decided to help her out. Birth and death and marriage records existed on handwritten pages in big leather-bound volumes. Property transactions, births and deaths, everything had been preserved. Names. Ages. Business and legal cases brought before local courts, requests by the Jewish community, reaching far back to Czarist times. His archive was a guidebook to the dead, and to the decimated Jews of the area. The record of their lives was intensely, almost overwhelmingly preserved.

So he'd set her up—young Charlie—in a windowless back room of his archive building with a copier and the old volumes themselves. When you opened them, dust rose from the pages like a movie effect. And the dust smelled, he had to admit, like the lives of many, many people who were gone. Charlie went to work. She asked him about hundreds of things—people's clothing before the war, the interiors of their homes, forms of transport, what people ate and drank. And back she'd go to her production company in Warsaw, to her set designer and location manager, to create what he viewed as a reliably accurate, historically ambitious project. This was, he thought, Charlie's goal.

Today's shoot is a scene calling for many babushka-wearing and package-lugging Jews. These bit players, in their carefully muddied and ripped rags, meander about in Radzanów's central square drinking coffee from paper cups while they wait for their scenes to be called.

Jankowski feels for the photocopied page in his pocket. It is evidence of one of the odder things he discovered following *Pani* Ania's visit, with her box of dug-up oddities.

Charlie waves, mouthing that he must give her one minute.

He retreats to a stoop not far from Ania's mother's house to wait. Later he might knock on the old lady's door. She was a fount of information about the village today, tomorrow, and sixty years before. She had the genes for recall, whatever they were. She seemed to have known everyone. Or maybe it was her parents who'd had dealings with villagers, farmers, travelling salesmen, the local Jewish craftspeople. And then there was the strange quirk of her holding onto a dead house on the square. From where Jankowski sits he can see its grey boards, its nickel-coloured tin roof. A typical Jewish house of the century before. Once, he tried the front door, but its ancient bolt held firm. He had dropped hints when talking with the old lady that he would appreciate a look inside. But she crossed her arms over her chest with a look that seemed to say *I'll punch you out if you raise this subject again*. So he dropped it. He had no doubt that a right cross from Ania's mother would send him straight to the hospital back in Mława.

Charlie is before him, her brown hair piled high on her head. A light-coloured scarf wrapped around her neck. She greets him with a girlish enthusiasm he finds endearing. If he'd had a daughter, he'd have taken pride in one like her.

"What are you doing in Radzanów?"

He takes the Xeroxed sheet from his pocket. "I have something for you."

"Really?"

"We need to sit. I'll show you."

"Okay. See that trailer over there? It's unlocked. There's really bad coffee and *drozdzówki* inside. Wait for me and I'll finish this set-up we're doing."

Jankowski heads across the square. It is livelier than it has been in decades, with what seems like fifty tech people and actors milling about. What was the village population? Less than a thousand. The film shoot created a temporary population boom. The director of photography sits behind his camera, waving and shouting at his assistants as they set up the shoot.

The trailer by the big church smells of cinnamon and burnt coffee. Jankowski sits in a white plastic chair. He places the Xeroxed sheet he has brought with him on one of the card tables covered in craft service food and paper plates.

Charlie opens the trailer door and settles down beside him. He hands her the sheet of paper, which she spreads flat on her knees. "Is it from here?"

"In a way. Not exactly." The Xerox shows two images, one atop the other. Jankowski points to one and says, "Recto." The other he calls, "verso."

"Was it a card of some kind? A postcard?"

"Of a very—how do you say?—explosive kind. It's one of the eighteen." His face is a mask as he awaits a response.

Charlie shrugs. She has no idea what "the eighteen" might be.

"It's a complicated story. I'll do more research. But here is the skeleton. The card was made in Germany. By a young couple. A factory worker and his wife. Otto and Elise Hampel. He, a fitter in a Siemens factory, and she, a servant in someone's home. Together they distributed cards like this, always with subversive messages. This one reads: *Der Hitler Krieg ist dess Arbeiters Tod*! Hitler's war is the workers' death."

Charlie nods, a little shocked. "What became of them? The couple."

"They were betrayed. It's possible someone saw them dropping things in a way that looked suspicious. But here's the crux. This is how you say it? They carried their project on long enough for the police to believe they were confronting an underground resistance movement. They were caught. In 1943. A bad year for everybody. They were interrogated, and it became clear that of the hundreds of cards they distributed, all were turned in but eighteen. The Hampels knew how many they'd printed, and the police knew how many they had collected. This tells us something remarkable. However many Germans there were who found these messages, almost all were the kind of do-gooding Germans who did just what they were told. Then, there were the mysterious eighteen. Who might they have been? Maybe, among these eighteen, there were some who, for whatever reason, destroyed the cards they found. Cut them into pieces and flushed them down the toilet. Soaked and ground them up in their morning gruel and swallowed them. Buried them in the garden not so far from where they'd buried their cat or dog. Think of it: as you gaze out over your kitchen table at the piece of ground where the provocative words were hidden, you couldn't help but wish you might retrieve them to read them again. It's a story with great possibility, wouldn't you say?"

Charlie agrees. It is. "But what does it have to do with here? With this place?"

"I don't know that yet. But I will find out and I will bring you this part of the story, too."

"Can you make me a copy of the card?" Charlie asks.

He offers the one in his hand. "I brought this for you."

The square has reverted to its characteristic quiet, as if shooting is done for the day. The old lady's villa window is dark. The bus awaits. Jankowski takes a seat and rides back toward the historic Mława front.

The Memoir of Jesse James

Nighttime on Cordova. Smells and sounds. A bit furtive but quiet. I put myself on the list at the Shop. Why I'm ready to play there, all of a sudden, I don't know. The other stuff's horrendous. How can he stand it? The loopy poets. There's the odd sensitive girl in a summer dress. I am interested in what they have to say. They seem entirely naked. None of the guys make any sense. It's like open stage is some sort of rite of passage for them. But it isn't easy. Some come up with a few too many beers in them. It's a little stage, the size of a dining room table. You've got to make sure you don't put your foot wrong or you'll fall off. A country and western swing band comes up, and the music is good, but they've got their instruments in each other's faces. The drummer hits his snare and looks like he might topple over on his back.

He's got staff now, a woman clearing tables and a young guy who takes names for the open mic. For once, I put myself on the list. I tell him: Nadia. I will play two songs on the dulcimer. I sit at the back deciding how authentic to make it. What sort of pressure to put on myself. I won't play the same things I played out on the stoop. That would be cheap. I take off my coat and put it under my chair. Before I go on, a longhaired guy plays some sort of performance chant piece on an electric guitar covered in electrical tape (what's the deal; is the thing a fire hazard?). I see a few guys in the back start to snicker and step out. Inadvertent hilarity. It comes out of nowhere at open mic.

I am not introduced. They don't do that at Simon's place. I get the signal and I just come up. The room is quiet but for a few clinking plates and clicking chess pieces. I can hear them calling out "check" at the chess tables by the window. When I hit the first notes, I know it's going to work. The dulcimer is so strange and strong. It resonates in the room, a rhythmic chiming, and everyone grows still and quiet. I play a klezmery thing, the way I imagine the guys might have played it in 1890 at a Polish nobleman's wedding. Rough and wild. I can tell I've got the audience's interest, so I give it an extra few verses. When I finish, there's a moment of silence, just dead quiet, then hooting and applause and talk and everything you'd expect from a room full of people who are a little drunk, short on money, and out for a good time on Saturday night. Then I take a chance with "Those Were the Days." The old Mary Hopkin chestnut. I can still see the Apple record label spinning on my parents' turntable. And I do something I hardly ever do: I sing, in my just-serviceable voice. "Those were the days, my friend, we thought they'd never end." It's just one of those songs. A heartbreaker. It is very satisfying to sing it out in that room with strange faces gazing up at me. I feel as if I've snuck into a secret cave and uncovered the genie's lamp. And that's it. I know the way out the back, so I gather my things and head that way. I disappear down the alley I came up in daylight. The locals are doing their stuff out there. Smells and sounds. Like the scene in *Dead Man* where Johnny Depp walks into the railroad town of Machine and gets an eyeful along the way. A real Old West free-for-all. The Shop might be one of those old-time saloons, with horrible poetry instead of honky-tonk. The neighbourhood, its cut-off quality, the way it makes people in the city titter, seems clearer to me than ever.

A Map of the City

Travelling with his father is a bizarre form of torture. First class all the way, and a never-ending stream of pugnacious, self-assured storytelling and world-repairing philosophy. A favourite tag line is "PIECE OF ADVICE," nearly shouted, as the entrée into whatever it is Simon's father decides he needs to improve in his life. In the old days, the "piece of advice" usually came with a relevant book or article title or museum show he *had* to see if he was going to understand *how the world works now*. But the world has changed, and now his father's final word is *Look it up, I'll send you the link*. On the crucial point of how to handle any personal challenge, the advice is always a version of: "You gotta get up every morning with a plan. You gotta walk through barbed wire and eat broken glass."

Was this sort of hardnosed worldview—more relevant to the boxing ring or a stock-exchange trading floor than family discussions—related to his father's uprooted youth? The lost connection with his childhood before Canada. Those unspeakable years, his Polish home, his parents, about whom he never said a word beyond a dismissal.

"Forget it, son," he used to say. "I forgot it all, and what I don't forget I'm working on forgetting, okay?" This, Simon imagined, was all connected with the need to remake himself in Vancouver, to set down a foundation with no one at all to help him.

Who knew? But as they sit in their wide leather first class seats he cannot help feeling depleted at the prospect of days in New York listening to his father assert that the answer to the widest variety of needs or desires is to dine on crushed glass.

★

For crushed-glass-eaters they treat themselves well. A gleaming Lincoln brings them in from LaGuardia to the Essex House Hotel near Central Park South. God. The people walking by on the street are a full-scale carnival of excess and want. While his father checks in, he stands in the heat on the sidewalk and lets it all go by. Business executives and delivery guys and a great groaning garbage truck.

Their suite is big enough to house an entourage, with a gigantic sitting room with a view of Central Park. He finds bathrooms inside closets hidden along hallways. The management sends up a complimentary table on wheels with salads and chopped fish and bread under pewter bells. His father lifts each bell, sniffing, but takes nothing, as if to spite the compliments of the house.

While his father changes, Simon drinks a tall glass of water with a slice of lemon from the room service offerings riding its surface. He stands by the window and watches Manhattanites walk and drive and bike down the great canyons in the distance. The wedding is late in the day, so his father insists that they visit a gallery where he has bought things in the past. They walk at his father's hopped-up rate, jaywalking and aggressively window-shopping the stores of the Upper East Side. The gallery stands out on the street. It is a high-ceilinged glass box pushed in between two old brownstones. On display inside are huge photorealist cityscapes, which are his father's latest passion. Four and five feet square, nighttime landscapes of river embankments along roadsides, bridges lit like wedding cakes, darkening skies catching the reflected light of a city or the moon behind a whiff of cloud.

"What do you think of this one?"

His father stands in front of the biggest painting in the place, a rectangle of dark purple and almost black shapes. In the foreground are six or seven teenagers sitting on a stone retaining wall that overlooks a lake, doing what young people do now: faces lit in the dark by the light of their phones. One has set a huge plastic jug of juice down on the wall. In the background, across an inlet or riverbank, lights shine silvery on the surface of the water. It's painterly and interesting but for some reason it scares the shit out of Simon. He wants to ask his father why he would want to live with such things. What's in the painting's story that pulls him? Maybe it's the god's-eye view of anonymous expanses. He bends in to read the price.

"Dad. $15,000?"

His father shrugs, gives him a familiar *Who cares?* look and moves on along the wall of art, his hands behind his back. "You have to come by my place. See what I've got. I think you'll find it interesting. You know what Christie used to say? It looks like fashion ads without the brand name. But she was wrong. It looks like someone else's life, under a magnifying glass."

Simon has been in his father's condominium twice. It looks out over Coal Harbour and Stanley Park from a very high floor. The millionth floor. It provides the same god's-eye view as the paintings. But he was there so briefly he remembers nothing about what was on the walls or how it was furnished. All he remembers is white and grey inside, the great green wall of trees surrounding the park outside.

They step back into the afternoon stew of humidity and idling cars and march back the way they came.

The wedding is far into Queens. They ride in the over-air-conditioned back seat of a Town Car. Its tinted windows veil the sight of the city, so they are hardly aware when they leave the crosstown traffic for the bridge that spans the river toward the outer borough. His father is agitated, even more talkative than usual. He is excited by the prospect of reconnecting with his childhood friend. He has not seen Mike in thirty-five years. Once he came up to Vancouver from New York, but after that their connection fell off.

"It was me," his father says. "I didn't answer his letters. He'd call me at the office and the little message paper would sit on my desk for weeks. Once the guilt takes over for not calling back, you never do."

"Why did you let yourself lose touch?"

His father fiddles with the window button. Humid afternoon air rushes in.

"I don't know. There's a time in your life when these sorts of things don't seem to matter. I figured I was on top of the world. Fuck the past. You know? But then you get older and it starts to look different."

Simon has no idea what to make of this but puts a hand on his father's knee. What a mess their family is. Everything broken. But then he wonders if this is entirely true. He thinks of himself as a young boy, careless, unaware of whatever these things meant to his parents or to his family. He was not unlike the Ray Bradbury kid, stepping out the front door of their home and snapping his fingers. *Get started, summer, nineteen-seventy-whatever-it-was.* All the possibilities of youth were there. He tries to imagine his father doing the same. Stepping from his parents' Polish village house, in the old-fashioned world that had disappeared from the little town north of Warsaw where they lived. This much he can imagine, but no more.

The wedding venue is a substantial, aging white clapboard synagogue on a neighbourhood street. They are among the latecomers, so no one greets them at the door. They make their way through the building to a tightly fenced courtyard out back.

"Dad," he whispers over his father's shoulder, "did your friend become a Chassid?"

His father snorts. He points at a single light-coloured suit in the crowd, worn by a grey- haired man with a tiny white *kipa* on his head. "That's Mike. Whoever's religious, maybe the groom, it's not Mike."

The ritual holds them rapt. They watch as the bride and groom, people they know nothing about, go through one of the momentous days of their lives. The *chupa* is hung with greenery, and the crowd leans toward it with great energy. In the outpouring of people after the ceremony his father and his old friend come face to face on the synagogue's front steps. They clasp each other tightly, like sportsmen celebrating a great victory. But his father's friend is with the wedding party and is swept away as quickly as he appeared.

It is early evening, the heat coming down just a bit, but people are red-faced and sweaty from the long ceremony. The sidewalk fills with wedding-goers. In the near distance, their car waits, engine idling. His father hands a card with the address for the wedding dinner to the driver, who ever so slightly raises his eyebrows. The next stage of their trip calls for some GPS nonsense. They travel up a street of identical postwar brick bungalows and hit a dead end. Back they come, following a dizzying map on the driver's screen, arriving at the padlocked gate of a rail yard.

"Don't worry," the driver says, sounding worried. "We're nearby."

"We'll be late," his father says. "But who cares? Right?"

No one. No one cares.

Another twenty minutes of twists and turns in the wilds of Queens and the car slides to the curb. His father pays with twenties. An elevated train runs above their heads. The block is lined with chop shops. The wedding venue's brightly lit sign reads "Queens Wedding Headquarters." The place is a huge red and gold conference barn. It feels, once they are inside, like a giant pinball machine. A pinball machine in a Martin Scorsese movie. There is a table with guests' names on cards to let them know where to sit. His father heads for the bar.

"Something cold. It's a million degrees outside," he tells the unsmiling kid in a shiny vest. "Gimme a tall glass of juice, with lots of ice, okay?"

No answer. Just the glass clanked on the bar top like a barbell.

They check their seating card and make their way to a table tight to the wall. They are the first to sit down. Soon their tablemates arrive. It's a single guys' table. Single, and except for Simon, old. One old-timer shakes his hand so vigorously he fears it'll snap. Another, upon taking a chair, swings around to call for a waiter. But service is unavailable until every chair is taken. This triggers the plates of roast chicken leg, mashed potatoes, and peas. Servers fling the plates down as if they are serving Frisbees or manhole covers.

The men at their table range in age from their seventies to their nineties. They are divorced or their wives are dead. Most of them are survivors, but not all. A few, like his father, came to America before the war. Their second lives have gone well. Some lost their first families in the war and then remarried. In the 1950s and '60s they bought third- and fourth-rate real estate, which they held onto until it turned to gold. One owns a hotel off Times Square that had been a flophouse for twenty years and is now worth too much to sell. Each one, it turns out, by some link, however near or distant, has roots in a place called Radzanów, not far from Warsaw.

"How far?" Simon asks, trying to include himself in the conversation.

A few of the old guys look at his father. Has he not told his son anything?

"We went by train," one of the men says, "but also by cart. It makes a difference which way."

His father doesn't like this line of talk. "Carts. By the time I left, no one went by carts."

A grey face sitting beside Simon's father asks, "In what year did you leave?"

"1937."

"So. You were a kid. And you were lucky. Did you even realize how lucky, leaving at that time? What's your family name?"

When his father says it, their tablemates go quiet. Their bantering energy simply evaporates. The grey-faced man holds out a hand.

"You're the son."

"I am. The son."

"Well, pardon me. I must say, meeting you is a pleasure. My name is Max Feinstein. Here in America. At home I was Feivel."

The two men shake hands. Max settles back in his chair. He fiddles with the handkerchief in his jacket pocket.

They eat in silence. After the main dish is taken away, a platter of pink and blue desserts is set in the centre of the table. One of them pronounces "Feh" and gives the plate a little push toward the far side of the table. His neighbour nods sadly. "Those we can live without."

His father asks about a family he knew, who lived nearby. The Grabowskis.

"From what I know," Max says, "still there."

His father's face falls as he takes this in. He has never seen his father cowed by anything before, the force of nature out-forced.

In a lull in the talk, he leans over to Simon.

"I'm going to find Mike. You stick it out here with these guys. Save my seat. Okay?"

In a few moments he's back, his old friend in tow. The old-timers around the table shake Mike's hand, extend greetings, along with a few side comments about the religiosity of the wedding.

"Back in Poland we were running from it. Here, they want it back."

"Listen," Max adds, "in the old country we were all mixed up in one family. My mother had a brother, he'd go off like a pilgrim to the Alexandrover Rebbe. Remember?" The others nod. "One shaved his beard. He was a middleman with the farmers. He'd buy wheat and bring it in to the mill. So, from Polish farmers to Jewish millers in one afternoon. Modern, religious, *Chassidish*. It wasn't such a reason to look at the ground when someone different walked by."

General agreement ensues, and Mike is eased into a chair pulled from a neighbouring table. He and Simon's father hold hands—actually hold hands, like young marrieds. While the others monopolize his father, Simon is pulled into a conversation with Mike. "What do you know," he asks, "about your family? In Poland."

"Nothing," he says.

"What, nothing? Your father told you nothing?"

He shakes his head.

"Well, it's something to tell. Listen. It's no small thing. Maybe you will appreciate this, and maybe not. But your family, they were impressive people. In Yiddish the word is *edel*. You've heard such a word?"

He shakes his head.

"Well, here's how I would put it. They were not big-timers in the area. Other people were richer and some were better connected in the towns around. In Szreńsk. Drobin. Bieżuń. Ciechanów. There they had a crusader castle. And I bet if you look in the memorial book—"

"What's a memorial book?"

Mike pauses to consider the ignorance he is dealing with. "Anyway, in the documents after the war they won't be mentioned. But this is to their credit. The ones who placed themselves at the forefront, editing newspapers or, once the war came, running the Jewish council, with lists and such, do you suppose they did these things for purposes of self-sacrifice?"

He shrugs.

"Listen," Mike continues. "What's easier to remember, that so-and-so was the area's biggest cloth trader, or that so-and-so was intelligent, a solid character, and when you talked to him he made you feel the world was worth living in? Who remembers that guy? Sit here with us long enough and listen. This one stole. That one cheated. Another abandoned his family and became rich in California. We all have a child's fascination with what's awful and strange, or larger than life. And uprightness? Who talks about this except Elie Wiesel and the Pope? Those clowns. A Jewish Pope is much, much worse than the real one. I can tell you that for sure."

Simon's father leans in to join the conversation. Mike tells his father about his wife's death. "Last winter. After a long illness. But I'll admit it to you. I'm enjoying this stage of life. I'm making the most of it. And this, this'll surprise you."

The heads around the table turn to listen.

"I've been back."

"Back where?" His father takes a long slow drink of juice.

"Poland."

The others around the table grow quiet. His father sets his glass down. No one says a thing, so Mike continues. There is a lot to report. The longer the conversation drags on, the more Simon fades into the background, unseen and unheard. At last his father drops his guard. His usual bluster gives way to pure curiosity.

"Mike, tell me. What's it look like now?"

"Parts are not so different from how they were. Around the market square. Those plank-front houses our parents owned. Some still stand. The church. Just the same from outside. Like it was yesterday. And the synagogue. I took pictures. Hold on." The hall has grown quiet. Most of the guests have left and the staff has settled down to their meal of leftovers. Mike produces his phone and pokes about at its screen. He hands it over.

"Here."

His father's eyes narrow as he concentrates on the screen.

"I know it's small. I can send it. You can look at it again yourself. But here." He pulls up another photograph and runs his finger along the topmost line of buildings, where the town meets the green countryside. What looks like a riverbank curves through the green. "Here was our town. Forget this." He points to a branching road that descends toward the bottom of the screen with warehouse-sized structures on it. "In the old days that was farms. So here, look. You see the church." He points to a white building, easily the biggest structure after the warehouses. "And this," he lays a finger beneath an ochre-coloured square. "That's the synagogue."

"Amazing." His father holds the phone screen in his two palms. His eyes seem to run from one side of the old town to the other, following Mike's guiding finger through what was the market square. Under his breath he mutters, "Holy shit. It's amazing."

"It is funny, isn't it, to think of them there all this time without us."

"Who's there?"

"Well, a lot of young people who don't have an idea about

anything. God, teenagers in Poland, teenagers in wherever. It's all the same once the government gets out of their way. They turn into beer-drinkers and what have you. But the Grabowksa. Remember her?"

A faraway look crosses his father's face.

"I thought you would." He takes the phone back and with a toothpick points at a small square off the market road. "See here? This was your house."

His father hardly looks so Mike offers it around. The tiny town in the countryside could be a toy model, the sort of thing train enthusiasts build out of finger-sized bits of wood and greenery, miniature pebbles and coloured sand.

"And I can show you one other thing." Mike looks at Simon's father. "Your son, he might want to see this. I brought it because I knew you would both be here. When my parents gave up their house in Queens, I found it. Let's let your son tell us who's in this photo."

Mike presents a black and white print, three-and-a-half inches square, from the early days of studio photography. On its back an address is written in florid handwriting, which is what landed it across the sea. The photo is a study in greys and silvers, like an etching on pewter, a neat white border around its edges. The scene it shows looks staged. Low in the picture there is a skiff, a high-sided boat. In it are two boys. Above the waterway on which they float is a bridge with a rail. Behind the rail stand a boy and a girl. The girl's hair is the lightest thing in the photo, almost white against the grey sky. Simon points to the boy on the bridge.

"Is this Dad? Beside the girl."

Mike takes the photo. He pulls a pair of glasses from his breast pocket and puts them on. And he laughs. "Of course! You're right."

"Then who are the rest?"

"Look." He points to the boy in the back of the skiff. "Me. I was, I don't know. Seven years of age. This is, as you guessed, your father. Now, the other two. The girl was our pal. A Polish girl. The Grabowska. This guy—" he points to the front of the skiff. "This one is the dead one in our little quartet. He was the oldest. It's crazy but you know his name."

Simon shakes his head. No chance. Even if it's a relative, he'll not have heard of the person. Not in his father's house.

His father smiles and shakes his head.

"He's in your business. Your father says you're an English professor? Well then, he's someone you know well."

"Who is it?"

"You know who J. D. Salinger is?"

Simon laughs. "What, is this someone with the same name?"

"This. Is. Him."

"Come on." They might as well have said they were looking at the young Julius Caesar or Charlie Chaplin's uncle.

"I know it sounds crazy. But it's him. He was older than us."

"What was he doing in the boat with you?"

"Well, that's a good question. Can you tell your son the answer to that one?"

Simon's father leans back in his chair. He looks toward the darkened exit doors, maybe for an escape route from this line of reminiscence.

"I'll tell you, if your father can't. From what I remember, Salinger's father was in the import business in New York City. Meat. Ham. And they had a supplier near Bydgoszcz. The slaughterhouse belonged to Oskar Robinson. You remember him?"

His father does not.

"What was it they called him? The King of Ham? The King of Bacon? Something like that. I had a cousin in Bydgoszcz who went to school not so far from the slaughterhouse. So, he hung around there, got to know the workers. In particular, one big slaughtermaster who told him that there was an American kid working there. My cousin was always on the lookout. What do you think he thinks when he hears an American is in Bydgoszcz? He thinks: escape. The slaughtermaster said the American was sad. He'd left a girl behind in Vienna. So my cousin suggests that he can introduce him around. And who should show up one day on the ham wagon but my cousin and the American. He was leaving in a few weeks. Back to New York. But for a short time, we were all friends." Mike holds the photo up as proof. "Your father, the future writer, the Grabowska, and me."

"And," Simon adds, "a cat."

Mike bends over the print. "What cat?"

"Here." He points to the gunnel of the skiff between Mike and the young future writer. Sure enough, there is a pair of triangles—ears atop a soft disk of a face.

"It belonged to Ewa Grabowska," his father puts in. "I remember when we said we'd take it in the boat she said not to, but we did it anyway. It was a smart animal. It rode like a pro and then we put it back on land."

With this his father stands. "Enough for one night. Look, Mike, we've got to go." And they do, his father and Mike having made plans to meet the following morning.

As they make their way through the pinball arcade of an entrance hall, Mike catches up to them and offers the photo. His father hesitates, his hands by his sides. So Simon takes it and pockets it. Somehow, he thinks, for the first time, he has the upper hand over his father. He has something his father might want but is too proud to ask for. The river, J. D., the Grabowska, and her skiff-worthy cat.

The Secret Place

When Simon wakes, he sees that his father's bed is empty. The red light signaling a message is lit on the phone between their beds. It is Mike. He's downstairs in the hotel lobby. Hadn't they agreed to meet?

At five to eleven Simon is in the lobby on the lookout for Mike, and there he is, in an overstuffed armchair by the lobby door. They shake hands like old friends. Mike grasps his hand, his arm, then his whole body, the way he did the night before upon greeting his father.

"Son," he says, holding onto his arm. "No sign of your dad?"

"When I woke up he was already out."

"Sure. He hasn't changed. You don't make it as he has by keeping needless appointments, right?"

So, Simon thinks, I'm the dummy who shows up when he says he will. Mike leads him to chairs at the back of the lobby, under a palm frond the size of a garden umbrella. They sit knee to knee, and Manhattan is made to disappear as Mike tells him what it is he has come to tell. He seems in a rush to tell it, as if he fears that Simon's father will appear and ruin the opportunity.

"Last night I started to tell you about your father's family. There's something more you should know. As Max said, they were impressive people. But I didn't tell you what I had in mind. It was a small place, Radzanów. We all knew each other. Things were changing by the thirties, when I was a child. One asshole had a sign up—I forget now what he did, mended pots or barrels or sold metals and things—that said, basically, screw the Jews. Buy all you need here. God, what was his name? I hated that guy. I hated his dog. Once I threw a rock at it and headed for the hills. But anyway, we were kids. You know. We didn't think about this stuff that much.

"As a kid I had a problem. Today they call it asthma. But before the war, in Radzanów, they didn't know what made it difficult for a strong kid like me to breathe. It was always worst in late spring when everything was breaking open. The orchards in bloom. Gardens full of herbs. The fields newly plowed. Animals and birds and you name it on the move. My head would feel like it was packed with mattress ticking. Like my throat was closing." He holds his hand out, thumb and forefinger almost touching.

"My head felt like it was the size of a house. My parents tried folk cures. And what they called a *feltsher*. In Poland a *feltsher* was an all-purpose character. A plumber and a barber and a magician all in one. Today, you find people like this on the TV. They're selling renewed hair. Renewed sex life. Renewed you name it. A *feltsher* today is on TV making a million bucks. A Polish Jewish *feltsher* was supposed to know how to heal. You know what they were originally? They travelled with the armies, with Napoleon. When a soldier had an injured arm or leg, the *feltsher* cut it off. He was a field shearer, so, a *feltsher*. By the time of my childhood, a *feltsher* had some old bandages. And maybe he'd mix you a *gogl-mogl*. A purging drink. Honey, cinnamon, a raw egg, valerian, and of course some *bronfn*. Even a kid can use a stiff shot. A *feltsher* might also serve as a midwife. Some were dangerous, and some not so. Once I was in the market square, with my throat like this." Again, the thumb and forefinger. "And my head like this." Mike raises his arm above his head. "One of the neighbours passed. Your father's cousin. His name was Aronek. He could see I wasn't right. He asked, *Bist krank*? Was I sick? I told him how I felt. Bad, but it would pass. He took me aside. We sat on the back of an open cart. This was our life back then. Horses, cows, chickens. You name it. Animals. What can I say? It was colourful. Anyway, he asked if I knew that there was a place in the forest. I should mention to my parents that we talked, because they would know that in this place the trees and grass, the herbs that grew there, even the wind, had a remarkable effect on the body. If you go to this place and stay through an afternoon and an evening, you are different when you leave. You take some herbs from the place. It makes you well."

It is strange to hear of these things in the gilded lobby of the Essex House. A woman passes them, smelling of cinnamon and nutmeg and tipped up on four-inch heels. As Mike talks, he is transported to his childhood places. He says that being allowed to visit the secret place was no simple thing.

"It had been in Aronek's family for a long time. They were its protectors and its proprietors. So their responsibilities were mysterious but also, it has to be said, financial. When someone like myself wanted to go to the Secret Place—and my parents agreed that we should try—they went, as I did, to the family's home off the village square. I was welcomed inside. I sat at a wooden table at the back of the house, as far as possible from any open windows. I described my ailment, the source of my unhappiness. Some visitors were told that their trouble was hopeless, not the thing the Secret Place was for, and were sent away. But the decision went in my favour. I could be helped. A date and time were chosen when I was to arrive at a little gulley off the road to Mława. It was near one of those roadside shrines to Saint John Nepomucene. Up high on a wooden pedestal by an opening to the woods. I went alone just before dawn. It was misty by the river. I waited, maybe a half hour. Then a voice out of nowhere ordered me to shut my eyes. A cloth was tied over my face. We walked in circles until I'd lost all sense of direction. At one point I was lifted into a boat and we floated. I thought it was the Wkra. With my eyes covered, I felt like a leaf floating on water. I was taken to the Secret Place—*der geheime ort* we called it. My guide sat me down against a tree. My palms were smoothed open and covered with grasses. I was told to chew slowly then swallow. Whoever it was who was doing this told me to breathe as deeply as I could. I wanted to be cured, so I did as I was told. I remember it like no other experience since."

After this, Mike said, he felt renewed. Strengthened. What transpired that day helped him survive the coming disaster. He found a way out of Poland, then far east. Like a spy movie.

"In the area around Radzanów—in Plock, Mława, and even further afield in Bydgoszcz—the Secret Place was legendary. Its true location was never revealed. These guys last night, whenever they see me, I can tell. They want to know. As if they might go back in search of eternal youth. But I can't say. Its secretness, in people's minds, this must have contributed to its power. And I can't rule out the possibility that Aronek's disappearance—nobody knows exactly what happened to him after the war—was connected with the Secret Place. Maybe there was a disagreement over who would be its keeper. Maybe someone asked him for it and it didn't go so well.

"Well, that's it. That's what I wanted to tell you. I was surprised when your father said you were coming. I don't know if you remember. I visited you and your family. It was in the early seventies. Vancouver was in the news. Something about visiting foreign officials. I forget why. So, I got it in my head to come up. Your father booked me at the Bayshore. Down by the water in view of the shipyards. It was captivating. I almost thought of staying. Calling my wife and saying, Listen, enough with the grubby eastern winters. Your father and I took long drives together around Stanley Park and over the bridge. I could see he wasn't happy, which struck me against the backdrop of the beautiful place where he lived. He said things about your mother. I can't say he sounded overly happy to be a father. What were you then? Two kids?"

"I have a sister."

"And he'd developed an attitude about the past. If I said anything about our childhood, he laughed and changed the subject."

"He never talked to us about it."

"It's a problem. If you have one thing—one big thing you cannot talk about—you cannot really talk about anything. So. I really did push him to come to this wedding. I saw it as an opening. I told him I'd take him around to the auction houses. He could pursue these interests of his. Pens. First editions. Art. It amazed me, really, when he said yes." Mike reaches into his jacket pocket and withdraws a handful of papers. "I was going to surprise him with this." He unfolds the papers and offers them. A plane ticket, via Frankfurt, to Warsaw. A map of the route north of Warsaw by car. A photograph of a white-haired woman before a wooden house with a pitched tin roof on a village square. A bundle of Polish money bound by an elastic band.

"I was going to give this to him. I was getting ready to go again myself, but since my wife died I couldn't get up the energy. I told your dad I could turn the ticket over to him. He never did get back to me about it. Now look. It can be yours instead. Just as good. So, I've got it all here, including a detailed description of the house."

"What house?"

"I'm not surprised, from what you've told me so far, that you don't know. Your father has a house waiting in Poland. The house he grew up in. This one." Mike points at the photograph of a wooden house with its aged guardian out front, arms crossed over her chest.

"How can this be?"

"It was not by his own doing."

"Well, then. How?"

"This woman. Our childhood friend. You will get the story properly if you meet her. This is the main thing. I didn't want to say it in front of your father last night, because it seems when it comes to the past, with you, he's been applying a scorched-earth policy. When I went back the most remarkable thing that happened, by far, was my discovery that your father's pre-war girlfriend was still dedicated to him. As if the war never happened. As if it weren't seventy-five years ago."

"She must have known a different guy."

"Yes. I think that may be true. He was—I'd agree—a different guy then."

"Aren't we all?"

"What?"

"Different, from when we were kids."

"I don't know." Mike puts his finger to the photograph. "Ewa Grabowska. When she was young, I knew a few things. She was pretty. And she was smart. She read books. After the war she had a family, a husband, two children. But here she stands. Look. In front of your father's family home. On guard."

"When was this picture taken?"

"I was there a year ago."

"What did she tell you? What was she thinking all these years?"

"The bottom line is she protected that house. She did it from when she was a girl. In wartime. The fucking priest. The community rumour mill. The neighbours. And after the war, the mayor, who, from what I can tell, under Communism was a real power grabber. It was dog eat dog in the apparatchik days. Nice guys got plowed under."

"Mike, you're sure about this?"

"I am. When I went to Poland. Last time. From Warsaw, with a guide. It was all by chance. She's got a daughter. Ania. I met her in the town square, which, I can tell you, is no damn good for anything the way they tried to bring it up to date. But we do things like that here too. Make something perfectly useful useless."

"What happened? With the daughter?"

"I went up with a driver and a guide. The hotel arranged it. It cost a fortune, keeping that guy waiting with his van as I rambled the countryside. Fortunately my guide was a very smart young woman. We still talk on the phone. She helped me out when I thought your dad might go with me."

"Mike. You don't know my father. He would never do that. With him, the past's dead. That includes my mom. And I have a sister. She lives in the States. His daughter. I heard him on the phone. *You crazy bitch. I never want to talk to you again. I'm writing you out of the will.* And that's what he did. If you asked him about a daughter, he'd probably say he didn't have one."

"That's harsh. What'd she do, join the Symbionese Liberation Army?"

"It's just one more piece of evidence that the old lady knew a different guy."

"What happened first was I nearly had a heart attack. In the town square. I see a young woman crossing the road and *she is our friend Ewa, still young*. The spitting image. I started to hyperventilate. It was like I didn't know if I was alive or dead. Old or young. I had to sit down. It's lucky that now, instead of a market, it's benches and weeds.

"She could tell something was wrong, so she came over and

asked if I was okay. She thinks, one more old Jew is going to die in our market square, maybe she can pull off a righteous act. I told her right off. She'd scared me. I thought I'd seen a ghost. She asked me—in Polish this all went, so maybe I'm understanding half—what I meant. I explained who I was. I'd come to see the place once more, before it was too late. And that I had been thinking, when she walked up, of someone I wished had joined me on this visit. He grew up—I pointed—in that house. And then it was her turn to turn white. She sat down. She said your father's name. She'd heard this story about him when she was a child. Not since. It was the only explanation for her mother's dedication to the house, a source of risk and some grief. It was a commitment that seemed to yield nothing but heartache and worry. So she and I sat there on that beautiful Sunday afternoon. Blue sky. Kids having ice cream. A funeral with all kinds of flowers in the church behind us. An old guy on a stoop drank what looked like a litre of beer and then stumbled off shouting into his phone."

"Nice."

"Yah. You're having the strangest conversation of your life and some drunk puts on a clown act. Anyway. This was the daughter. Of the old lady. But I shouldn't call her that. When we knew her she was 'Grabowski's girl, Ewa.' That's how she was called. In Polish, Ewunia. The father was kind of a big guy in town. He owned land opposite the synagogue. He got along with Jews and Poles alike. So the girl had a certain freedom. She crossed boundaries others never managed to cross. But I didn't understand all this at the time. It comes into focus with the years. So, if I had not bumped into the daughter, Ania, I would know nothing at all. Wow. Very impressive. Just as the mother was. We all kind of loved her. But your dad."

"He didn't love her?"

Mike says it with a look. He loved her.

"So off we went to see her mother. That was something. That's when I took this picture. The Grabowska, in front of your house."

"Does the daughter live in the village?"

"No. Warsaw. But she's in town often to help out the mother. And from what I understand she was the reason a film shoot chose Radzanów. She had connections in the city and worked it out with the local mayor."

Mike pushes the package, maps, money, something handwritten on a pad of lined sheets, across the table between them.

"If you go, and you should, I can tell the travel agent to turn the ticket, you name it, over to you. She'll make the necessary changes."

Simon eyes the doorway, as if he half expects his father to appear. He would gather up the Polish money, the maps, and details on scattered sheets, and throw them out into the street. But it is New York that comes roaring back; the Secret Place in the woods outside a town called Radzanów is dispelled, disappearing like a flock of birds scared into the sky.

The Weapon on the Wall

Simon is in the back room cutting carrot cake squares. He lifts each square with the flat of a knife, lays it on a small white plate, then wraps the whole thing in plastic. He likes this job. The students he hires to put dishes in the machine, to take orders and gather the names of those who want to go onstage, cut pieces too large. They also eat while they cut—as does he. It is delicious carrot cake. He wonders if he can bump the price up a bit and gain an edge on the electricity bill. He finds himself daydreaming about what Mike called the Secret Place. He can hear old Mike describing the way it operated in his oddly lilting New York Polish-Yiddish English. What kind of place heals people? In Vancouver, people sought out the water for this purpose, or the mountains, or the islands.

His father had tried a Gulf island for a while, after he walked out on them. For a number of years, because his mother forbade it, he never saw the place on Galiano. When he was in university, living on his own, these prohibitions fell away, and he'd gone out with a girlfriend with the idea of showing the place off. The house overlooked Active Pass. The ferries and whales passed in perfect cohabitation. Deer gathered at night to eat whatever grew in the garden.

They arrived on a rainy afternoon, the sky like cement and the island sodden, silent, dark as night. The key to his father's place was in the mailbox, left for them by a neighbour. Inside, half the bulbs wouldn't light, while those that did seemed to top out at forty watts, leaving the place in shadow. His girlfriend said the place was "soporific." What, he asked, was that? "Sleep-inducing," was the answer. Where had she learned that word? Well, in her childhood reading of Tom Thumb books, of course, and off she went describing a youthful love affair with Beatrix Potter in a way that was itself perfectly soporific. Magically, as if the combination of the word and weather had cast a spell on the place, they both dozed, snoozing on his father's threadbare, dog-smelling couch like a couple of island retirees after a long walk.

He'd never heard what his father did with the place. A knock at his front window summons him from his daydream. It is his father, nose against the glass, on the Cordova Street sidewalk, his head crowned by the crisp letters Simon paid a sign painter to add to his shop's front window. His father's mouth opens and closes without a sound coming through the glass. Not such a bad arrangement.

He lets him in.

"Simon. Holy shit. I haven't really looked around down here in ages. What a shame. You know, this neighbourhood had its charms. What was it, sixty years ago?"

His father sizes the place up. Scouts the back room. He stands with his hands on his hips and pronounces, "Nope."

"Nope what?"

"I never owned this. I had a place up the way, just west of the Hildon Hotel. God, what a bedbug palace that must be these days. With that hole-in-the-wall bar in the lobby. Who would go in there for a drink? But I remembered about this place. 36 West Cordova. It's got a story."

"My economic demise, right?"

His father smiles. "Well, sure, yes. You're hurtling toward bankruptcy. I don't have to tell you that."

Simon takes a chair and sits in front of where his father stands.

"Listen. I knew the guy who had a pawnshop in here. In the fifties, into the early sixties. I had a building nearby. I told you. I bought books around the corner. Remember?"

He does.

"Well, this guy—God, the name will come to me. He was by far the softest touch on the street. They had a nickname for him: the Gentle Jew. Lots of other Jews had shops. It was real Jewish down here. You know? Nobody talks about this anymore. But this was a Jewish district. Strictly business. These were the outposts for guys coming up in the world. They couldn't get hired in banks or insurance companies so they opened shops where they could afford rent. The guy who had this place, he gave out easy loans. And from what I remember, he didn't need the pawn business anymore. He lived in Kerrisdale. He dressed like a business guy, no windbreakers. A vest and a tie and a hat. These other shop owners, some of them were straight out of the war. If you haggled with them they threw you out of the place one-two. It was as if you'd questioned their reputation by asking for a few bucks off some lousy thing. *And don't come back!* That was the final insult. What a joke. Like one shop mattered. You had umpteen others to choose from. But Batzanoff—that was his name. Izzy Batzanoff. We used to talk real estate. He had some fourplexes and he was building an apartment block in Shaughnessy. I asked why he didn't let someone else run the store for him. He told me he liked it down here. He was trying to get his sons to do an honest day's work. Sometimes a younger brother helped out. I heard about him because he wasn't so reliable. He would not show up when he was supposed to. The area was getting dicey. The rule was two people in the store at all times. The day it happened the brother skipped his shift. As I remember he wasn't at the funeral either. But that was something else. You know. Not easy for him.

"Two guys came in. They ask to see watches. They tell him to hand over the day's receipts. He says no. Get out. First time he ever told anyone to get out of the shop. Maybe showing them the watches was a mistake. Maybe he should have said he had sold out his jewelry the week before. They grabbed the watches and I guess he tried to stop them. I think they got $200 from the cash box. One took hold of a pop bottle. What's the Brando film where he breaks a bottle and uses it like a weapon? Is it Brando? They beat him with it. Very bad. The next person who walked in called the cops. They found Batzanoff conscious, and he described the two guys that did it. What they wore. One had a scar. Their height. These guys robbed the most observant pawnshop owner on Cordova. Three days later he died. I went to his funeral. When they drove his body by the synagogue on the way to the graveyard, they opened the front doors wide. Jesus. That made everybody cry. It was big. In those days, like I say, everyone had a little shop. But this scared them. And to top it off the city started talking about razing skid row. The city was going to do them a big favour by knocking down the neighbourhood that gave them a living."

"Jesus."

"Yah."

"They murdered him. In here?"

His father seems to be counting off paces.

"Here. His counter was here. I would stand here and he would open two bottles of pop and we'd talk. We talked about Poland. His father had come to Canada in the twenties, when they were still letting people in. He came, I think he said, with a wooden suitcase. No one else I knew wanted to tell me their story. I was curious back then." Simon's father stands where the cash counter was. He is out of steam. He waves a hand in the air. "History. Like the pyramids, right?"

Simon doesn't know what to say. It's bad news. Bad old news.

His father steps forward with his arms wide and they hug. His father steps outside and waves through the glass. Simon watches him go. There is a new store opening just to the east. Its perfectly of-the-moment name is WANT, which is printed in stark white block letters on a crisp black awning.

Simon thinks of the dulcimer girl. Nadia. Better to call her by her real name. She'd not been by. He must consider, now, what it means to hold an open mic in a place where a man was killed. His dad sure had a way with the old stuff. Save it for a hundred years then drop it like a bomb. From under the cash counter he draws the bulky package Mike passed him in Queens. He lays it on a table and sits down, removing the contents of the envelope—the airline ticket, hotel recommendations, maps, photo of a Polish house, money. Using a currency converter on the Shop's computer, he realizes that he is the holder of Polish *zloty* worth more than $5,000. Well.

God, the rain. It begins early and the city turns dark for weeks. From his window overlooking the park on Comox, Simon watches as all the brown and dry stuff of summer turns green. Fall in Vancouver is a whole new growth season. For the sunflower in the community garden the moisture is too much—it fades, its yellow head bent like an old man's.

The neighbourhood around the Shop changes with the season in a patchwork way that makes Simon uncomfortable. In the WANT boutique they are selling thousand-dollar handbags made from pony skin, and luggage with logos too specialized for him to be able to decode. He finds himself wishing some drunken late-night carouser would break in and make off with all this high-end loot. But no such calamity befalls the two young high-heeled owners of WANT. They lock up like clockwork at five p.m. and clatter off on their heels like a couple of runway models. One morning he opens the newspaper's "Lifestyle" section and finds they are featured. He feels gutted, but he knows it's stupid to feel this way. Even if the newspaper had come calling when he opened the Shop, he might well have blown them off, mistrusting the mainstream credentials a feature might have lent his efforts.

At the window, his hands in his pockets, taking in the volume of rain running down the roadway, he turns as the phone rings.

It's Mike. "Mike from Queens. You forgot me already? Listen. You passed the things on to your father?"

Does mumbling mean yes or no or maybe?

"I did. Yes." He can see the packet from where he stands holding the phone.

"Well, what's going on there?"

"Here? Rain. You?"

"Oh. I've been thinking of you two. Your father. His peccadilloes. Is that the word? And you, what, you've got a new business? The first two years. You know the rule. The first two years are killers."

He finds himself telling Mike how much he enjoys his routines. The regulars. Even the unpredictable side of it all. Trouble in the back alley, or graffiti on the front of the place, or drunken open-mic performers, or blown speakers when some punk poet turned the volume way up *and then* plugged in his busted old guitar.

"Listen. There's something I should have spoken to you about when I had my chance. I wrote to the old lady. The mother of the daughter. The Grabowska." He pauses. "I told her your father might be coming."

"Really?"

"Yah. But if your dad changes his mind, and that wouldn't surprise, me, you should go. She'll treat you well. She's getting all the recipes out."

With the phone at his ear, Simon stares out at the street and waits for whatever's coming next. The cars roll by. A couple passes, each with a cigarette and paper coffee cup in hand.

"She'll open up the old house."

This is quite a thought, exchanging his view onto Cordova for a little wooden house on a Polish square. The rain is hitting the pavement in great splashing waves. It has driven every last soul indoors. Even the cars have thinned out and he can see far up, past the Hildon, almost to the edge of what he thinks of as the real downtown. Under shadow of rain he glimpses the street as it might have looked to his father, newly arrived, his Polish romance something that needed to be junked, like his accent and the too-formal cap and coat he'd brought with him, the last things his parents could give him before he left with the American ham distributor's son who was destined for greatness.

The Typewriter Girl

Ania sits at a café table on the *Krakowskie Przedmieście*, opposite the man she is dating. Called Marek, a housing and skyscraper construction manager, a few years younger than she, he is an exemplary New Polish male. Born in Lodz, he grew up in an apartment with a view of the old ghetto neighbourhood, Bałuty, where the city's roughest working-class toughs lived. He'd excelled at wrestling as a schoolkid, taken advantage of the opportunity to travel to international matches, and then made a go of learning three languages when it was finally safe to expunge Russian from his mind. Spanish, French, and English. Next in line, for obvious reasons, was Mandarin. He started out as an agent selling shoddy villas on the outskirts of Warsaw, but gradually worked his way up the ladder in a German-owned construction company. He has made it, and having done so, he is glad to pay the same amount for two espressos that Polish families used to spend on a day's meals. He drives a tiny, shiny sports car noisily over Warsaw's cobblestone streets. If someone asks, Ania's mother or a friend or even her assistant at the office who receives his many calls, checking first to see if Ania is free to talk, she says that she is "dating" Marek. She does not think they have a future. Her impression is that he feels the same way, but he might think she can be brought around, that she might be turned in a more conventional and materialistic direction, into the right kind of woman to adorn his otherwise full-scale success. On the surface, she supposes, their lines might seem to meet—they are two busy professional people of a certain age. He is a sharp dresser, if a little trendy for Ania's taste. But for it to work out she is sure she would have to give up her very public career, which she has no intention of doing. Why, she wonders, has he got her so wrong? In some crucial way, he is not paying attention.

When she talks with Marek she is aware of her own voice, as if she is partially, or even mostly, speaking to herself. She has meant, for some time, to tell him things that she has kept to herself, thinking they might be what will drive him away. And now maybe this is what she is trying to do. They talk in a mixture of Polish and English, mostly at Marek's urging. She cannot tell if he likes people nearby to hear them switching languages, or if he simply takes advantage of the opportunity to practice with her. This is one of their compatibilities. In her government job, English is a necessity. To Marek, English is the language of global money. Because his spoken English is less than perfect, he ends up listening more than usual. Ania's English is British-lilted, with her accent acquired when she studied philology and linguistics at the university in Krakow. There, in the shadow of Renaissance churches and the resurrected Jewish quarter, she pursued her training so diligently it allows her, to this day, to recreate from memory the phonology chart of the "Received Pronunciation" system favoured by her teachers. It was a period in her life that formed her. She spent hour after hour in the old libraries of the Jagiellonian University. Her garret—it really was a garret, nearly furnitureless, and cold at night, with one dormer window and a view of the turrets of the Cloth Hall in the old market square—was a perfect student's haunt. During those years she was transformed from the country girl she'd been, full of yearning and romantic misconceptions, into the woman she is today.

Marek asks about her ambitions. This is a word she usually doesn't consider. She has accomplishments, but ambitions?

"It isn't entirely straightforward," she says, "being a woman in my position. At the museum, it was different. A woman's intelligence about art was appreciated. I stayed away from the more provocative collections related to war and the nobility. There was a fussy, tight-lipped man who oversaw the armour. And another really crazy one who catalogued the artillery pieces and horse tack. The men on staff viewed these things with special interest. But my move into politics took some adjustment. My upbringing was very specific. My parents never talked about the socialist view of the world. By their silence they seemed to accept things as they were. My father was never a Communist Party member. But he had good connections and he had the respect of the people he worked with. I think he played the role of an honest broker between the apparatchiks and the non-joiners. This made him valuable. Even though he was a rural official for much of his adult life, he was important to others. So, he was not happy when, as a teenager, I became dedicated to Radio Free Europe. And his status suffered when a nephew accepted a fellowship to study in the United States and never returned to Poland. You know, this was not anybody's fault, but if someone wanted to question your reliability, your dedication to the way forward ... "

This chapter changed things for their family. It all descended like a dream, the sense of threat and vague guilt, as if anything her father might do could be reviewed for its doubled, untrustworthy motive. And then there was her brother. Such a loser. Nothing could be expected of him. So she became the target of all her father's hope and worry.

"I listened to Radio Luxembourg after midnight. I carried my worn copies of Orwell's *Animal Farm* and Aldous Huxley's *Brave New World* in case some like-minded stranger wanted to discuss how these books told our story. My image of myself—it's funny to think of it, and a little sad—was of a warrior with books as my weapon. I expected to hold them up before Russian tanks the way the American students strolled up to their National Guard and placed flowers in the barrels of the pointed guns."

When she thinks back on it all, the past is vivid. Shops were empty and so many Western things were out of bounds that when she found her way to the objects of her desire—a record album, a certain kind of blue jeans—it was an accomplishment. Memorable and very meaningful.

"Did you ever go to the record stores? Like the one behind Marszałkowska—*Sklep Płytowy* Hey Joe?"

Marek shakes his head. Of course he didn't. He was busy pinning some lightweight to the mat in a Gdańsk gymnasium.

Ania pauses, feeling a tightness in her belly as she describes her youthful doings, her beginnings. But her expression does not shift. She looks past Marek. On the sidewalk a civic worker picks his way along, scooping cigarette leavings and trash into a black plastic sack.

"Coming to work at the ministry was a struggle. I had many dark nights over it. My mother was against it, but she felt that the link with my boss at the museum, who wanted to take me with him into the government, was too valuable. In this way she was thinking the way we did in the old Poland, when things relied on connections and surreptitious dealings. It wasn't easy, coming to work for the government. But I am viewed as irreplaceable. Can you imagine that? So, I can travel whenever I need to see my mother. And through the office I have taken on the role of gatekeeper. This is not my only job. But certainly it's one, and this makes others willing to help if I have a favour to ask."

Why, she wonders, is she telling Marek all this? But she cannot stop. It is the public interview she should never ever give, because it would cost her her job. Whether he is unimpressed or intimidated or uncomprehending, it will help him understand where they stand.

"Then, unfortunately, my fifteen minutes of fame. All because of typewriters! A dead technology, right? Something for the antique dealers in the Old City, like amber necklaces and war-era caps. But not so in the back rooms of our government offices. Because all the old *teczki* were prepared with typewriters. And my building is bursting with these security files. Those that people did not manage to bribe someone to destroy. The investigations into people's pasts, exactly who they dealt with, whether they offered meaningful information or were simply priming their security minders with fairy tales in order to seem to be behaving like good socialist soldiers, these are all intimately tied up with typewriters."

What she is explaining is the underlying problem, the trap, into which her otherwise sensible job has thrown her. Authenticity of the *teczki* has become a fetish. A kind of internal industry. And Ania recognizes that her role in the industry must place her in some danger. If not personal, at least professional danger. Some files have been found to be fraudulent. The real files replaced with false ones. Or a file that never existed suddenly appears. This is what many believe happened with Wałęsa. But she is the one who guarantees authenticity. Ania, her boss says, as he brings the goods in a fat folder, let me know if this one looks okay. Inside the folder she holds not only a person's past but their future. It is a strange, powerful role to play. But she tells herself that it is non-partisan power. She is not looking for a particular outcome. Nor does she provide avenues for falsification. She is the final say. In Kafka, this person is always sinister. But she is not.

She is serious and accomplished. She obstructs the trumped-up charges and foolhardy efforts. She confirms provenance, the age of the documents; and she does this by way of what she calls her Master List. She has thorough knowledge of the machines used in each office by each security agent at any point in time. This was easy to discover, since the files for buying the machines, repairing them, even destroying them if they were unrepairable, were all intact. And when computers replaced typewriters, some parsimonious civil servant arranged all the newly abandoned typewriters on shelves up to the ceiling in a utility room high in their office building. A treasure room of aged, incontrovertible evidence.

Marek loves machines. Cars above all. But if enticed, he will talk for hours about construction vehicles, elevator specifications, the measurable hardness of steel girders. For once she has something to say on this front that he's not up on.

"One of the quirks in this story," she tells him, "is that typewriters in Poland were manufactured in factories that had produced armaments. In the 1930s we even had a brand whose name signaled this link as a mark of distinction. They called themselves *Fabryka Karabinów*, Factory of Guns. We also imported machines from Yugoslavia and the East Germans. These places were given official permission to manufacture what our Soviet overseers considered strategic materials. Getting a typewriter for home use required an official okay. It sounds unbelievable, but this is how it was. You needed permission from the police to do so. The typewriter was a well-controlled tool. It's true, people bought used machines on a flourishing grey market of old German models. These are always easily recognized. They are better built. Some of the machines used by our security people in the bad years, the 1960s and '70s, they were like elephants doing a hummingbird's work. If you hammered away too hard they simply shredded the paper. But some of the models, they served a clerk's purpose in the same way they might serve the maker of a *samizdat* manuscript. A piece of carbon paper—remember carbon paper?"

Marek shakes his head. Of course he does not.

"With carbon, at least three copies could be made from one typed sheet. It must have been very satisfying."

The rest Marek knew because it had played out in the press. Ania became known as the Typewriter Girl. The *maszynistka*. It always reminds her of another word: *magiczka*. And maybe there was something magical about it all—her circumspect work. It came out (and this should never have happened) because her boss came under attack for playing one political side against the other. The president ordered an audit of the ministry's methods. When the press went looking for interesting stories she turned out to be one. The smart girl from the countryside who was running the whole show. The minister kept saying, in interview after interview, I must ask *Pani* Grabowska about this. Ania's mother, who learned about life in the bad old days, feared that Ania would end up in prison. What will they arrest me for, Mama? Ania asked over the phone. Having the biggest desk, or the coziest view? But her mother was an old woman with too much time on her hands.

Abruptly, as if to save him from wherever the conversation is leading—a political lesson, some sad story about a lonely old mother in the countryside—Marek's phone rings in his jacket pocket. He grabs it like a drowning man, combating the poor reception by yelling at whoever it is on the other end. For some reason, today, Ania cannot listen to him talk business. He embarks on an incomprehensible discussion in English about a real estate deal. He stands but hovers near the table. As he talks on, Ania drifts off, into a daydream. As an antidote to what is in front of her, she conjures a scene from long ago, a centrepiece of her youth, when her father sold her hair.

It was a lovely summer, her thirteenth. Living where they did, they saw no unrest, even as political demonstrations overtook life in the big cities. Many of their neighbours worked at a shoe factory or at the TV manufacturing plant near Mława. But whatever their response was to the shipyard strikes and the rest of the chaos, life in their town continued blissfully free of it all.

Her father's desk job for the local government kept him quiet—not happy, but quiet—and he overcame the feeling he had wasted his life by dedicating himself to daily late-afternoon drinks with his crowd at the *kufelek,* the makeshift bar in the centre of their village. He nursed a beer, smoked a handful of cigarettes, stared at the TV, and listened to his compatriots' inane opinions. Possibly this is why the traveler pinpointed him as a mark. The quiet, solid-looking man in the corner, once handsome, thick now around the face, hands wrapped around a mug of Zywiec.

The *kufelek* was the kind of place where anyone on the lookout for suckers—or even better, drunk suckers—went. The traveller's name was Olewski. He was a line surveyor from the city, sent to check the village service. But as a sideline—something that came his way as he visited far-flung places—he acted as a buyer for a hair processor in Mława. The notable thing about this Olewski was the thick bundle of bills he kept in his inside jacket pocket. He showed it when he paid the woman at the counter for his beer. American dollars on the outside, Polish *zloty* and German marks on the inside. Once he waved these about, Ania's father was a hooked fish.

What followed was her first lesson in how events outside one's own life, over which one had no control, could change the future. There was nothing magic about this, or tragic, or even mysterious. It was simply the way things were. Her father might just as easily have seen an advertisement for the hair processor's agent on a telephone pole. Instead it was a meeting over a beer that presented him with the opportunity.

"Everything in Poland now is shit." This was one of the traveller's favourite lines. "I'm not for or against the new politics. I simply want people to be able to feed their family and stay out of trouble. Out here in the countryside everything happens without anyone knowing why."

The traveller knew not to reveal his true interest, so he patiently tried other subjects—Wałęsa; the local economy; he even indulged her father's willingness to discuss the weather—before he asked the all-important questions about family.

Her father had little to say about his wife. Their marriage was a big mistake, undertaken in the bleak middle fifties, when life was one challenge to survival after the next. Their first-born was a boy, stupid and lazy. How had he ended up with such a son? But the girl was a lovely thing. Ania was smart and took no shit from anyone. She would run the whole show one day.

What did he mean by *the whole show*?

Her father expressed great hope for Ania. Out came his battered black leather wallet—a gift upon reaching his fifteenth year of service in the local bureaucracy. Inside were twenty *zloty*—enough to buy a drink, a loaf of bread, and a lotto ticket—and photographs of Ania. He chose a baby picture, but the traveller asked for something more up-to-date, and there it was, ready to change her world: the school picture, in which the photographer's light seemed drawn to the blonde braid on her chest. The traveller offered him a hundred American dollars, with the promise of $25 more if, once he'd seen the hair up close and examined it for softness and highlights, he was assured it qualified as Polish Gold. The best there was on the market, worth five times what her father was paid for it once it found its way to the hair-extension market in a high-end salon in Saint Petersburg or San Francisco. The outcome, after the deed was done, was that another woman, in some strange way, would feel improved, more desirable, wearing Ania's hair, while she, stoic but so angry at what her father had done, would be transformed into a different person. For good. Were there fairy tales, children's stories, about such things? If not, someone should write one. The story of the stolen Polish Gold.

Olewski and her father agreed to meet at the same time the following day. That night, while Ania slept, her father crept into her room with a pair of her mother's sewing shears and cut her hair off. She woke the next morning and felt a strange sensation of lightness. When she saw herself in the mirror she began to scream.

Her father had already left the house. It was an early departure for him, even on a work day. Her mother screamed when she saw her.

What had she done? her mother asked over and over as she came close enough that Ania could smell the bread she'd been baking. They held each other in the morning light, not knowing what to say. Then her mother let go and left the house without a word.

It was a wonderful sunny morning, warm, calm, fresh, like a fairy-tale version of a country morning. The sky was soft blue and white, the air full of the scent of warm fields, peonies and phlox. Ania sat on the front stoop and put her fingers to the ends of her hair, which stopped by her ears. Cars, horse-drawn carts, the bus to Mława entered and left the square. Everyone else was having a perfect day. She could smell it, feel it in her gut.

When her mother reappeared, she was dragging Ania's father by his coat, as if he were a child. Once he'd told them what he'd done, he went out back and lit a cigarette, staring at the smoke as it rose to their roof.

At age thirteen, what did Ania know? She did not know that marriages became unhappy. She did not know that the children of unhappily married people became misanthropes, like her brother, or wickedly competent, self-contained successes in an adult world they'd never imagined, as she would. What she did know, all of a sudden, was that when a girl had wonderful blonde hair, but came to school with it haphazardly chopped off, the class was sure to erupt in laughter so raucous that the notion of a just world became ridiculous. It was vain and childish to hold on to such ideas. The haircut turned her in a new direction. Of course she didn't recognize this at the time, but later she would, with great satisfaction. When she went alone to visit her father's grave, which lay in the countryside outside their village on a treeless hill looking east, she always said a quiet thank you for this unintended redirection in her youth.

While she daydreams, Marek stands on the sidewalk, the phone stuck to his head. He is, she thinks, a phonehead. This will be her new secret nickname for him, and may signal the end. Pedestrians and trams and cars roll by so that in the blur of it all, Marek, in his grey suit and tie, evaporates. The city in its hectic way swallows him up. It is her opportunity. She gathers her things and slips out a side door of the café. Halfway down the block, she notices her father's car—one exactly like the one he drove before he had his last heart attack and was told by the village doctor that it was fine if he wanted to kill himself, but driving meant he might kill others, too. So, he was to stop. And he did. His car sat in the field beside their house and became a home for rats and wildflowers. A Moskvitch. Same colour as this one. Sunflower yellow. She rests her hand on the roof and looks inside. The same faux leather material covering the seats, cracked in the same places. A block heater like a hair blower under the Bakelite dash. She looks up from the interior at the passersby, as if her father might ramble up and take her in his arms, saying, as he once did, "My sweet girl. Ania, my sweet, sweet girl."

But the street is full of strangers and Ania turns for home.

PART TWO

The New World

Simon carries his guidebooks and maps in a knapsack, glancing through them when he sits at café tables and at airport gates. Holding pride of place among them is the bundle of materials from Mike, with its remarkable array of gifts—an old map of Poland and a newer one of Warsaw, a hand-drawn map of the village where his father's Polish real estate stands, and photographs of the house itself. He has, too, the Polish currency bearing engravings of musicians, scientists, and religious heroes. Stapled together are the lined sheets of handwritten notes entitled "Guide to Radzanów and Area." This is the Radzanówer's rosetta stone, codes and customs meant to unlock the place for Simon. Simon is, Mike insists, a fortunate traveler, since not so long ago the kind of trip he has undertaken would have been more or less science fiction, an impossibility. Even in a spy novel the plot would not have held together. Maybe, maybe, in a superhero comic book, say, in a Schimanski story where the hero took on the whole police apparatus of Communist East Germany with nothing but his broad shoulders and two days' growth of beard.

Simon feels heroic, light-headed, and bulletproof all at once as he steps onto the pavement at Warsaw Chopin Airport and smells the air. It is a kind of low-grade miracle, or, at least, a bizarre sort of happenstance that he is on his way to hail a car to drive him into the centre of the city. At his hotel, he rides the glass elevator to the top floor to see the view it offers over the city, of the sky and the great flat expanse of neighbourhoods that have been built upon the destruction caused by war.

The first thing Simon does is stall for time. A tourist is entitled to this, isn't he? He takes a bus trip out to the royal castle at Wilanów. There he gawks at statues in the garden and ogles King Jan III's four-poster bed. He rides Warsaw's electric trams on Jana Pawła II Boulevard and walks the wide Soviet-style thoroughfares. Marszałkowska and Elektoralna. In the Empik bookstore across from a huge Stalinesque skyscraper he buys a paperback translation of Stanislaw Lem's *Solaris* and sits with it on his knee in the Old Town square. Instead of reading he watches the crowds, locals and tourists and restaurant hawkers and balloon men. Group after group of schoolchildren pass him as he wonders, what do their teachers tell them? Time for another ice cream?

He walks downtown to look at Stalin's bizarre "gift" to Poland, the rococo Palace of Culture and Science, with its wedding-cake turrets bristling with cellphone towers. On its thirtieth floor there is an observation terrace, where he goes to look out at the city, first to try to trace his own wanderings. There, down on Marszałkowska, was the Empik store, but then he scans the far horizon borderlands, confident he is looking north and west, more or less in the direction of the village he is due to visit. The city fades off into a haze of white and pale blue. Lost there in the haze is his father's place. Why, he wonders, is he up here looking out at the countryside instead of where he's meant to be? Well, obviously, because he is procrastinating. If it takes him a week or a month or a year to see Radzanów, what difference does it make?

Back on the ground floor he investigates the *Sala Kongresowa*, a concert venue famous from Soviet times, where crowds came to carouse in front of Leonard Cohen or Frank Zappa, icons of the freewheeling West. The room is under renovation, so nothing is booked, but the ticket office is awash in alternate entertainment options: pamphlets and coupons for a circus, nightclubs, and out-of-town possibilities. In Łódź there is the Manufaktura complex developed from a great nineteenth-century industrial factory into an all-out consumption zone with shops, galleries, and cinemas. In Kraków, the salt mines, Wawel castle, and, of course, Auschwitz. Poznań, a city he has hardly heard of, advertises a museum devoted to musical instruments, including antique, folkloric Polish dulcimers. These are not, it seems, the kind played by Nadia, not the instrument beloved of coastal folkies and Appalachian crooners. The Polish dulcimer is more elaborate, resting on legs, with many strings, which the player hits with hammers. A promotional video runs on a screen above the shuttered box office. The hammer-wielder almost dances before his instrument. It looks to Simon like something worth seeing on Poznań's rebuilt Renaissance square where, at noon, a pair of clockwork rams pop out of the town-hall clock to butt heads. Why not go? He might impress Nadia with his exotic dulcimer knowledge, if she ever showed herself on his side of town again.

Across from the *Sala Kongresowa* is the main train station. He considers first the cigarette-strewn floor and then, for a long time, the remarkably low price for a ticket that would allow him to travel to Poznań. It is feasible to leave Warsaw early in the morning and return in the evening. Just a day trip, so only a temporary postponement of his departure to Radzanów.

Early the next day he goes. The train platform is a dead zone, like so much of what the Soviet years left to the city. It is a long, wide expanse of weed-ridden cement covered by tin canopies. The trains pulling in are electric, silver and red, with one great eye of a headlight mounted on the nose of each engine. He stumbles into his train and chooses, stupidly, too late to make a change, what turns out to be a smoking car. Because he has no Polish language, not one word, not yes or no or hello or goodbye, he offers his seatmates a kind of international salute, open palm raised at an angle. Three sit across from him and two beside. One young woman is glued to her phone screen. It is her cigarette, her opium pipe. If Simon had a choice between old-fashioned drugs and the phone, he would choose to smoke. But he needs neither. He is intoxicated by the countryside. In the morning light, as the train breaks out of the city limits, it is lovely. Most of it is green still, in summer richness, but maples, here and there, have turned red and yellow. The first clouds he's seen since arriving in the country appear on the northern horizon. The woods fly past, breaking into meadow and cropland before returning, soft, their high crowns brushed by the wind. Up close, the woods do not look entirely wild, as if they have been picked over and mown through many times. This makes him think of war—a subject he knows little about—of partisans finding things to eat in the undergrowth, collecting firewood.

At train sidings in whistle-stop towns he spies buildings in greater need of paint than any he's seen. The old red-brick stations, once impressive, are tumbledown, with the names of towns announced by a variety of precarious lettering. The fields look prepared, but for what? Two seatmates get up to stand in the narrow corridor beside the compartment and smoke out the open window. Now the corn shows itself, immense fields of it. Then one spread-out suburban neighbourhood after the next. Stucco villas with satellite dishes. The mysteries of other people's lives. On the horizon line, groups of trees like families on the move. The train's rhythmic clatter, and insistent voices in the neighbouring cars.

The outskirts of Poznań take shape and then the city swallows the train whole. From the station, he makes his way to the old central market square, which is a wonderful confection of medieval house fronts, some rebuilt since the war, but many, too, that survived it all and have now been polished and accorded great love and attention with the rise of a new tourist economy. The dead Soviet years are being scrubbed out of this old city.

The music museum has a Chopin room, to which he gives a cursory look. In it, a piano played by the composer himself stands like a well-loved ancestor. He had read somewhere that Chopin's heart resided in a Warsaw church.

Folk instruments are what he wants to look at. He remembers Nadia describing the kind of rural trios she was interested in. Drums and whistles and the much-loved Polish dulcimer. The museum collection appears to include a hundred of these. The most spectacular are table-sized instruments. None resemble the one Nadia brought into the Shop. Supple and thin as a little ship, hers is tapered at both ends, its sound holes carved in the shape of sunbursts.

A video on a hanging screen shows footage of groups playing antique instruments. This is followed by an instructional video on how to care for a dulcimer, using orange oil in a spray bottle. The gift shop inside the museum is shuttered behind a Plexiglas sliding gate, which means that if he wants to buy a gift for Nadia—maybe the little toy dulcimer he sees on the counter, just out of reach—he will have to make a return trip.

It's noon and a crowd gathers by the town hall where the clock tower presents its pair of mechanical goats who butt heads on the hour. Children clap as their minders take photographs with their phones.

The return train, as it turns out, is a milk run. Maybe this is why the ticket was so cheap, and he feels, once more, that familiar foolish traveller's recognition of having made a decision without understanding what he was doing. The train stops in one town after another, as one or two passengers get off. Swarzędz. Września. Słupca. The light grows gold in early dusk. Remarkably, as the sky goes dark and the countryside disappears from view, no lights come on in the compartment. Simon gets up to see if he might change to another, but one carriage after another is full, doors drawn shut, containing families and couples with heads resting on companions' shoulders, while those doing the shouldering stare out the window at passing crossing lights, which flash away behind them.

When Simon returns to his compartment, he finds a new face across from him. The man is around his age but dressed in an outmoded style, his hair cut short, his shirt buttoned at the neck. He has one arm in a sling made of blue cloth, and he smokes with his free hand, slowly, almost ritualistically, raising the cigarette to his mouth in one slow arc, holding it there for a long drag, then resting it on his knee. As the train rolls on, the compartment is shrouded in smoke.

Darkness envelops them. Others in the car drift off to sleep, and sleep tempts Simon, too, but he fears he will sleep through the Warsaw stop and be carried on further into the night, over the castle-and-cornfield countryside to the east. Russia, Samarkand, then straight into the ocean.

He closes his eyes *just to rest*—and sees in his mind's eye the man across from him, with his smoking mouth and his sleepy eyes, for who he is: he is the Night Jew, who has ridden the Polish trains for a century, as long as the rail lines crossed the countryside, his pack above him on the rack, his nicotine-stained fingers in his lap.

The Night Jew asks, "What are you doing here, my young friend?"

Is it English he's speaking?

Simon explains why he has come to the country. It is his father's birthplace. His own solitude in Vancouver makes it possible, almost any time, to head out on an adventure like this one. He describes the Shop as a venue for all kinds of strange performances, including the eastern-inflected dulcimer girl. Simon wonders, what is she doing right now? Is she playing something chilling from the stage, the eyes of the surprised audience members turned up to her, her fingers moving smoothly along the rail line of her instrument's strings? He had hoped to get something to send her from the Poznań museum, but this fell through. The shop was closed. Now Simon dreams of something more grandiose, something hallowed and old. He dreams of Chopin's heart in its case.

Simon is startled by coughing and the Night Jew says something roughly in Polish, which, of course, he cannot understand. The man across from him, recognizable only in Simon's dream, gets up abruptly, so that Simon knocks knees with him. He steps out of the compartment, drawing the door shut loudly behind him.

The iron wings of the rooftop of the station, *Warszawa Centralna*, are visible beneath tall white light standards. The train heads underground. He has arrived.

Moskvitch 412

Mike's handwriting is small and spidery, lines running to the edge of each sheet. His "Guide to Radzanów and Area" begins this way: "You must make the most of your time there. Go it alone. That's the only way. This means, I guess, get a car and drive. Take it all in slowly. If you do it right, you'll feel like a new man." Though it is unclear what this means, Simon feels that it is a good proposition. His visit is a beginning, he thinks, the beginning of something, whereas the book Nadia gave him in the Clandestine Book Room was in some strange way the end. Z.

Mike's travel advice begins with basics—currency exchange, Warsaw sights, the weather, and ten key words in Polish (*tak, ni, dzień dobry, do widzenia, jak sie proszę, dziękuję*). In a *Warsaw in Your Pocket* magazine taken from the bedside in his hotel, Simon discovers the existence of the Motorization Museum on Warsaw's far southwestern edge. He sits with the magazine in his hands, gazing out at the city skyline. He must make his way to Radzanów soon. That is why he is in Poland. Once he has left the city, having a car will ensure a method of escape. He stands by the window, hands up to steady himself before the view. The city is unlike any place he's seen. It's full of young people, international business types, new skyscrapers rising in view of what was once the ghetto. Hooray for the new era, the whole place seemed to scream. Communism is dead. Let's live. We squeaked through. The liars and backroom apparatchiks went back to Moscow. Let them make people miserable there.

Simon finds his way to the Motorization Museum, making use of a map in the *Pocket* guide. Then a long walk past shuttered garages and what looks like an endless walled cemetery overgrown by forest. He is on an adventure in the Polish urban hinterland, in Warsawian exurbia. He pays his entrance fee—ten *zloty*—and finds inside a pair of bright red double-decker buses parked alongside a New York City Checker cab and, according to a guy who wanders over to greet him, the Popemobile John Paul II used before the assassination attempt by that crazy Turk.

On a whim, Simon points at a butter-yellow sedan with square headlights and an ill-fitting passenger side front door. Its finish reminds him of his kitchen table back home. It is, the staffer says, a 1960-something Moskvitch 412. It was the Polish Beetle. Or Lada. Or Trabant. The car that even losers acquired on their way to something better in the 1960s and '70s, when it seemed that Communism was around for good.

"How much for this one?" Simon asks. The car is one in an array of similar 412s in neon pink, avocado green, and barf beige. Nothing is said in any of the museum's promotional material about selling cars, but he assumes they might be willing to let go of one in their collection for the right price. How much Moskvitch colour variety do they really need on display? The kid goes off to ask someone he calls Yuri. Time passes. Maybe Yuri is on his lunch break.

The key is in the ignition. Simon opens the driver's side door, sits on the big couch of a front seat and starts the car. It runs rough. Conks out. He starts it again, runs it harder, and the telltale blue smoke from hardened seals rises to the ceiling of the museum's hangar. He kills the engine and opens the trunk. Inside he finds a spare battery, a rusted set of jumper cables, one spare hubcap, chrome pieces in need of reapplication and a drift of dry fall leaves.

The kid reappears with the price in *zloty* scribbled on a scrap of paper. In light of the Mike-supplied wad of cash, it is a piddling amount. There is so much cash he hardly knows how to carry it—big bills, little bills, and in-between bills, sporting etchings of Chopin and Marie Curie and Polish kings. Spending money in Warsaw is a regular history tutorial. In the Westin, for the first time in his life, Simon has made use of the room safe. Once in the countryside he will have to decide what to do with his Polish money. Maybe bury it in the backyard. Do it at night. Pick the place beforehand and mark it off. Dig with a trowel. How deep? Lay it in there. Inside of what? Plastic? Maybe a big old tin can. Who knew if Polish money held up the way Canadian bills did. If Polish money went through the washing machine did it come out intact?

In order to hide what he could afford to pay, and to avoid acting like a gangster, peeling bills off a wad in his hand, he says he will take a walk around the grounds to think the price over. In a far corner, beside a twisted metal fence and the front end of a farm tractor, he counts out the bills and sticks them in his jacket pocket. He makes his way back to the car. In an exchange that reminds him of an old-time game show, he offers a handful of money while the museum guy holds out the keys. He bends himself inside and as he pulls out of the hangar the car backfires, loud and sharp, in an excellent impression of a gunshot. In the rearview he sees another worker with his arms over his head.

This is the start of his career as a driver in Poland. It does not occur to him until he is behind the wheel to wonder if a Canadian license entitles him to drive. Back he goes to the hotel to collect his things from the fourteenth floor. On his way through the lobby, like a real tourist, he buys an *International New York Times* at the little souvenir kiosk. Out front, a concierge in a brown uniform with gold braid on his shoulders looks over the car with a mixture of admiration and malice. He waves a hand at it. "Your car?"

Simon tosses his bag in the back seat. "Mine."

"My father had one."

"What colour?"

"Blue. A kind of washed-out blue. I've never seen it since. Once the car almost poisoned us. Somehow the exhaust was blocked and routed inside under the dash. We could have all fallen asleep and crashed on the highway." Delicately, he opens the driver's door for Simon to get in.

"Enjoy Poland," he calls as Simon pulls off.

He is a driver in Poland. Unlicensed and free. Mike's guide lies on the passenger seat. In it are details on how to find his father's house on the square in Radzanów. "There is no street number on it," Mike writes, "because no one has lived in it for decades, and in the old days, who needed numbers? They would say, by the Krystals." Using Mike's photographs, Simon will recognize it by sight. He imagines himself in a rocking chair inside, or walking in the woods, stumbling upon the Secret Place. Mike writes: "It will be like that old story where the children are playing and discover an intact synagogue buried in the ground. You will sit down in the clearing the way I did when I was a boy, and you will feel like a new man. No, that's advertising language. You will feel better than that."

So. What will it feel like? Simon wonders. He'll know when it happens.

In an instant, he changes his plans. Why run away from Warsaw? With the car, he is part of the place in a new way. He can cruise the wide Soviet-style boulevards. He will roll down Marszałkowska and then Jerozolimskie and Jana Pawła II. If he can find an Internet café, he might be able to connect back home, see what his father is doing, let Mike know everything's okay. And Nadia, the dulcimer girl, what might have popped up on her blog during his Polish interregnum?

It's a balmy late-summer day. The sky is full of clouds piled behind each other like great pearl-coloured battleships. He overshoots the centre of the city, somehow taking a side route that lands him on the bridge over the Vistula to Praga, Warsaw's left bank. He gets himself back on track, crosses the bridge that leads to the lower part of Old Town, and up, onto the *Krakowskie Przedmieście*, the Royal Route. He parks the Moskvitch on a cross street and behaves as if he and his nostalgia-inducing car belong on this street of boutiques and galleries, government palaces and hotels. Up the street he walks, looking for a good place to sit. To taste Polish coffee and send a few emails, if his lousy laptop will work, to Nadia in her west-side room with the smell of grass cuttings wafting from the yard. He thinks of the book she gave him, like a period at the end of his father's collection.

Simon takes a seat at a café table on a wide piece of sidewalk in front of the Bristol Hotel. The young waitress takes his order in formal English. Shoppers and students hustle past. Four women stand together on the sidewalk. One, in a peaked cap, holds a coffee in one hand and moves her cigarette between lips and an arm's distance from her hip. Up walks a bum. He is one of the grizzled old street guys lost in time. Grey hair. In a bulky overcoat, too heavy for the weather. Maybe he had a role in the old system, but his life came unmoored. He was purged, told to beat it, so he did. Now he was beat, Warsaw-style. He hovers around the women, especially the one in the cap. He looks steadily at the ground, as if searching for butts. The woman notices him. He straightens up and looks at her from behind his matted beard. She hands him the half-smoked cigarette. She nearly smiles as she does this. He takes the cigarette and walks off, holding the lit butt before him, as if it is too valuable to actually smoke.

A woman sitting at a neighbouring table notices his attentiveness to the street drama—this, and whatever else is obvious about him, leads her to ask where he is from. Simon over-explains: Vancouver, on the west coast of Canada. This elicits a smile; he has made a faux pas, assuming a Pole has not heard of his city. She turns her chair in his direction, looks at him over her glasses and says that she is Magdalena Borowska, a student at the Łódź Film School. She is in Warsaw to attend a festival. Magdalena holds out her hand to shake. She is happy in her program, even if David Lynch's plans for a studio in Łódź have fallen through. Walking in everyone's footsteps—Polanski, Wajda, Kieślowski—makes things interesting. Magdalena speaks perfect, almost unaccented English. His peculiar story raises her interest. Why is he in Poland? Where is he staying? For how long?

Simon's answers, though she receives them politely, clearly astound.

He has spent the past few days in the Warsaw Westin with a view of what was the ghetto. At night, when the lights come on in faraway neighbourhoods, they remind him of memorial candles. The blue bank tower in the distance is like a beacon to all that's taken place in this city in the last century. To change the subject, he says that he just bought a car. A Moskvitch.

A Moskvitch! Her father drove one when she was a child. It was, she says, pea green. Or pea-soup green, as they used to joke when the car needed a good wash. Black seats. When Simon says he is on his way to Radzanów, to take up residence in a hundred-year-old house on the village square, she looks concerned, as if he has said a truly crazy thing. She shakes her head, very slowly. Almost whispering, asks, "Are you a prisoner of memory, Simon?"

This shocks him. He has no idea what to say in response. Instead he tells her that he is, in some ways, a prisoner, though a happy one, of his business in Vancouver. It is in the hands of employees he would describe as well-meaning but not entirely competent.

Why would he take such risks, she wants to know. And why now? Does he not value his business?

Certainly, he values what he's made back home. He offers to show her the Shop on her laptop, since his will not pick up a Wi-Fi connection. On the website, there is a view of Cordova at dusk, with its cozy grey- and red-brick buildings, and not a soul in sight. He shows Magdalena a photo of the interior, with its wooden tables and chairs, and is surprised at the surge of pride he feels when she says she likes it.

"Here," he says, "this is this week's set list."

It is even busier than when he left, with slots through the afternoon each day. There is a new feature. A chalkboard where someone confirms who's due to play. On Wednesday: Michael. Juliana. Endrick. Galen. Mississippi. On Tuesday: Mary-Grace. Virginie. Aiensley McEaneley. Gabriel. Amelia. Eva Werner. On Friday: Dr. Z. Jesse Speed. Davie. Bruno and Manu. Everything is running fine without him.

But no Nadia. Sometimes she ignores the set list and hangs around till there is a gap when someone doesn't show, and up she steps with the dulcimer, looking like a musician airlifted in from another place and time.

"You see," he says. "On it goes without me. Jesse Speed. Amelia. Virginie. They come and play and eat and drink and everyone is happy, more or less."

Magdalena gives him a long look, then back she goes to the screen.

Simon explains that he has opened a new chapter in his life

without knowing entirely where it will lead. He feels the need to argue in favour of what he is doing.

"If there is anything I can do to help while you are here, you must just ask. I grew up in Warsaw, so I know my way around it."

And so there is. Though he has a computer with him, it will not connect at wireless hotspots. Could he use hers to check on things back home? Magdalena pushes her laptop across the table and opens her email program.

"Go ahead," she urges. "It's all yours." The screensaver is a photo of colourful objects set out on a countertop—shoulder bags, shoes, hats—painted in Day-Glo colours, tangerine and blood orange, mauve and bright green.

"Do you make these?"

Magdalena looks at the photo and nods. "It's a project of mine. I invite visitors to my web site to send an object they value. I promise to return it, but first I paint it. As you see. I use spray paint the graffiti guys like. And I ask them to answer a few questions." She slides the computer back towards herself and pulls up a questionnaire. "You can see here. Really, I am creating a community of women with this work. If you know someone who would be willing to send me something, okay, send this and ask her to join the project. I call it Everyday Things. Don't rush. I am going up the road to do some errands. I'll be back in less than an hour." And off she goes on her heels. The sound of them on the cobbled walk reminds him of the backfire at the Motorization Museum, which caused the young worker to take cover.

Simon gazes at Magdalena's questions. They include the most basic details: name, address, age, work life. And a self-portrait. How would the sender describe herself? How does she like to dress? Does she read women authors? Which ones? What grows in her garden? What is the special meaning of the object being sent?

He proceeds to Nadia's blog where there is one new post since he last looked. It is called "33 1/3-Sized Lions." It is longer than most. He gazes at his street-side surroundings and feels that he has slipped entirely free of his life back home. So, what is the point, he wonders, of reading Nadia's blog now? Still, he leans forward to see what she's written:

> I didn't know it at the time, but we were suburban folk. I thought, in some naïve way, that everyone lived like we did, in and out of the car, everything bought at the mall. My mother took me there on Thursdays. That was our night out, the night my father taught till late. To the library we went, where I chose volumes of Norse myth and scratched copies of Leonard Bernstein's music for youth. Then we'd have dinner. I'd order a cheeseburger with a slice of pickle and fries and a strawberry milkshake. Soon our subject of discussion became the fact that I'd outgrown my music teacher, who taught out of a windowless cubicle at a music store in the back end of the mall. He was well-meaning but short on ideas when a student had her own interests. Mine were developing in a very particular direction. I was happy to perfect the classical pieces we attended to each week, but my father had bought me a Hitachi transistor radio the size of a paperback. It pulled in local AM and FM stations from far away. I lay awake at night, the radio beside me on the bedside table that belonged to a set of colonial furniture my parents gave me on my tenth birthday. Great things came in on that little radio. The Temptations, in all their symphonic loveliness; Alice Cooper, hollering in his malevolent way; soft-rock anthems from southern California. Jackson Browne, Seals and Crofts. Joni Mitchell: "In France they kiss on Main Street / *Amour*, Mama, not cheap

display." Wow. I was smitten. I wanted to understand the nature of these things, how to make a pop song, with its verse-chorus-verse-bridge-chorus pattern. At school I passed the time in class by running "Diamond Girl" and "Take it Easy" through my head, trying to pick out melody and key signature. What would a song sound like if you moved it out of G and into D? This was something I figured my dad would allow me to follow up on. My mother wanted straightforward performance and decorum out of me, in an effort to recreate herself. She dressed me impeccably in pressed skirts and patent leather shoes, which became a point of conflict around the time I turned twelve. On the outside I was as well put together as she, but on the inside I was *disorderly*. That was her favourite word for me. Nadia, she would say, you are so *disorderly*. Fashion trends fascinated her. Social outings, club memberships, and bridge parties. But my father, in a kind of absurd contrast with the person he'd married, was increasingly talking like a suburban Weatherman. The whole game, as he liked to put it, was rigged. No way was his daughter going to join the rest of the social climbers. Without telling my mother, he found me a more off-the-wall teacher by way of the music school at UBC. Her name was Martha. She was the wife of a professor, but she was somehow too idiosyncratic to land a job teaching university students.

The twist in my new teacher's life was that she and her husband were loaded. Her father had made money in West End high-rises in the sixties. He'd torn down the great old rich-people's mansions, with their colonial-era names like Braemar and Gabriola, and built twenty-storey orange and beige towers ringed with balconies, dubbed Hacienda and Malibu. When the house crusher died, his wealth went into a trust and then into a savings account for freewheeling spending when Martha turned thirty. With all that money Martha and her husband bought a ramshackle mansion in the heart of Shaughnessy, a wood and stucco house with too many rooms to furnish, a coach house with a family of feral cats, a yard that required a team to take care of it, and lilac trees which, in spring, the season when my father first took me there, smelled so good they might have been a drug—a nectar that might turn you into an angel. And I did feel I was a transparent sort of magical being when I approached Martha's house, my music in my bag, the snack my mother had packed for me half-eaten, my homework forgotten. Martha told me she was named after someone famous out of the Weimar golden era of modern music. She was, certainly, my first crush, with her peasant dresses and her chestnut hair down to her waist. She had wide-set green eyes and a knowing smile that suggested a lot of inward thought that she was not going to pass along to a girl my age. Her piano was a Steinway grand, naturally. It was well tuned. Sometimes it had supper plates on it, à la Thelonious Monk, and although it was huge, with a huge sound, it was dwarfed by the big living room where it stood beside leaded glass windows that overlooked the backyard trees and gardens. After we'd gone through my pieces, Martha fed me cake and milk at the kitchen breakfast table. Or ginger ale and ice cream.

Sometimes when I arrived she was involved in a long, uninterruptible phone call. Unseen, I snooped around the house's front rooms, turning over books and pulling out record sleeves. There I first saw the haunting cover of Miles Davis's *Kind of Blue*, the weird psychedelia of Cream's *Disraeli Gears*. I pocketed a metal souvenir that I later learned was a piece of metal type from a music publishing company in New York City. I still have it.

We had fun. We played serious music. We talked pedal work and posture. Arms straight from the body and not bouncing. But we went deep into the kind of music I was falling in love with, and I became an improviser, a freewheeler all over the keyboard, a kind of radical musical youth. I waited and waited for Martha to make a pass at me, because I was young and teachers did that to their students, didn't they? But it never did happen. I pined. I fell far into a private musical world that battered back all the social competition of junior high, so that by the time I was in high school I could entirely reject the stuff we did in music class in favour of things I did with friends, who formed bands. I had no plan.

Simon taps out an email to the address listed as "Site Manager" on Nadia's blog: "Nadia. Here is something funny. Maybe I should use it at the Shop to screen out the crazies." He copies the questionnaire and the array of painted things and sends them to her. He considers trying to explain whose email he is using, but instead, looks up the town hall address in Radzanów and sends it with the shoe query. It is: Urząd Gminy w Radzanówie 06-540 Radzanów n./Wkrą, Plac Piłsudskiego 26. That is where he is meant to be. He sits back and waits.

Magdalena comes up the street and sits beside him. Simon explains that someone from Vancouver named Nadia might email back. He offers his email address, though he can't be sure he'll be able to access it once he gets to Radzanów.

"Then let's meet here and I'll pass on whatever comes. You tell me what time." She packs up her things. "I am here anyway, for the festival and then a few days after that."

Everything is Horseshit

Once the city's outskirts give way to farmland, the drive to Radzanów offers a tableau of Polish countryside. Simon passes one little town after another, each marked by an introductory sign in green and white, and then, upon leaving, a sign with the town's name struck through with a diagonal line. The outskirts of Radzanów are lush and green, irrigated by the Wkra River. The roadway runs through sparse pine forest until a puzzle of buildings appears, one and two storeys tall. Then he is in the central square and parks at an unmarked corner. A crowd is gathered in the centre of the square. Equipment is being loaded out of white cube vans. A film crew is in town. Some hover around the craft services table, sampling sandwiches and drinking coffee from paper cups.

A woman stands on a sidewalk near to where he is parked. She is dressed in office-professional black and is marking something on a clipboard. She is the only figure on the square not wearing the film crew's de rigueur semi-camouflage. Simon feels that he knows her from somewhere. But this is impossible. He watches from where he sits, parked at the curbside. It's a remarkable scene. The town square is packed with vehicles, a forest of lighting equipment, actors in costumes meant to look like some old-fashioned kind of dress. They are familiar too, but in a wholly stereotypical way. There are women and children and grizzly-bearded men. Are they dressed as wartime refugees? A few look distinctively like religious Jews. The women wear long skirts, down to their ankles. The boys wear caps. The girls have their hair in braids, which lie on their chests. Some of the male actors wear long black coats and paste-on grey beards—an approximation of Chassidic garb. These made-up Jews huddle against the stoop of the old brick synagogue. Simon knows it's the synagogue from Mike's handwritten guide—"Look for the red-brick building across the square from the church," he wrote—though Simon could have guessed this on his own. In Brooklyn, Mike had told the story of a wedding in this synagogue before the war, which was interrupted when the women's gallery collapsed to the floor below. The brick building, standing opposite the big church on the other side of the square, is distinctive in its surroundings. Its Moorish flair, the round windows high up in its façade, signal its Jewishness.

Something is holding up the shoot. Cars pass on the far side of the square where the road is not blocked. The drivers rubberneck, slowing to witness the scene. Simon wonders if what's being filmed is a scene out of the town's past. A horse-drawn cart laden with hay trundles by. The cart driver raises a hand in salute. Was he from prop services or the real thing? Who is he saluting? The fake Jews? The carnival of city-dwelling film techies and their spending power? No one takes any notice of Simon, as if he and his car are invisible.

With the window rolled down, he takes a deep breath. The square smells like bus exhaust and mown fields and horseshit. From where he sits in the ticking car, Simon can see "his" house. He confirms this by pulling a photograph from Mike's packet of papers. He has looked at the photograph of the house many times. In Vancouver, he kept it propped against the windowpane behind his desk. There, he thought of it as a kind of icon, an image to meditate on. This after he'd decided to say nothing to his father about the proposal Mike had made. On the plane from Frankfurt to Warsaw, he'd taken out the photograph of the house so many times that the woman seated beside him asked what it was. She was, she said, on her way to promote a skyscraper development, thirty storeys high, in downtown Warsaw. New money. New Poland. From what she understood, the building she would be financing was not far from where the Jewish ghetto had been. Did he know anything about that part of Warsaw? Simon shook his head and put the photograph away without explaining its backstory.

Now he slides it out of the envelope full of maps and *zloty* and sets it on the dash where cab drivers once positioned the medallions of their patron saints. The house where his father was born—really, born, with the *feltsher* arriving by sleigh in the snow at night—stands behind the crowd of actors, across the narrow roadway from the square. It looks, compared to many others on the square, prehistoric. It is pinned between the walls of two larger houses. It is fronted in wide planks. The peaked tin roof is the colour of tarnished nickel. The neighbouring house on the left is nearly as scruffy as his, but the one on the right has been fluffed and turned into a modish market-town house, with new wooden window frames and a coat of banana-coloured stucco, topped off by red Mediterranean-style roof tiles.

Simon reads from Mike's guide to the square. Piłsudski, its namesake, is a hero for his military campaigns, for the miracle of the Polish defeat of the Soviet Red Army after the Russian Revolution, even for General Piłsudski's willingness to build a modern Poland made up of all ethnicities. Jews too. There is a Piłsudski Square in every little town in central Poland. Sometimes the general's bust sits on a plinth, but not in Radzanów. "Your Piłsudski Square," Mike writes, "is the centerpiece of the village with its

850 souls, fifty miles northwest of Warsaw, in Plock County, Mazovia Province. The place has been run over by war again and again. One of Napoleon's generals is said to have a slept in a house, still standing, a few kilometers to the west. This borderland was among the first places the Germans saw in Poland. Not far west of the town, using bunkers whose ruins can still be seen, the Polish army maintained a hopeless struggle along the Mława Front. After the war, with barely enough time to lick its wounds, the countryside fell under the power of a second political and social lie." In Mike's words, "The whole pathetic garbage pail of Soviet Communism."

Could this be Radzanów's final historic chapter? To be merely a mundane village in the countryside, nothing more? On its website were photographs of houses for sale, a beauty contest with teenagers in bikinis, a newly built playground, and news of upcoming saints' festivals. Add to this, most absurdly, a film with fake Jews. Simon's head buzzes with the surprise of driving into town for the first time, on this lovely summer day, blue smoke trailing from his car into the light in the trees and over the housetops, the air as sharp in his nose as silver dust, to find that a deportation was going on in Piłsudski Square.

He decides to let the film set shut down for the day before trying the door of his house. Hoisting his knapsack onto his shoulder, he crosses the square and ducks into a little corner store. A confectionary. He wonders what the Polish word is for this. Like so many things in this country he has no clue. He gathers up lunch—a box of juice, a couple of buns that resemble bagels, a tin of Polish luncheon meat. He mistakenly places Euro bills on the counter, but the proprietor—an aproned grandma of indeterminable age, somewhere between sixty-five and eighty—stares at him until he realizes his mistake and exchanges the overvalued bills for *zloty*. Now he knows something about the square, besides the fact that it has been transformed into a film set full of fake Jews. The woman who owns the store nearest the church is honest.

He crosses the square, passes the impressive white church, follows a sandy road that leads to a green hilly landscape, a view out over fields, like the one on the way up from Warsaw. He walks along the roadway. What he looks out at could be a set for Beckett's *Waiting for Godot*. An angular leafless tree. A single cow with a bell on its neck. The melancholy of the cow; the blighted suggestiveness of the tree; the loveliness, like a trap waiting to be sprung, of the grasslands and hills; a few little farm outbuildings along fenced property lines. Simon sits by the crippled tree, opens the tin of meat spread and makes a sandwich. Just as he bites into it, mouth watering after the drive, the pause in the square, the mystery of it all, who should step into view but the woman who held the clipboard. She is walking with a lanky guy, at least six inches taller than she is. He has a pair of cameras over his shoulder, one with an extra-long lens that reminds Simon of a sniper scope. As he chews on his sandwich, the two arrange themselves on the remains of an old wall. The woman sits, her hands in her pants pockets, in a kind of alert slouch. She lengthens her back and brushes the hair on her forehead to one side. The photographer goes to work, moving from side to side. He backs up, adjusting the focus on his lens. With the digital camera, he might be taking hundreds of shots. Then, when they are done, and the man has swung his cameras over his shoulder and onto his back, they turn toward the view, out past the contorted tree and the cow and Simon, whose mouth is full. The woman hesitates and gestures, ever so slightly, almost a wave. For a moment, it seems she will walk over and introduce herself. But something the photographer says shifts her interest. He is forgotten.

At this moment, as the two strangers turn back toward town, the new reality he has entered comes into focus: his aloneness, having appeared on the scene from nowhere in a car out of the dark lands of the Soviet past. Simon watches the pair move off toward the village, the woman's hair a straight line across her back, the man with his camera lenses pointed at him, as the butter-coloured sunlight fills the space between the three of them.

Open House

When he returns, the square is empty of activity.

He is in his father's ancestral town. Here his father was a boy, and Ray Bradbury-like, stepped off his parents' front stoop with a snap of his fingers to get the summer started. It had remained a hidden place for so long. His father had prospered on Abbott, moved uptown, met his mother, married, fathered children, raised a family by the sea and then moved on further, abandoning what he'd built as a family man. Never, not once, had he talked about this place.

Some of the older houses on the square—not his—are decorated with a bit of gingerbread, frivolously cut wood trim. His is bare. This is the word that goes through his mind as he approaches. A bare house. Once upon a time it was stained a mustard yellow like its neighbour, but now its wood planks are a weathered grey. Their shade reminds him of photographs he's seen of Haida Gwaii, of the wooden house fronts built for the heads of clans facing the Pacific. Simon wonders where all the film people have gone. Back to Warsaw? Or over to Mława where there might be enough hotel rooms for them all.

Two locals stand, hands in pockets, not far from the church. Simon puts his foot on the rotten wood stoop of his house and tries the doorknob of hammered tin. It turns. On the floor inside, he finds an envelope. He picks it up but sets it on a table in the middle of the room, forgetting it as he is drawn into the weird vault of time that has been maintained for his father's hoped-for return. He is his father's stand-in, a role he's never played.

The front room is dark. It smells of wood and water. The windows, set deep into casements, allow little light. The ceiling is low, built of three massive square beams, roughly hewn, on which lie pine planks. A table and four wooden chairs stand in the centre of the room, before an elaborately painted armoire. At the back of the room, in the darkest corner, is a tile stove with an ash-coloured iron cooktop and metal doors. Inside the stove is a rusted grate. On the stovetop, there is a dented kettle and a tool the size of a pot, meant to do some kind of grinding. On a crooked shelf to the side of the stove sit an enamel pitcher and ladle and a bundle of wooden spoons, one of which has a handle carved in the shape of a bird.

Where, Simon wonders, will he get firewood if the nights grow cool?

At the back of the house, he finds a bedroom. Its corner windows and whitewashed walls make it brighter than the front room. Its ceiling beams are decorated with stenciled drawings of holly and mistletoe. At the back of the room is a door with an intricately carved frame. The bed is narrow, built for a child or someone very thin. Over it is draped an embroidered cover. He sits on the bed and peers into the light that falls through the windows.

In the front room, he pulls a chair from the kitchen table and places it by the window. High up the little panes are broken, and in the corners, stuck to the glass, are the upturned carcasses of flies, wasps, moths with transparent amber wings.

He reaches for the envelope with his name on the front. Inside it is a neatly folded sheet of paper, which reads:

Dear Simon,

I am helping my mother by welcoming you to her town. I am the daughter of Ewa Grabowska, a childhood companion of your father. We invite you to her place for dinner. My mother is a very good cook. She tells me (she says it in Polish, because this is the language the two of us speak together) that she "looks forward to feeding the boy." I know you are not a boy. But to my mother, everyone who looks like they are under a certain age is a boy. And so you are. My mother read English a bit when she was young, but she is rusty. In the meantime, I offer to operate as your go-between. I live in Warsaw, but I am often here to see my mother and I am helping with what you see in the square, the film set in the wartime.

My mother's house can be found as follows: step out your door and, to your right, walk on your side of the square until the road bends, just opposite the church. Her present home (I was raised in an older house, further from the town square) is yellow. It has a red roof with an upper balcony where she grows geraniums. Knock and introduce yourself any time. Friday would suit us. Maybe we will see you. If not, another time.

With our best wishes, Ania and Ewa Grabowska

Night comes on. He has nothing to do so he does nothing. Radzanów sleeps beneath a sky the colour of fountain-pen ink, a deep blue with a flash of stars. The house is dark, sealed like a box. When he's had enough of the darkness, he lies on the sagging bed. The surrounding world is incomparably silent. Somehow this makes it impossible to sleep. He feels his back in the concave mattress and his feet are cold. He is overcome by a kind of sleeplessness that allows self-doubt to rush in. He considers his directionless adventure, regardless of the pleasures of surprise it brings, and this takes him back to his point of departure. He dreams of his street back home. It rears up before him like a pop-up illustration in a children's book. The yellow of his building, the green of the park across the road, a bright red fire truck idling at the curb. He sees it all from a bird's-eye view. A car—in dream logic he recognizes it as Nadia's, though she does not own a car—traverses the puzzle of West End blocks. It stops on Davie. Nadia gets out. She walks by the seawall where she seems to be looking for someone. She stands with her hands on her hips. The water is boldly blue and still, the tide far out. She turns and heads up the rise on Davie, continuing along Barclay, where she turns and approaches his building. From above she is head and shoes, a white T-shirt like a lacuna on the grey sidewalk. She mounts the stairs at Simon's building and disappears inside. She inhabits his absence this way.

In the morning, dying for a coffee, Simon makes his way into the front room of the house. There, the envelope with its invitation stands propped on the table. It is a fine welcome, crisp, white, and bearing his name. He holds it in one hand and hangs out his front door. He cranes his neck up the roadway and there it is—the yellow villa with its balcony of flowers.

I Begin to Sing

Nadia is waiting for Joshua, her best music student. He reminds her of herself when she was thirteen, visiting her teacher's big old house in Shaughnessy where music seemed to grow in the garden. He is tall for his age and lean, not a man yet, but he is through with being a boy. She knows this partly because he had his bar mitzvah the previous winter. Learning for it got in the way of piano lessons. She does not really know how these Jewish things work. At any rate, he does not talk to her about what he did at school, or about the peculiar challenge of chanting Hebrew before a synagogue congregation. He rarely speaks about his family, as if he has none and lives alone, a teenage hermit. This, too, reminds Nadia of herself at his age, when she thought she was a creature *sui generis,* as if she had emerged barefoot out of what was left of the old growth at Stanley Park to listen for music in the world around her.

When Nadia was thirteen, music offered an escape from family life. Piano lessons were the first thing she did on her own. After an hour at her teacher's Steinway, she hopped on the Granville bus headed downtown, away from her home in the suburbs, to walk the streets below Georgia. There she explored record stores and instrument shops. Standing out front of nightclubs she read the posters advertising upcoming bands, as if she might actually go inside. She talked to people, acting like she was part of the crowd; too young to join the scene but open to invitations. Once she got home to discover that her mother had caught sight of her on a downtown street corner, but by the time she'd driven around the block to nab her, Nadia was gone. *What,* her mother wanted to know, *was she doing? If this happened again, she could kiss her piano lessons goodbye.* But Nadia's father intervened, and the threat wasn't mentioned again.

It was this exploration, her secret adventures, as her mother called them, that prepared Nadia to move out when she was eighteen. She moved downtown, sharing an apartment with a woman called Rosemarie, who provided her entrée into the punk scene. They met at a music bar called the Railway Club. Rosemarie's band had just finished a short, raucous set. Four songs, each one two minutes long. After which they destroyed their instruments. Rosemarie introduced Nadia to musicians, many of whom had grown up, like her, in Vancouver's far-flung suburbs. In faraway flatlandia. But their new homes were the clubs like the Smilin' Buddha on East Hastings, and Luv-a-Fair. Irregularly, but with great fanfare, Rosemarie performed at these places with her band the Punk Assholes. It was her job to shout "We're punk assholes!" from the front of the stage as they launched into a song that approximated the sound of power tools applied to electric guitars. The Punk Assholes' big night was an ear-splitting opening for D.O.A. at Luv-a-Fair. That night Nadia took in the punk paraphernalia—the safety-pinned shirts, the butchered hair, even the power tools—with a careful eye. Joey Shithead was their chieftain. Their big man. He fired up his saw onstage and Nadia thought, so that's where they get the idea. She could not stand this sort of stuff. She could handle noise, and she wanted to be unconventional as badly as anyone else you might find at Hamburger Mary's after midnight, but music was music and noise was noise. Rosemarie was surely going deaf from all the punk noise she made, but she was living wild and this made her happy.

When Nadia moved out, her father had staked her with a gift of five crisp $100 bills. He gave it to her as she packed up. Kissing her on the forehead, he said, "I wish you well, Nadia." The money bought her a few months in Rosemarie's spare bedroom on Broughton, with its view of a back-alley rooming house. After classes Nadia cast around for a job, something to pay her half of the rent, which was $225. She waited tables at Binky's Oyster Bar, but this demanded a put-together wardrobe of more crisply ironed white shirts and black skirts than she could afford or aspired to own. She lasted one day behind the counter at the Avis car rental outlet on Georgia. She had not, she saw immediately, moved downtown to meet tourists' Toyota requirements. She tried to get on the Parks Board crew that tended the roses in Stanley Park, but that was all sewn up by union guys who got their girlfriends cushy jobs.

Then one day Rosemarie took her along for support to visit a friend known as Crazy Janie, who was dying at St. Paul's Hospital. Nadia did not want to go, but Rosemarie pleaded. Crazy Janie had been a kind of Punk Assholes patron. She lent the band money when they needed new equipment. She was, according to Rosemarie, dying of some new virus no one understood. Down to eighty or ninety pounds, she was so bitter it was nearly impossible to sit and talk with her. She'd bitch at Rosemarie for bringing the wrong kind of ketchup to supplement the horrible hospital food, or for forgetting the newspaper section with the crossword puzzle. The last time Rosemarie visited, Janie had crabbed at her so much she left crying.

Nadia waits for Joshua in front of the music building on campus. The trees tower over her, cedar-smelling, leaves rustling as students cross in and out of their shadows.

Joshua is too young for the sort of musical adventures she'd pursued—eighteen-year-old adventures were barely in his view—but he seems eager, as she'd been at fourteen and fifteen, for a life of his own, out of his parents' control. He tells her stories that remind her of her younger self, but what reminds her most of herself is his habit of finding music in everything. In traffic, in a flock of birds rising from the rooftop of a condominium building. The differences between the two of them are accounted for by the fact that he is male and born some fifteen years after her, in a different world, really. Time, she recognizes, is everything.

If she were going to have just one student, he is certainly the one she'd choose. She'd been taking students for a few years by the time they met. Most were six- or seven-year-olds who played their instruments without care or interest. They played as if they were music boxes, wooden in their rhythms and brittle on the keys. But she was dedicated to them all the same. Her punk days were long gone. Rosemarie was just a memory, and late nights at Luv-a-Fair might be stories someone else told her about fun *they'd* had when they were young. By the time she met Joshua she was living alone in Point Grey on a street lined with beech trees and Audi SUVs. She had no piano in her apartment. She had her dulcimer and a popgun for scaring the pigeons in the eaves outside her window, the rotten electric stove—a dead ringer for the Betty Crocker play stoves that were popular when she was a girl—and a four-poster bed painted dark red by an optimistic previous tenant. She knew she'd sleep better if it were another colour, but somehow she never got around to the job.

In order to teach, she booked time at the university where, against the strict rules of the music department, she snuck Joshua into the portholed practice room meant for her.

She enjoyed meeting students. It was work focused on someone other than herself, and she learned from them, especially the good ones. Her practice room arrangement would have been discovered if Joshua had not been so talented, because no matter how soundproofed the place was, someone would have noticed the racket of an inept kid playing Scott Joplin with no sense of swing or rhythm, and would have asked what was going on. She thought he was as competent—innately, instinctively, if not in rote learning—as some of her university music-program companions who were ten years older than he and had been taught by professionals. He picked things up quickly, and always returned with some advance on what they'd worked on the week before. He was not a prodigy. But this may have been because he did not apply himself in any disciplined way. She had known a few prodigies. One on piano and another on violin. They were serious and single-minded. They practiced, unremittingly, forgetting to eat or to go to the bathroom. She did not think Joshua practiced at all. He went home and lay on his bed with an old guitar playing Neil Young or Muddy Waters. His forte, when he was not sitting in front of her being asked to play, was to find himself in what he called "situations." These involved music, often found in the streets in unusual places. Vancouver offered a rich supply of situations, especially when the sun shone, but she expected he found them in the rain, too.

Finally, Joshua runs up, fifteen minutes late for an hour-long lesson, a bottle of Coke in one hand, his school bag half open on his back. As they make their way up to the practice room, he tells her that it was a situation that made him late.

Nadia shushes him till they are inside the practice room. She shuts the white windowed door, with its rubber soundproofing. Joshua sits at the piano but turns to face her rather than the keys.

"You know those pianos?"

"Which pianos?"

"Those pianos they're putting around. On the streets."

"Oh. Those."

"Yah. I pass one on my way over here. It's orange and it's all grafittied up. It's on the dock where the little ferry pulls up in False Creek. You know?"

She has never ridden on the ferries that pull up at the dock. Why would a dedicated walker like herself pay four dollars to skim across the creek when the bridges all around provide a much greater adventure, up high, with views of the city, the water, and the sky? She has seen people banging away on the piano as she circled the sea wall beside False Creek.

"Well, today there was a guy playing it, you know, not that well. He had a tin can out, and I wanted to see if anyone gave him any money. Which they didn't. Nobody. He played, I don't know, for maybe half an hour. Music from the movies or TV."

Nadia thinks of Joshua sitting there, watching for coins to drop in the tin, while she waits for him in the sun on campus, their practice time slipping away.

"When he gave up I asked if I could go next. 'Be my guest.' That's what he said. 'Be my guest.' Is that an old-fashioned kind of line?"

Nadia smiles as she considers this. Periodically he treats her as his guide to the olden times, to that mysterious era known as "back in the day." He'd ask her about the 1960s as if she were eternal, a wise old stump of a creature who'd seen the creation of time.

"I guess. It's true, people don't talk like that any more."

"Anyway, I sat down and played, and he listened to me."

Well, of course he did. Here was this kid playing beautiful music and there was his empty tin.

"What did you play?"

Joshua hesitates. "Uh. Well. You know. The blues. I fooled around. Improvised around. Remember that bebop scale you showed me?"

She nods, smiling her fake teacherly smile, because, of course, why would he bother trying out the difficult rag they were working on, which, she guessed, might have felt like chopping wood, when fooling with the blues made him feel like the wood was all in a pile in the yard, waiting to be picked up?

"He listened for a while. The hobo? And he comes over and drops some money in his tin for me. Isn't that funny?" Joshua reaches into his pocket and pulls out a toonie. He holds it between thumb and forefinger, his first money earned from music. His initiation into the guild.

While Joshua makes his way smoothly through the first two sections of Joplin's "Pineapple Rag," she finds it difficult to keep her mind focused on what he is doing correctly and what needs improvement. She thinks of the total absence in her own youth of a found piano, an instrument placed for anyone to play. There was the cordoned-off player grand that showed up each year, around Christmastime, at the Oakridge Mall. How badly she'd wanted to duck under the rope on poles that circled it to try the bright white keys, but her mother held her hand tight. At home they had an old upright, always a little out of tune at its high and low ends. Her father would hear her practicing from the kitchen and shout, "Nadia, remind me to get that thing tuned, or I'm going to give it away to the Salvation Army." Another threat not followed through on, heard and forgotten.

When she asked her music teacher about finding a piano tuner, Martha said she'd try to think of someone. But Nadia never did learn who could tune their piano. Certainly not from Martha, who was a wonderful musical guide but no source of practical information. Martha was like no one Nadia had ever met. She would forget to show up *at her own house* for a lesson, then call Nadia's home at ten p.m. to apologize and say that next time they'd do four hours! Six hours! We'll play all night, Martha promised, and catch up and race ahead so Nadia would realize that music was not about scheduling but about joy!

Suddenly she hears Joshua playing, loud and clear, the freshness and the bounce of his rendition of "Pineapple Rag," the spring in his right hand and the steady rhythm in his left, just as she'd shown him by tapping it out on his knee. And she notices that their time in the room is up. She lets him play all the same, until he slows down on his own, like a watch that needs winding. He turns to her, swinging his leg off the bench, saying, "Well. Yah." The perfect fourteen-year-old coda to a wonderfully played Joplin rag.

As Nadia comes down West Tenth, the buses and cars roaring past—did they always make this much noise?—she sees that there is some sort of lunchtime open mic jamboree going on in the café opposite the antiques place above Alma. Two guys are cramped up against the front window like bugs. She has her grocery shopping and banking to do, but the music pulls her inside. She orders a French press coffee, which is the place's specialty, and sits by the door for ease of exit. Her seat provides a perfect listening and viewing spot. The café is empty except for a few students in the back who read from thick paperbacks. Dostoyevsky? Hegel? Dickens? Universities make people do all kinds of remarkable things.

The two open-mic guys play like the room is empty, looking at their shoes. Sometimes they seem to be making eye contact with the insides of their skulls. They are terrible in so many ways. They are like an instruction manual in how to be terrible at music, and, she thinks, if you studied them with some care (though not *too much* care, because their terribleness is obvious) you would learn about a hundred things to avoid: the willingness to sit on anything while playing—an amp or a box; the custom of drinking out of a jam jar; the microphone set-up, done so both musicians lean down, stretching their necks, even their lips to get close to the mic; the spidery way one of them strums his guitar, with showy effect but no rhythmic regularity.

They are twenty years old at most. They wear railroader dungarees and their hair is long on the sides and thin on top. They are young but they're going to be old in about fifteen minutes. No one claps when they finish a song. It's like a scene in a Bugs Bunny cartoon, but without the crickets in the wings. After listening to Joshua in the morning, this is the wrong thing.

Nadia takes the last drop of coffee on her tongue, the one that holds the sugar she dropped in the cup. As quietly as she can she heads for the street.

She feels her phone buzz. For once she's glad she has caller ID. Jess. She considers letting it ring but doesn't go this far.

"What do you want?"

Jess sounds out of breath. Wheezy. She hears him take a long drag on a cigarette.

"Nadia. I've got something for you. I think you'll want it, okay? I don't want to talk about it on the phone. Can we meet?"

She shakes her head, not even saying the thing she means by her silence: no.

"Remember the Wilder Snail? On Keefer? That place with the awning. By the park?"

Nadia lets out a sigh.

"After work. Around five. Okay?"

"Today?"

"Yes. Nadia. Okay?"

Once she's hung up she feels her day is shot. She stands at the corner, winded. What can he possibly have for her? She has no good reason for what she does next, except that like a crow, she will be traveling in the direction of the east side where Jess is pulling her, taking her from her own path one last time.

She walks through Kits, across the Burrard Bridge toward the West End. Her old neighbourhood; as Joshua would say, from back in the day. It beckoned. On the bridge, she gets herself on the wrong side. She's out of date with these things—the walkway on the south side is reserved as a bike lane. She steers close to the cement railing as she marches across the bridge, then up Burrard and left into the crowds on Davie. Some things remain exactly the same—the gay clubs, the little dry cleaning shops and Asian food spots. But where there had been a building, the lot is now being used as a public garden. On the corner of Bute, a Starbucks has appeared, with wire chairs out on the sidewalk, doing a poor impression of Paris. As she nears the corner, she sees a familiar face at one of the sidewalk tables.

"Eddie?" She stands before him as he looks up from a tall paper coffee cup.

Eddie's expression is vague at first, then his face lights up. "Nadia." He stands to take her in his arms but bumps the table. Coffee spills down the storefront window. "Nadia." He stands back and looks at her. "God. How did I recognize you? You've gone . . . straight?"

"Straight. Yes. And what's new with you?" It takes all her presence of mind not to say the first thing that occurs to her, which is: I thought you were dead. He looks very much as he did a decade and a half before. The startling blue eyes and fluttery lashes. He has put on weight. When she last saw him, he might have weighed ninety pounds. He was a friend of Rosemarie's. The partner of Crazy Janie. Nadia had first seen him at St. Paul's. He made a furtive appearance just as she came to see if Rosemarie was ready to go, and she had watched him collect something from Crazy Janie. A handout from his dying girlfriend? Then he slipped away. He was obviously sick himself, but he would not check himself in for any kind of treatment. Nadia heard about this sort of thing from an AIDS ward nurse who said the government, in its wisdom, had figured out a way to dock welfare in favour of hospital-fee payments. So people like Eddie stayed sick on the streets.

On a few occasions, Rosemarie begged her to join her on errands, shopping, a bookstore visit, a get-well card. Crazy Janie had asked them to send her devastated boyfriend a get-well card. They chose one with a picture of Elvis on the front. The inside was blank, and they wrote "You ain't nothin' but a hound dog" on it in black marker, then handed it over in Eddie's squalid room off East Hastings. It wasn't much wider than the bed itself. The four walls were bare but for two ancient paper calendars someone had pinned up years before. She'd assumed that he'd died there, looking up at the month of June, 1969. But here he is. Looking fine. As healthy, in his offbeat way, as Joshua.

"It just gets worse over there," Eddie says. " I haven't lived on the east side for a few years. I'm on Comox. On the way down to Denman. Remember the old houses along there? Can you believe they still exist? The landlord likes to garden, cut the lawn. He's not interested in a windfall. He sits out front on his lawn chair and watches the yuppies roar by in their SUVs. He'd throw eggs if he could get away with it. He kind of keeps us, like we're his family. Do you want to see my place?"

This is an astonishing invitation from a man out of her past, the long-ago past she'd loved for its unpredictability and freedom. It is an invitation from someone she thought was dead from a horrible disease that swept young people away. Of course she wants to see his place.

So they walk along Davie to Broughton, and then down Comox to the stretch where the old houses stand behind their hedge of holly. The big porch out front is shadowy, and as they step in at the front door Nadia thinks she smells Earl Grey tea or nutmeg. It is a house with tea and spice floating in the dust motes and streams of sunlight pouring down from the stained glass on the landing. Eddie shuts the front door so the sounds from the street fade away. They've stepped into some sort of vault of time.

He leads her up a stretch of stairs and turns at the landing. Eddie produces a single key from his pants pocket and unlocks the door. His apartment is huge, barely furnished, with books on board shelves. The floor is an expanse of shining maple. Wide windows look out at the monkey tree in the yard. She feels strange, something tightening in her gut, as if she's entered her own past. Has she been in this house before? On a rainy day, full of expectations? She's tempted to turn and go, but he's shut the door behind them.

"Here. Let me show you something." He takes her hand. This startles her at first, but she remembers that in the days when he was sickest, she brought food or medicine to him at the SRO hotel where he lived. Week-old newspapers were spread by the bed and the windows were wide open so the bus noise came roaring in. He always took her hand as she got ready to go. He was like that. Innately youthful and kind.

"Look."

At first, she can't tell what it is he's showing her. It is under glass. A kind of display case at hip level. Inside, on a bed of black satin, are clothes. A pair of black boots. Something with studs. A T-shirt that reads *D.O.A. Rules!* A book. She can't focus on its title. Record albums. These she looks at with more care. The Clash. *London Calling*. She realizes that she is looking at a shrine. Crazy Janie's shrine. A very beautiful and strange way to remember the girl who snapped at Rosemarie when they brought the wrong ketchup.

Eddie has nothing more to say about what he is showing her. He lets go of her hand and goes over to the sink. He runs the water and fills a glass. He gives her a moment to consider what he's shown her.

"Do you want something? Glass of water?"

Nadia shakes her head. She doesn't know what to say. She must get going, but can she drop by if she's ever nearby?

"Sure." Eddie sets his glass on the edge of the counter and turns to her with his hands wide behind him on the counter's edge.

She goes down the lofty inner stairway like a cat, as quietly as she can. She opens the big wooden front door and pulls it behind her with a careful click. As she steps out of the holly onto Comox she begins to sing.

A Girl I Know Who Steals Everything

Nadia spots him from across the park. Against the backdrop of the Wilder Snail. The awning over him in the almost-evening. Cigarette ever-present in his left hand, though Nadia knows he is right-handed. At his feet, a box. Or is it just outdoor café furniture—a stool? With his bad eyesight, she has the edge on him. She stands at the far edge of the park between Keefer and Georgia, screened by a growth of bamboo, and surveys the old neighbourhood. What a shift. Once it was dockworkers and barrel-makers. Jews and Japanese. Chinese laundries and Ukrainian corner stores. Now it's reborn, full of artists and house-proud professionals.

    She breathes. Even here, not far from the viaduct and the truck throughway on Prior, it smells good. Green. Golden at sunset. Lucky people, the ones who live around this park, breathing it in with their breakfasts and dinners. She smiles. Shuts her eyes. Her hands rest by her sides. She thinks of her father in her teenage years, walking everywhere at his remorseless pace. You couldn't keep up if you tried. It seemed to be his way of being alone. But as far as she knew, he never came marching over to this side of town. Where she stood wasn't far from where his family had started out in the city. She had a clearer picture of that now. Though he'd never said a single thing about those years. Not a word about Reliable Loan. She'd learned about that herself, how it was one of fifty pawnshops in a neighbourhood of barber shops, book stalls, psychics, and Chinese groceries. She'd come across no photographs of Reliable Loan. There was a vogue for Vancouver street photos, in high-colour Kodachrome and black and white; they appeared in newspapers, on postage stamps, in gallery windows. The old streets erupted anew, bouquet-like, and it was in a gallery that she noticed one photographer's genius for shooting a big shop window so the dark behind it included a reflection of what stood out of sight *across the street*. The unseen thing, a shadow photo, haunted the main subject. Sometimes what lurked there was mundane: power lines, the tops of trees, rolling cloud. But in one of these, mirrored in a plate glass window, were two figures in a doorway. One was short and bald, hands in the pockets of his vest, a smile on his face. The other was tall, a book under one arm. His head was turned from the camera. Planning his escape: Nadia's father, with his brother. The turned head defined him. It predicted everything that happened years later, his urge to flee, to walk right out of the picture. She'd been his good girl. Not one thing would she learn about him until she was handed the calling card: Reliable Loan, Marine 3647.

She settles on a wooden bench, hoping that Jess will not see her from where he stands. What role does Jess Portman play in all this? He raises a hand to his forehead and calls.

"Nadia? Nadia!" Here he comes, carrying the box. He crosses the field in his untied runners. He sets the box down gingerly on the bench and opens his arms. For a hug? Something really is up.

"Listen. Nadia. Sit." They settle beside each other. "The cops called on Tuesday. What's today? Thursday? I didn't know they did that. Call you on the phone. 'Sergeant Detective So-and-so.' And he says, 'Is this Jess Portman's residence?' Scared the shit out of me. Like a knife in the gut. Nobody calls and asks for Jess Portman. Here. First. Look." He strips the tape off the box's flaps. Nadia lifts them herself. Inside: newspaper as packing material, which she pushes aside. And there it is. The pop bottle.

"It's the one. I took it. For you. First I had it under the bed at my place. My boss, he has no reason to think I took it. He had me call the cops to report it. I thought that was funny. Reporting my own theft. But I thought it all out in advance. Before I took it, I'd got in the habit of not turning on the video camera attached to the alarm system. So there was nothing odd about it not working the night I needed it to not work. I broke a window in the back bathroom from outside and dropped a couple muddy boots through. It looked like some kid had slipped through, you know, and fallen on the tiles before making his way in. I grabbed a few things a druggy thief might go for. A mobile phone we kept by the cash, and, for fun, a set of steak knives that had belonged to Roman Polanski. We were just getting those evaluated. That would distract everyone. Those I threw away.

"The cops came and photographed the empty vitrine with its pot lights pointing at our card describing the bottle. 'Murder Weapon, Cordova Street, 1962.' They were nice, relaxed Vancouver cops. They might have gone to my high school. Then nothing. No follow-up. I figured my little caper was a success. A crime that would never be solved, like the murder with the bottle itself. I was going to sit on my booty—sleep on it—for a few weeks. And then I was going to call and say 'Nadia, I've got something for you.'

"So Tuesday, right? They told me to come down to the Main Street station. Two p.m. Heading over, I thought I would flip. My head felt like I'd inhaled a bunch of helium. You know me. Always late. But this time I went down early. Too early, so I sat out front. I figured it might be illegal to smoke anything within, what is the law now, three metres? But I lit one up all the same to relax. I watched the action on Main and Hastings. It's grim but I love it. I can't say exactly why. I worry, am I as grim inside as those streets?"

"Jess."

"I know. A horrible thought. But it's exercise to fit in there. It really is. Human exercise. You know, Nadia. You tried it for a while. It's a place full of people that other people can *just not stand*. I know the city has been looking for ways to disappear it all since the sixties. So far no one has figured out how. The Empress, the Balmoral, the Hazelwood Hotel. The Regent. Vancouver's Tower of Babel. But tell me, Nadia, what am I going to do if things really start to change? Start a revolution?"

She shakes her head. Jess is no revolutionary. He is a bystander. Nothing more.

She looks down into the box at the bottle wreathed in its halo of packing paper. Her gut feeling is to tell him to screw off. *Screw off, Jess. What a creepy thing to do. Don't ever call or write to me again.* At the same time, she thinks of him getting up the guts to enter the police station on Main by watching the street carnival of wanderers and do-nothings. Dealers and cops in their cars crawling along the curbside. And Jess, for the first and last time, a desperado. Fearing he might lose his job and end up out on the street with his cat in a cardboard box if the truth came out. He'd risked it all, like Clyde for Bonnie.

Jess gives the box a nudge.

"There's one more thing." He reaches into his pants pocket and pulls out a scrap of paper. "I went over to see Detective What-have-you. And there he was, a totally pleasant-looking guy, not too buttoned-up, a reasonable head of hair, not the usual Dachau buzz cut. I sat in a chair in front of his desk. He said he was interested in the theft. But it took me a while to realize that I was not a person of interest. Like they say. Person of interest. There was nothing in his voice that suggested this. And then I thought, if I'm not a suspect what the hell am I doing there? He asked if I knew that the bottle was evidence for another crime. I did. A murder on Cordova half a century before. Then he asks if the bottle was cleaned. Cleaned. I'd unpacked it when it arrived in its old Woodward's shoebox. I'd installed it in the showcase. No. The answer to that question was no. We didn't clean old things that came to the showroom. They were valuable *because* they were dirty. Then he asks, did I know how long DNA could survive? I guessed four hundred years. It's thousands. Well. The bottle was more than sixty years old. He would have liked to do a DNA check on it. He was working on a murder case connected with it. A super-cold case. He patted a file on his desk. He'd pulled it when he heard about the break-in.

"Then things got really weird. What sounded like a gun went off. Somewhere in the building or outside. And my guy dashes out of there with his hand on his gun. It was like a movie. I sat there and watched as the office cleared. They left me there. What did I do? I thought of you. I got up and spun that file around for a quick look at your family story.

"The funny thing was I knew a lot of what was in there. It never occurred to me that the materials we put together to try to sell any old disreputable object might resemble a crime report. JR Auctions. I know what you think. Creepy. Dead people's stuff bought by weirdos who like to waste their money. But who knew that it supplied me with the same job training as a cop? Their file had clippings on the crime back in '62, on the plans to level the neighbourhood, the shootout with one of the guys in Osoyoos. Norman Diablo. One of them was 'scar-faced.' I'd seen most of it when I prepped the bottle for auction. About how the second guy got away. Never caught. But there was one thing in there I hadn't seen. A name with a question mark typed and underlined.

Witness? scrawled after it. Ace Bailey. But he was not found. Or not properly looked for."

Jess opens his hand and offers Nadia the slip of paper with the name. It is written in his nearly illegible writing alongside the words "Patricia Hotel #411."

"They all came back laughing. A car had backfired. That was all. A car cleared the room for us, Nadia. They said I could go. I went downstairs and outside and smoked a great life-giving smoke. Oh man. It was one of those desert-hot days on Hastings. It was Las Vegas on West Hastings. The rest of the city was southern California, but the old downtown streets were burnt to a crisp, as if they were on another planet where they'd never heard of air. Buses barrelled up to the curb like army trucks. There was a buzzy, anxious energy on the sidewalk. With those guys who set themselves up curbside to sell incredibly bad, or maybe it's better to say sad, cast-off stuff, so jumbled that the question always seems to be: who is going to buy that iron? Who's doing shirts down here? And whose library is in need of one more book on the Third Reich, or a battered porno magazine? It was like a comedy sketch version of somebody's favourite possessions. I headed home. A free man."

Jess's last words. She takes the scrap of paper with the name written on it and drops it in the box, which she picks up. She turns to walk up Keefer into the violet, pot-smelling evening. As she leaves him behind, she feels sorry for him. Just a little. Without meaning to she'd drawn him into something he couldn't possibly understand, going all the way back to their unrequited wanderings, their itinerant way together in the city. He'd teased her about having a walking disease. One of the auction lots was related to a Frenchman who'd had it in the nineteenth century. The guy could not stop walking. He was some sort of medical cause célèbre.

The box is awkward in her arms, but she is not about to junk it and hoist the bottle like a hand weight. She wants it out of sight. The cops were not going to learn the meaning of Jess's crime from her. That it was a crime committed for Nadia the night walker, the girl who stole everything. That's what Jess had called her. When he left messages for her he would say, "This is for Nadia, the Girl Who Stole Everything." She'd given him the full portrait, offering it up as they drank their coffee on Commercial; as they chose their steps on a Mount Seymour hiking path; as they sat in the dark at a cinema on Burrard, waiting for the show to start. All the way back to the start, May 7, 1978, Vancouver General Hospital. Her parents brought her out of there into the city as she would come to know it: a green, fresh, self-renewing place. Her parents, each miserable in their own way. Her father, worn down by academic failures; her mother, obsessed with a certain kind of self-possession expressed through clothes and season's tickets and dinner invitations, neither of whom the arrival of a child was going to change. She was lucky, baby Nadia, that they didn't forget her on the roof of the car as they packed up to drive home. They lived then not far from the hospital, in a wooden house that today would cost $2 million to knock down. But back then, its value was as a home. It had a big backyard with fruit trees—cherry, plum, and pear—and a cement-floored basement where the previous long-time owner had abandoned wine-making gear and a Bendix washing machine. There was a shaded front porch where wisteria grew, and Nadia never could understand why they sold it to move to the suburbs, so far away from where they'd lived till then. When she was small she asked her father why they'd moved. She begged him to drive by the old house, but he never would.

Her parents' divorce opened an avenue; her family broke and she could make her own choices. No one told her otherwise. Her mother was planning to winter down south. Her father's troubles were overtaking him, the likelihood that he would have to stop teaching all the more real. For weeks at a time, after he moved out, they would hear nothing from him. Her mother's lawyer would report: "Dr. Baltzan AWOL. No fixed address known. One report suggests he may leave town to beat support order. Any information you can supply would be appreciated." Well, Nadia thought, they're going to have to watch the off-ramps and mountain trails on the North Shore, because that's where the next manic walk will be taking him.

She did not know then what the impact of her father's breakdown had been on her. His example was an odd mix of anarchy and intensity, fierce and dark. But an overwhelming element was his view that no one should be told how to be or what to do with themselves. He had told her that when he tried to teach *Lolita* he would be routinely visited by young women who told him they could not read the book because something along these lines had happened to them. It made them sick or angry to try to treat Nabokov's version of this story ironically. So he told them to forget it, throw it out. Bake it in the oven. Read something else. One outcome of this was a student had gone around to bookstores in the city to steal the novel. What had she done with the stolen copies? Nadia did not know.

Theft. It had the power to reorder the world in interesting ways.

The first theft: her father's wallet lay on the table beside the bed. Inside were ID cards and cash. She took two $50 bills and hid them in her school bag with her pencil case and Kleenex. How many records could she get with two fifties? Six? Seven?

The second theft: money was cold comfort. The things she coveted, the library in their neighbourhood mall let her borrow. But she wanted to keep them. Enough with the return deadlines and fines if she was late. She pulled the magnetic strips from the back page of her favourite book of Norse myths; from the label in the centre of side one of the Beatles' *White Album* and *Freewheelin' Bob Dylan*. Then, because these all bore the mark of theft—the library stamp on every available blank surface—she hid them. But they were hers. And this, she recognized, with little appreciation of any larger meaning, turned her on. Stealing turned her on. It pointed in new and exciting directions. Adulthood. Did adulthood equal taking what you wanted? This seemed in opposition to her father's approach to things, but he wasn't around to ask, which made things easier than they might have been.

The third theft: though meaningless to its victim, it might have had repercussions for Nadia. On an afternoon when her music teacher excused herself for what seemed like an hour—where had she gone? To the bathroom? To answer the phone?—Nadia went to the wood-paneled room that held an immense record collection. She knew where to find an original pressing of Miles Davis's *Kind of Blue*. Martha had played it for her once as a treat. Slow, cool modal chords. "Freddie Freeloader." Improvisation was theft. You grabbed things, unpredictably, out of nowhere, and then ran with what you'd found.

The day of the third theft Nadia came prepared. She brought her outsize gym bag instead of her knapsack. The record just fit. And then, by some absurd coincidence, Martha suggested they listen to a particular point in "Freddie Freeloader," exactly two-and-a-half minutes in. The record's absence puzzled her. Had she lent it to someone? She stood before the shelf where Nadia, moments before, had taken it. She turned and gazed at Nadia, considering. Whatever it was she was thinking passed. Brightly, she told Nadia, her musical theft artist, "I'll get another copy. See you next time, Honey."

The fourth theft was the first one that had repercussions, but not for Nadia. Nadia worked at many half-decent jobs, but she hated them so. The bosses with their insinuations. Uniforms with kerchiefs. Punching the clock. Being told to talk less and to do the thing she'd been hired to do. This stream of obnoxious expectations came in perfect time with her own search for a new attitude toward the world, a purposeful hatred of what seemed to her to be pointless rules, which was an outlook that made her mother furious. Why, why, why, her mother would ask, did she have to think this way? What had the world done to her? This was about the time that she and Jess had met. She had landed a job waiting tables at the Bayshore Inn through a friend of her mother's. It was meant to keep her out of trouble, and the tips were certainly worth her while. One of the perks of working in the hotel restaurant was the view out back, past the pool, through the forest of sailboat masts, to the mountains far beyond the lush green richness of Stanley Park.

In those days Vancouver didn't offer such an array of plush places to stay, and celebrities came to the hotel. Karen Magnussen had skated on a rink in the lobby. Howard Hughes took two whole floors through a long spring and summer visit. He was up there, the papers said, collecting his urine in Mason jars. The press gathered in the restaurant to interview whomever was in the house. Nadia learned how to do her work and not disturb the scene, discreetly filling coffee cups and clearing ashtrays. It was surely an imp of the perverse that led her to apply her skills for quiet invisibility to lift—as she removed a mountainous ash tray—a notebook which sat on the tablecloth to the left hand of the day's interviewee. She didn't even know, at the time, who it was. The notebook captivated her, not the person who'd set it down in order to face the microphone and TV camera positioned before him.

The beauty of Vancouver back then. On a clear day. The sea in the air. Once her shift was done she sat with the notebook overlooking Coal Harbour, the railyards, the gasoline stations floating in the bay. The boatworks clanged and ground out their special musical setting for the late afternoon weather. She saw that it was a poet's notebook that she held in her hands, full of short tryouts and redraftings. Titles were reused but marked with a "#2" or "#3." She had stolen a poet's thoughts. On its cover was scribbled a date and the words, Bayshore Inn. The notebook signaled where the poet was headed next. It was his set of directions. She had a strong urge to get up and run back to the hotel to see if the media scrum was still going on. She would hand the notebook over. But this was a crazy idea. She'd be fired. She put it back in her bag, took it home and hid it where she thought her mother would never look. At the same time, she wondered what it felt like to write something that might be great—a symphony, a detective story, a suite of poems about the failure of a marriage, brutally personal and honest—and have it vanish. Unrecoverable. Like a lead weight dropped in the sea.

Heirloom

The rain lets up as Nadia crests the hill on West Tenth. A big rush of a downpour has filled the gutters and left everything dripping. She's thoroughly soaked, her shoes like a pair of sponges. When she turns the corner on her street she sees the ambulance in front of her place. From the corner of the yard, she watches as attendants bring another of the house's tenants out, strapped to a gurney. She is an old woman, rarely seen, about whom Nadia knows nothing. When the ambulance doors have been shut and the attendants have taken their seats, ready to go, she makes her way across the soggy lawn.

Her landlord is in the doorway, one hand on the doorpost.

She asks, "Is it okay?"

He shrugs. Landlording, his shrug says, has its ups and its downs. Today is down.

She takes the stairs to her place, makes a cup of coffee, and lets it cool. She stops in front of the computer to check her emails. Joshua writes to say he can't make his next lesson. Could they change the time? And, oddly, something from Poland, sent via the tech person who helps her with the blog.

She carries the coffee over to where she's been storing the pop bottle, high up in her kitchen cupboard. She gets on a chair to take the box down and sets it on the counter. Reaching inside, she removes, if everything Jess has said is true, the murder weapon, circa 1962, with its fault line in the glass where it struck her uncle's skull. She turns it in her hands and reads the slogan on its orange shield. Out of its vitrine, standing on her counter without a pot light casting a halo of importance around it, the bottle looks like something that should have been thrown away long ago.

Nadia thinks, *Jess, you idiot. What have you done? Why did I ever tell you anything*—anything—*about myself?*

In the bottle's neck a note is rolled. Nadia pulls it out and looks at Jess's crabbed writing, with the name Ace Bailey. At the Patricia. Hastings and Dunleavy. #411. She knows it as the building they fixed up for Expo, kicking out a crew of down-and-outers.

She picks up the bottle, using a dishtowel so she doesn't have to touch it, and makes room for it in a cupboard behind her egg cups and tea saucers. Then she sits before the beckoning screen to see what could possibly be there for her from faraway Poland.

The Train South

Magdalena is on the train from Warsaw to Łódź. She sits by the window with her work open on her lap. It is late afternoon and the sky is turning orange at its edges as the sun begins to drop. It is the time of the afternoon she likes best. Something in the look of the landscape reminds her of fall, which has not yet arrived. And the day is winding down, so the rush is over. Across from her sits a schlub in grey who is shouting into his phone. She puts on headphones to drown him out and watches the stations slide by in the countryside, men and women waiting with their little bags. It's some sort of human scene, but she doesn't know its meaning.

As if in answer to this musing, an email from Canada appears on her screen. Her first instinct is to leave it unread. It is not for her. But who could do this? Only a saint. And anyways, on the *Krakowskie Przedmieście* she heard the beginning of the Canadian's story; the email is the continuation of the narrative Simon told her. She opens the note meant for her Canadian abroad—her *Canadien errant*—and reads.

> pl on your email means, I guess, that you are in Poland. I wondered. It's true, I don't know you that well, but I wish you'd let me know where you were. I have been to the

Shop a few times. They are running it okay without you. Some of the people who show up for open mic need to be in prison or out in some pasture getting some fresh air.

I am easing up on the blog. It may not have a future. I haven't decided. I will write to your mailing address from the place pictured below. It suits my purposes now.

A photograph follows with a cutline, which reads "Regional Assembly of Text." The photo is of a narrow room. Its ceiling is hung with little yellow flags as if for someone's birthday. On the back wall are shelves that display writing pads, notecards, rubber stamps, and ink pads. Down the centre of the room, at a long table, young people sit, their heads bowed over manual typewriters. Some of the machines are big and black; others are sleek and painted shiny shades of red and gold. Magdalena gazes at the people typing. Beneath the photograph is the following: "The Letter Writing Club has been gathering to write letters to their loved ones since September of 2005. Join us the first Thursday of every month at seven p.m. No need to sign up ahead of time. No cost. Supplies provided."

The email from Vancouver continues:

I will put my old pair of walking shoes in the mail to that woman in Łódź. Maybe they will arrive there next year. I have nothing else worth sending. I don't know if they'll live up to the other objects in her collection. I am well-practiced in self- portraiture, via my blog. In answer to her questions:

My name is Nadia Baltzan.

I live in a few rooms above a green lawn on the west side of Vancouver, a city by the ocean. I have stopped paying attention to my birthday. Nobody else does. Father dead. Mother retired in Arizona, tanning herself to a crisp. Her second husband cannot be believed.

I play music. Sometimes I teach. I am back at school like a little girl. I am a walker in the city when I find the time. I have brown hair. When I was young I turned it inside out and coloured it, but now I leave it alone.

In the garden behind my place you can find caragana. Morning glory. Holly, too.

I read the music that women write.

My dream is a very long and colourful one. It has a musical backing track and takes place in late summer, on an afternoon reminiscent of a day or two in August when I was eight. My father is there. I have not yet taken anything from anyone. I am his good, good girl.

We go out walking.

If the walking shoes arrive Magdalena will paint them, photograph and mail them back to Vancouver, care of a girl called Nadia. It will be the first time she has sent a pair of shoes across the ocean. This introduces a whole new angle to her project, one that interests her.

A Girl's Responsibilities in Wartime

Ania sits on a stool by the open back door and watches her mother get things ready for dinner. The windows are open and the breeze is wonderful, fresh, scented with what Ania first takes to be wildflowers. But her mother corrects her. Barley. Once upon a time it would all be turned into liquor. By Jews. That's all it is. Shorn barley. No romance. Soon it will be bread.

Ania finds her mother's hyperpracticality, her fierce irony, troubling at times. But today it seems true to the state of things. No horseshit romance, she seems to be saying. The farmers grow a crop to survive. We eat bread to live. Period. Her mother has a cup of bitter coffee on the counter and a piece of apple strudel, which she nibbles at as she moves around the kitchen. The cat, a tortoiseshell with very long legs, bounds in over the back steps.

"I have something to show you, Ma." Ania goes to her bag and brings back the boy's box. There is a flicker of recognition, of rising interest, when it is set on the kitchen table. Ania carefully moves the dishes and cloth napkins out of the way.

"This is what the boy gave you?"

Ania nods, opening the box's top. It expels its own smell. Wood and must. Inside are the things that Ania showed the archivist. She sets them out one at a time. The postage stamps. The photograph. The handwritten card. The rolled onion skin paper with its Jewish writing. Her mother breathes in a long, slow breath. Like an athlete before great exertion.

"You know these things, Ma."

Her mother nods. "From long ago," she says. "From the wartime. I'd entirely forgotten. I put them in the ground."

"Ma, what are they?"

Her mother takes the cup of coffee in her hands but does not drink from it. Then she tells her story with great calm, remembering, it seems, everything.

The boy was gone. He had left for America a year or more before the start of the war. His parents were gone too now, as was every other Jew in the village. The house where they had lived was dark as night. She was sure there were others who felt as she did, but people weren't talking. She felt gutted every time she went past the empty house. Like a fish that had been hooked and cut open. People had been brought in to live in the abandoned houses on the square. Some were Germans. They arrived with the Gestapo from Ciechanów. Often they were delivered in staff cars, their luggage unloaded by an officer as if they were royal visitors. They set their leather bags down on the ground lightly, with the utmost care. Others who moved in were from the surrounding towns and countryside, locals who fancied themselves *Volksdeutsche*. These were the worst. Worse than Germans. Because everything they did was a lie.

A man from Germany, Fischer, lived in the house off and on. He disappeared just before the Stalingrad winter. After that she took it upon herself to guard the house. She intended, in her childish way, to prevent it from being squatted in, taken, though she had no idea what she could have done to prevent this. Fortunately, nothing happened. Birds nested in the eaves. Squirrels opened a hole in the front wood cladding. One spring evening she slipped round back and tried the door that led into the house's back room. To her surprise it swung open. She stepped inside and saw that the German had left behind things that were precious in wartime. Work boots. A stack of paper. Pencils. Pots. And to her great amazement, sheets of what looked like postage stamps or customs stickers, and a radio. These had been taken away—first from the village Jews and then, too, from Poles who were not doing their share for the occupation. In a kitchen cabinet she found two bottles of beer, sediment settled at their bottoms. They looked hopeless, but she took them, putting everything in a canvas sack that hung by the front door. She was ready to slip out back, the way she'd come, when she remembered that the boy had told her his family kept valuable things in a box behind a curtain, which hung by the brick chimney near the stove. She set her sack down. She took a quick look out the front window to see if anyone was passing. The moon had not risen so it was very dark. She moved quickly across the room. The box was where the boy said it would be. Once opened, she found that the man from Germany had been using it. It contained German money and a weapon, some sort of pistol. Buried beneath these things was the photograph. She pointed at the photo of herself and her pals. And the map—Ania's mother pinned one corner of the onion skin with her thumb and unrolled it, shaking her head. And the card. She assumed it belonged to the German but she wasn't sure. She could not read German and the handwriting was strange.

She put everything into the bag and over her shoulder. She slipped out the back door. Pushing it closed, she stood in the high grass and looked for something to lean against it to keep it from swinging open. She set a stone on a brick and with her toe she pushed the door shut. Afterward her shoe bore a mark as long as she wore it. And there would be no new shoes till after the war.

Ania is amazed. "You've not told me anything about this before."

"While your father was alive, he didn't want to hear about it. *Jewish things*."

"And since?"

Her mother shrugs. They both jump at the thump on the door. Ania opens it and there is Simon. It is six on a Friday. The village is quieting down for the weekend. A bus labours by in the square. Shops are open but empty. They had invited him but had not heard one way or another, and here he is.

Ania takes Simon's hand and guides him inside.

The house bears no resemblance to his. It is a modern place, with normal furniture and white walls. "Here," Ania says. "Come meet my mother."

She is in the kitchen. The old woman takes his hands in hers. She is stout, but she has bearing. She is someone to be reckoned with, even in her eighties. She lets go of his hands and steps back to appraise him. She smiles, satisfied, at her daughter. "*Proszę*," she says, directing them to the front room.

"In fact," Ania says, "my mother used to read English. Especially the American press. There are headlines from after the war that she remembers like her own name. Isn't it true, Ma? But she's rusty. I will be our translator. She told me to tell you that you shouldn't feel obliged, but whenever you want to visit you may. Her house is open to you."

Ania's mother slips out of the room, and the two women call to each other in Polish.

"Tea?" Ania asks.

"Sure. Yes."

"Do you have what you need? In the house? No one has lived there since the war."

What's there, he assumes, was arranged by Ania's mother. So

he hesitates to list what's lacking. He does not know how to operate the oil lamp on the table in the front room. "Firewood. I'll need wood for the stove."

"But you have. In the red-brick building at the back of the property. My mother hired a man to deliver it. She made sure he stacked it neatly." She goes to the kitchen and returns with two cups smelling of gingerbread. Simon sniffs and drinks. From where he sits he has a view of the square out the front window. Ania's mother is in the kitchen. He hears her open and shut her cupboards. Cutlery and plates are being gathered.

Simon, on his best behaviour, asks Ania what she does.

"A government job in Warsaw. I'm a small-town girl who made good."

Simon asks how Ania learned such perfect English.

"It's far from perfect. If we come to know each other you will see. I went to London when I was young. I worked as an au pair, which was no picnic. That was an education in itself. I also managed some teacher training there. When I came back I taught English, which had not yet become a big deal. It was the late stage of Communism, so I had my taste of the Soviet way with things. What about you? In Vancouver, what do you do?"

"Have you been to Vancouver?"

Ania shakes her head.

"Well, I taught at the university. But there were cutbacks, programs they just lost interest in. Along with that, the idea of what a professor is changed. They sent me packing. I floated a while. Vancouver is a place where you can do not much and feel pretty good."

"Here you have to be drunk or very old to accomplish that."

"Understood. I think. But then I took a leap."

He describes the Shop, what to expect on open mic nights, the oddball customers.

"I would like to see it."

Ania sounds as though she means this. Her enthusiasm takes Simon by surprise.

"In Poland, in my adolescent years, music was a safe form of rebellion. We had our would-be rock stars. *Trubadurzy*. Four guys in Sgt. Pepper suits. I think they all played the bass. But it was the western music that seemed to offer the key—how do they say it in the blues song?—to the highway. The situation, when I think back now, was so strange. It was designed to make us crave everything we weren't supposed to have. This was one of the sicknesses in the system. Everything was a shortage, everything rationed, and the things that were prohibited, of course we wanted them most. For the longest time you couldn't buy western records. Then, right near the end, as late as 1988, they allowed ten each year. Legally released, as they would say, by Polskie Nagrania, the government-owned label. It would be interesting to know what the apparatchiks were thinking when they made their lists. Some of the releases were good. Even a little risqué. Pink Floyd's *Dark Side of the Moon*. Leonard Cohen's *I'm Your Man*. But then there was pure entertainment. Michael Jackson's *Bad*. George Michael's *Faith*. Something by Madonna. Sting's *Nothing Like the Sun*. Kim Wilde's *Close*. Do you remember that one?"

Simon shakes his head. He has not heard of Kim Wilde.

"But there was also a guy on the radio. Piotr Kaczkowski. He would play a complete record, and he'd tell you side one was this long and side two was this long, so you knew when to flip your tape and press record. My father caught me late one night taping Pink Floyd's *Animals*. These tapes were like currency. You copied them and circulated them. It was an old-fashioned black market." Ania laughs at herself, remembering this. "I haven't thought about it in a long time. It was strange and sad in so many ways, but we got what we wanted." She is quiet for a moment. "Who comes to play on your stage?"

Simon describes the potpourri quality of it all. The weird unpredictability of a typical night. The second-generation punks. The semi-musical trios, a trio being the most substantial group his stage can hold. Batting at snare drums. Squawking on horns. Tearing up the place on out-of-tune guitars.

"But once in a while it tips over into the sublime. For instance— " he hesitates, about to describe Nadia playing her dulcimer, but Ania's mother interrupts, quietly, in Polish.

"The meat," Ania says, "is not tender. So there is no rush. You were about to say."

"About one of our musicians. I call her the dulcimer girl. But I can't describe her. It would be better to show you. It turns out that one of our regulars filmed her and put it up on YouTube. He shouldn't have. But there it is. Can we use your computer? I'll find it for us."

Ania goes to her bag by the door and takes out a laptop. They set it up and wait as the dark square on the website transforms itself into the shape of Nadia on a stool, the dulcimer on her knees, her face serious. She strums her instrument with big sweeping motions. The roomful of people in front of her is silent, transported.

When it's done, Ania looks at her hands and is quiet. Then she says, "It's an old folk song. We knew it here. It made everyone sad. Because, where else but Poland under Communism, could it break your heart to sing, 'Those Were the Days'?"

"She's remarkable. But I know I shouldn't call her the dulcimer girl."

"Why? From what I see, that's what she is."

"Well. Girl. It's not a good word to use when you're talking about a woman."

Ania makes a face. "Oh. Well, I was a girl once and I don't

mind being reminded of that."

"I suppose Nadia might agree with you." He begins to describe what Nadia's dulcimer sounds like, but Ania interrupts.

"We have our own version here. More elaborate, but from the same musical family. We call it a cimbalom. You know *Pan Tadeusz?* Our national epic. So maybe it won't surprise you to hear that there is a dulcimer story in Radzanów, right now."

"Tell me it."

"Oh. It's not that interesting. You saw the film set as you arrived. It's one of the more lively things to take place here in a long time. I helped the crew with permits, since I have contacts in Warsaw but also here, with the local governing people. The mayor is the son of an old friend of my mother's. They want to include a scene, maybe more than one, with a *kapela*. An old-time Polish band from the countryside. Drum. Fiddle. And do you say squeezebox? But the truth is, this music is awful to our ears today. It sounds like one song—not even one song—one musical idea, played over and over with no ear for melody or rhythm. Like a box of spoons being shaken. So, the director has some idea of how to enliven this with a dulcimer. Which has its own Polish character. But he's not happy about the musicians he's auditioned."

"Incredible."

"Why?"

"I don't know. It just strikes me that way."

Ania shrugs. Before they can say more, her mother appears from the kitchen with a platter in each hand. She sets these down and heads back for more, until the table is covered by an impressive array of dishes. Ania's mother sits at the head of the table and points to each one. Ania provides the English description of each: there is the meat that kept them waiting; mushrooms, picked nearby, marinated in oil and vinegar; a Russian salad of cooked vegetables; sliced cheese, tomatoes, and onions. Simon samples everything except the mushrooms, which look to him like they are half alive and ready to slide out of the bowl.

The inevitable bottle of vodka stands at the ready. Ania holds it up and reads the label: *Zubrowka*. The bison insignia, she explains, means that it is flavoured with sweetgrass eaten by bison who graze the Polish-Belarusian borderlands. "Usually," she says, "it's the man who offers this. Tonight, I am the man of the house."

Ania's mother smiles and nods at this, as if you couldn't possibly say a truer thing.

Ania fills three shot glasses. They drink and Ania follows the custom of immediately filling the empty glasses. Once they've had a few refills, and they are all a little light in the head, Ania announces, "You have your dulcimer girl. Here I'm the typewriter girl."

"Ach." This is Ania's mother's response before getting up to clear the table.

"Well, we don't have to talk about that. Here is a pleasant topic." Ania reaches out to her mother as she passes, hands full, but the old lady dodges her daughter's touch.

"How," Ania asks, "does Poland strike you?"

Everything, he explains, is still rolling over him. He feels like a kid learning to swim whose teacher throws him in the water. And he has a hundred questions, since everything he has seen, right down to the grass and the trees, is a mystery to him. The little huts, neatly sculpted and fitted into the landscape, on the drive in from the airport. The Warsaw spectacle, the Old Town, its miraculous postwar reconstruction, undoing what the Germans did during wartime. The skyscraper economy turning the city into a place with a future, not just a past. He'd walked down Marszałkowska, opposite the Palace of Culture and Science, just to see the kids buying things, and everyone coming home from work.

Ania nods. Does he plan to stay long?

This is a funny question. He knows it and they know it. But no one is laughing. Ania pours another round of vodka, even though Simon has waved off more of the stuff. He came on a kind of lark. He doesn't want to say that he is here because his father rejected Mike's offer of a return visit. Tickets sent his way that no one else would use. This, he thinks, would make him sound foolish, worse than a thoughtless tourist.

Ania's mother says a few words over his shoulder, which Ania translates.

"You have come to watch us for a while. You know, your presence in town puts things in people's minds. Things they haven't thought about in a long time. My mother's house on the square, for instance."

Simon thinks, for the first time, of himself stalking the countryside, ghostly and uninvited. A Night Jew.

Ania's mother has something she wants to tell. She sits. As she speaks, Ania struggles to keep up, translating what her mother says into English.

"There is a man. He has come to our town. Four times. He came first when he was young. Then seven or eight years later. Then a few years after that. With different Polish guides each time. An aristocratic older man. A young woman who carried a big bag full of books. In one case he spent time talking to people. Once he sat in the church and talked loudly about the wartime. He ate a sandwich on a bench in the square. Then, each time, he disappeared."

Ania's mother looks at her hands, which rest in her lap.

"Do you know who he is?" Simon asks.

Ania's mother looks at him as she answers.

"Mother says maybe. He is someone's son. He must be a Jew. She has a guess who he might be. Now we talk about him and wait for him to return. He seems to make it here on a Sunday.

Usually around eleven. He often leaves at two or so. If you stay long enough, you might meet him." Ania considers what she has said. "Mama. I find that a creepy suggestion. It's time for your poppy-seed cake."

Ania's mother gets up and claps her hands.

The cake is layered and moist and spreads itself on the plate and it may be the best cake he has ever tasted.

"Wow."

"That's a compliment, Mama."

He nods.

"This is just one of the old recipes," Ania says.

Simon pushes his chair back, not exactly ready to go, but signaling that he won't outstay his welcome. To which Ania's mother says something in Polish.

"My mother doesn't want to let you go. There are things she's anxious to tell you. About your house."

Her mother begins in Polish and Ania listens, taking in as much as she can. She puts a hand on her mother's arm when she needs her to take things more slowly. The telling proceeds this way, in blocks of Polish and English. Ania translates but speaks in her mother's voice.

"I was a girl in the war. Day to day, we made our way. In my family, the dangers were unusual. My father had livestock and land—we grew barley—and the Germans were always demanding things from him. But my father was not inclined to collaborate. I know, everyone says this about their parents. Their grandparents. But I can tell you with us it was true, and it put us in danger. A whole new set of powers came into existence during the war. In certain cases, it removed people like my father, who had been a village leader, and set other people in their places. None of these things could have happened if the Germans had not come. They turned the world on its head. So, the power came from the Gestapo office, which was not far off, in Ciechanów. They didn't want to visit us in our little towns. They wanted people in the area to do their work. For this they chose *Volksdeutsche*. Some from around here.

"They organized night watches. Hunts in the woods for Jews. They also strong-armed peasants and people like Ania's grandfather to make what was called voluntary payments. Livestock. Barley. Liquor. It was organized robbery. And it went on for years. Can you imagine? In cahoots with them were the Blue Police. Blue for the uniforms. These were Polish boys, or men who could not be expected to behave better than boys. Do not," here Ania imitates her mother's finger wagging, "*do not*, my mother was told, talk to these guys. If you see one walking in your direction, go the other way.

"In each town and village there was an elder, a spokesman, who dealt with the Germans. Around him the whole thing turned. He knew the territory, had the ears of townspeople and farmers. . ."

The Polish version of the story rushes forward and Ania is quiet. Then she interrupts her mother and looks over at Simon.

"I have never heard all this." Ania carries on, in her mother's voice.

"I went to the Germans' man in our town. I remember he was bald. A big dangerous animal. Really. I'd seen him at one of the saints' festivals drinking beer out of a bucket. As a girl, this sort of thing disgusted me. So it was not like going to ask the priest for forgiveness, or to your teacher for help on your lesson.

"So, I went. I stood by the gate and his wife came out. She told me she would check with her husband. The witch of a look she gave me scared me to the bone. The husband came out. At the gate, he reached for me. Ewunia. This was what the adults called me then. I showed him a single German mark. He took it in his fingers and held it up to his face, as if to smell it. I said I knew where to get more. And I would bring him some each month if he would assure the security of my house on the market square— not the one my family lived in, but the one that belonged to the Harbst family. This was certainly a strange request coming from a child. And who said there would ever be a time without Germans, when you could protect anything that was or wasn't yours? For the time being it was all theirs. We were theirs. We were their slaves.

He agreed. He took the mark. He patted me on the head. Ewunia, he said, say hello to your parents. Tell them I am keeping an eye out for you. So, this was how it started. In a time of great dying. I kept the house safe."

The cat jumps on the table to lick for scraps and Ania waves it off. Simon has no idea what to say in response to what he's heard.

"Maybe it's time to go? Mama, would you pack some food for Simon to take?"

Once this is done, Ania's mother gives him a hug and looks into his face, pleased. She tells him, "*Dobranoc.*"

"Goodnight," Ania adds helpfully.

Ania leads him down the house's front steps. They stand together on the sidewalk where it bends away from the main square, around the church and off along the country road. The evening is coming on, but the day is still warm and there is light in the west. Simon takes in the lines of colour in the distance: green farmland, another shade for the treetops, the soft blue and grey of the evening sky.

"It's a very peaceful scene." Simon recognizes the cliché in his words as he says them. To say this on a Friday evening in the countryside. But he feels it all the same. Ania looks toward his house and offers to walk him back. A small-town courtesy, to escort someone ten or twelve doors along the way. At his door, he offers his hand. She gives him a government-approved handshake of impressive firmness.

But he has one thing left to ask. About the Secret Place. He recounts what he heard from Mike.

"What is it? Have you heard of it?"

Ania looks puzzled. There are many things, besides her mother's girlhood adventures, that she's not yet heard.

"I was told by someone who knew this place well that my family had a dry-goods store on the square. Tobacco, spices, and flour. We had a leasehold where we gathered peat. And a mill. Would it have been on the river? The Secret Place was along the riverside. At least that's what he thought."

"A mill. On the Wkra. You'd have to ask my mother. There are ruined mills along the way."

"I've yet to see the river."

Ania points south behind the houses. "The banks are dry now. We've had so little rain this season. I can take you down to the bank. If you follow it in either direction, you can walk to neighbouring towns. But what does it mean, a secret place?"

"It was believed to have healing powers. You were vetted. I'm not sure if this is the right word. You were interviewed, regarding your complaint. Whether it was physical or emotional. And if you had the sort of thing that could be healed—"

"Healed by the place?"

"Yes."

"I've not heard a word about this. But my mother is very devoted to things growing nearby. Valerian. Willow bark. St. John's wort. She's an expert brewer of teas and maker of poultices. When she's doing that sort of thing, a bomb going off wouldn't distract her. But what you're telling me, it sounds like a folk tale."

"It does. But the guy who told me, he knew your mother when they were children. He seemed to me the kind of guy who would know the difference between a folk tale and the real thing."

"Will you wait? I'll go ask."

He sits on his stoop like a local watching the evening go by. He has a view of the curving roadway. No sign marks its name. The power lines are double the height of the old low-slung houses. There is a parking sign he can decode, and then a pair of yellow signs he cannot read: a yellow diamond inside a white square above a pair of dashes, like an equal sign. It might as well be Morse code. He will have to ask someone what the sign means. Attached to a two-storey red-brick building, the most impressive old structure in view besides the church, there is a grey radar dish.

Ania reappears, holding the wooden box. "Here. Let me show you something."

She sits beside him on the stoop and opens the box. He cannot at first see what's inside. Gingerly she lifts out a sheet of paper, tightly rolled. Setting the box on the step, she unrolls the paper on her knees.

"It is a map. I'll show you the other side in a moment. But here. Can you read this?"

He looks closely at the writing alongside the sketched shape of ground and what might be a riverway. The writing is Yiddish. He knows this much.

"No. Not one word."

Ania sighs. "It used to be half the people here could. Now no one at all. Okay. First, just look. I will make you a copy. But I can't give this to you. It was given to me. And I'm not sure who is the real owner. I have to think that through."

Simon nods. "Okay. These markings, they could point to a secret place. This one"—his raised finger traces a curving line—"could be a riverway. And the teardrop. An island?"

"The Wkra has many little islands, further upstream, but also down the way, toward Warsaw. Upstream the Wkra meets another river. The Narew. We're in river country here, with the Vistula and the Bug not so far. And what about this?" Anya points at a thick line with inverted arrow points crossing the line that snakes like a riverway. "A bridge?"

Simon peers at the marks on the unfurled sheet. Practicing, he says "*Vk*—ra."

"I know of a few bridges. And your guy, he said a bridge near a mill? There is a lovely one, intact but utterly forgotten, near Śniadówko. The mill's weir remains as well."

He shakes his head.

"A weir. Am I mispronouncing it? In Polish we call it *jaz*. It's where they have built up a kind of barrier so the mill wheel can work."

Now Simon has a goal: a river bridge by a mill, and an island, teardrop-shaped. Ania turns the paper over and reads what is written, translating the crabbed Polish words into English. "This was written in October, 1941. 'Best regards from family. I have a grievance to you, because you do not show us any interest. Mother frets. I cannot imagine why you don't send. Aronowitz gets packages from America, tea, meats. Why don't you write more detailed letters? We borrow money and have lost the house. I remain'—" but Ania cannot decipher the signature. "I have shown it to an archivist friend. He tells me the writer lived on the square. There." She points toward one of the shuttered old wood-fronted houses. Curtains in its peeling window frames. A tin roof. Not one lick of paint on it anywhere. Like his own, with its hundred-year-old weathered wood.

"They were communicating with American relatives. Well into 1941. But this letter was not sent. Instead"—she turns it over—"someone made the map."

"If you could send a picture of this that would be great. But I have something to go on now."

Ania rolls the sheet, carefully fits it back inside its box and closes the top. Something tugs at him inside. A stitch in the ribs he remembers feeling as a child when he'd run far fast and needed to breathe.

House Museum

Simon has lived in the house on the square for a week, all the while resisting the urge to flee the countryside for Warsaw. Thinking, *okay, I've seen enough; I can say I was here.* One hour's drive by Moskvitch is all it would take. But so far, he's held tight, while making certain domestic breakthroughs. Having started a fire in the stove, he thinks there must be a bird's nest in the chimney. He has no idea how to deal with this. In his pocket Polish-English dictionary, he looks up "chimney." It is a *komin*. And what he likely needs is a *kominiarz*. A chimney sweep. He has a basket full of bread and greens from the shop in the square. The woman who runs it obviously views him as a big spender. He has candles, and an oil lamp made of brass that he found tucked away in an armoire, but no oil to burn in it. He has toilet paper, and the outhouse seems to do what it's meant to do, at least in good weather. The latch, which could be seventy-five years old, works. He has Mike's guide, which he reads as he might the local newspaper, finding surprises and advice. But there is nothing in it about the river, as if this is not a subject worth raising, or rather, as if the Secret Place was not a subject to be discussed openly.

Simon has placed the most comfortable chair in the house—an armchair that smells faintly of tobacco or coal smoke—by the window in the front room. From there, he can see the square where the film's people busy themselves with the day's set.

Suddenly, a knock on the door. Simon's first thought is: ignore it. Someone has chosen the wrong house. But it recurs, a bit more insistent. He opens the door and there stands a young woman. She has one foot up on the stoop and the other on the sidewalk. She is dressed like her workmates in camouflage, her hair piled on top of her head, a white scarf wrapped loosely around her neck.

"Hi." She holds out her hand. "I'm Charlie?" She introduces herself using the uptalk favoured by his students at UBC. "I'm the production manager." She aims a thumb at the crew in the square. "English, right?"

"That's it for me. English. I have no other options."

"Well, I'm glad to hear that. I need a break from Polish. I'm enjoying speaking it, but it's hard work. Like long distance running. On my days off, I visit my cousins near Bydgozsz. My family is from there. Originally. Can I come in?"

Simon is embarrassed to welcome her into his dark house, but in she comes. The light in the doorway is startling. Everything inside is in shadow.

"Wow." With both hands on her hips, turning on one heel, Charlie repeats herself with greater enthusiasm. "Wow!"

"It's old."

"Sorry. Did you say your name?"

Simon introduces himself and she proceeds to use his name at every opportunity.

"Simon, this place. It's one hundred percent. Authentic." She peers through the doorway into the back bedroom.

"You mean unchanged."

"*Un*—changed. You said it. The guys on the set, they always feel they should insert a 'fucking.' Even in Polish. Un-*fucking*-changed. Do you know this house's story?"

Simon knows that his father's parents owned it. And that a girl, now an old woman with wonderful recipes, known as the Grabowska, preserved it.

"Listen. I've got someone with me who'd like to see inside. He can tell us a lot. Can I ask him in?" Charlie ducks outside and beckons toward the side yard, as Simon thinks of it, though he has no idea if this is an appropriate word for little fenced areas in Polish villages. *Look it up*, he tells himself: side yard.

The man who follows Charlie inside is dressed like a retiree, in a cap with a polo shirt buttoned to the neck. His pants are frayed at the knees. He is chewing on something. He shakes Simon's hand and speaks to Charlie in Polish.

"This is Ryszard," Charlie explains. "Ryszard Jankowski. He is the archivist at the museum in Mława, west of here."

Simon knows where Mława is from Mike's notes. It is the nearest small city, where a person can buy a pair of shoes, a cellphone, a razor, any little thing that is unavailable in the stores on the village's Piłsudski Square. In Mława, you can buy an espresso and pastry to have while you read your *Gazeta Wyborcza*.

"We've hired him as a consultant for our shoot. He was hoping you had some Polish, but it doesn't matter. He learned his English on an archivist's training project. Maybe in the service of the government?"

Charlie's witticisms are of no obvious interest to their visitor. He shakes Simon's hand and gives his full attention to the house's interior, eyeing its back rooms.

"You have chives in your garden. Garlic too." Jankowski says this, all the while holding firmly onto Simon's hand. "Did you know this? They're fragrant. Someone's tending them. And they've been divided in the past few years. Good in soups and sauces. You are in good shape. You can make us lunch from what you are growing."

Jankowski holds his hands behind his back as he moves from the front window to the table and chairs by the stove. There he surveys each object hanging above the stovetop, almost fingering them, but stopping at a millimetre's distance. Simon and Charlie follow him into the bedroom where he quite audibly catches his breath as he runs a finger over the carved door frame at the back of the room. He turns, brings one hand from behind his back and places it on Simon's shoulder.

"This place is a miracle. It is unchanged. Not just from the war. The 1920s. Certainly the thirties. I would venture that there is no house museum like it in the country. I've gone to some of the open-air museums. And of course Sierpc. There is a good one near Katowice, where they've brought buildings from around the country. But these places are always hodgepodge. Is this the right phrase in English? New and old. This and that. Local and brought from many parts of the country." He turns to Charlie. "I think we should sit somewhere and talk."

"Let's sit out back."

Simon leads the other two through the side yard, where Jankowski points authoritatively at the garlic and chives, and then at the flat-cut stump of a tree with ample room for two to sit. Simon and Charlie settle while Jankowski stays on his feet in order to say his part. He is, as Charlie suggested, at their service.

"This house belonged to your family for a long time. We have the records for this at the archive. I found a title document from the nineteenth century. It is one of the very few unchanged houses on the square. There are outbuildings in this area, on nearby farms, that are not so different from how they were, fifty, sixty years ago. But what can we find in such places? Pitchforks. Ladders. Milk buckets. Here—" Jankowski seems to lose his composure, then recovers. "Here, you have a story. It's one I have some small personal connection with, since I was born here. After the war. But these stories remain fresh in my mind.

"In the past few years, new research has been done. Really, a kind of flourishing in this area, by Poles and Germans. Even Americans and a Canadian or two. So what I did not learn growing up here, I am learning from the historians. Archives like the one where I work, which were once thought of as useless backwater storage rooms, places for lazy people to take a safe job, have become important resources. People are amazed at the kind of documentation we hold, which, for a long time, nobody cared about.

"If I may be so bold, I think I understand how a village like this one worked before the Germans. And then, what they did here. It's possible, too, to trace the borders of the Mława ghetto, even though much of the city where the ghetto stood was destroyed. And I can tell you a great deal about what happened here once the Jews were taken, their homes stolen, their livestock, and the place, like many other towns near to the *Altreich*—this is how the Germans called the territory newly included in their country—was repopulated by Germans from the west. The records show very clearly that this region of Poland was to become not only empty of Jews, but of most Poles as well. Things began to move in this direction by the end of 1939. When the war started to turn, after the defeat at Stalingrad and the United States entered the fight, our German friends rethought their plans for our countryside. They had killed many, many Jews. Those who remained after the emptying of the ghettos hid in the forest, in rafters, in cellars and barns. What can I say about such things?"

This is one of the few noticeable rhetorical flourishes in Jankowski's speech. From time to time, whether to provide himself with a rest, or simply to highlight the nature of what it is he has to tell, he repeats the phrase: *What can I say about such things?* Under the great maple, in the shade thrown by its crown on the house's back property, Jankowski embarks on an impressive performance. He raises his arms and points in different directions. He pauses, at times at length, to gather his thoughts or to contain his emotions. He sometimes picks up sticks and rocks and arranges them in the grass to create a kind of impromptu map of the village, before the war, in wartime, and after. How, Simon wonders, can he retain what this man has to tell? He cannot. He may retain nothing at all, which would put him exactly where he stood when he took the wheel of his Moskvitch. But then, years from now, he will think, *did I really sit on a stump and listen to a village history lesson?*

"You sit on a tree stump in western Poland. But if things had gone otherwise, this—" he bends and places the palm of his hand in the grass—"would have been swallowed up by the *Altreich*. This house—if I may, your house—was given to an import from the German lands. From the *Altreich*. We know this from the Ciechanów Gestapo archives, most of which survived the war. I've seen these materials in Warsaw. Under the Communists these files were impossible to access. But things have changed. The man who took over your house had a family back in Stuttgart, who did not join him here. He may have split his time between this place and his old home. He shows up at this address, in the Gestapo files, accused of *Judenfreundlichkeit*. I think you can guess what this means. Certainly, in the Gestapo's eyes, he was guilty of *Polenfreundlichkeit*. This had to do with his drinking pals. Someone informed on him. And he was ultimately found guilty of something worse: *staatsfeindlichkeit*. What do you think this means, Charlie? This a good test for you."

She shakes her head.

"Well, more studying is required. *Staatsfeindlichkeit*. Hostile attitudes toward the Nazi state. This could get you sent to Auschwitz. I apologize for raising this spectre, because we, here in central Poland, are far from that place, and, in fact, our *Altreich* gentleman was not sent there at all. It's interesting, I think, and telling, that this German, brought all the way here, to this faraway village, in order to contribute to the depopulation and then repopulation of these territories, was not entirely—do you say, on the job?"

Simon nods, and Charlie gives her assent to Jankowski's way of putting things. She has taken a notebook out of one of the camouflage pockets in her pants and is writing notes with a tiny pencil.

"So, your house's good fortune, if I can put it this way, is that later in the war, our man from Stuttgart attracted the attention of the Gestapo at Ciechanów one final time. It seems he might have been involved in helping Poles smuggle Jews through the countryside to Warsaw, but I cannot confirm this yet. He was betrayed. The snitch's name is in the records. I know his son. The child of a local woman. The full story does not seem to have been discovered. Still, our friends at Ciechanów had heard enough and sent Herr Fischer—that was his name—to a work camp not so far away. The house, at this point, fell into a kind of limbo. About this, I think, we need to ask the neighbours." Jankowski waves in the direction of the houses on the square.

"It's all interesting." Charlie puts her notepad and pencil away. Jankowski slips his hands into his pockets and reverts to his savvy onlooker stance, gazing about the property in amazement, as if he's discovered something he has waited years to see. He goes back to sucking his teeth, in search of garlic and chives from the side yard.

"Should we go back inside?" Simon asks.

Jankowski leads the way around the side of the house and inside.

"The thing I want to ask you." Charlie works a cigarette out of a shirt pocket. "Don't worry. I won't smoke it. Just holding it gets me by. We'd like to know—"

There is a knock at the door. It's a morning of knocks. Simon opens the door and finds a lean, long-haired version of the production assistants in the square, standing with a laptop under one arm.

"Oh, Marek," Charlie waves him off. "I'll look for you in a while. Okay?"

With a courtly bow the knocker is gone. Charlie starts over, at the point where she was interrupted. "We'd like to ask if you would let us film inside your house. We'd pay, of course. We would only need to be inside for a few days, but lighting would be a challenge, so the place would be turned a bit upside down. I'm in charge of the production budget. We could pay a thousand a week. Dollars. Not *zloty*. What do you think?"

Simon is not tempted by the money. His stack of currency is in the trunk of the Moskvitch, under the spare tire. And he is not drawn, for the moment, to being uprooted. The Secret Place still lurks, unfound. He says he'll think about it.

Charlie looks surprised. She might have to raise her offer. "Okay. Let us know. I'm always around. You see that white hut?" She points out the window at a mobile trailer parked by the big church. "That's the production office. Would you mind, sometime soon, if Marek looks in and asks you a few questions? He's one of our writers. We've decided to follow up on some of these local stories. Ryszard is helping us with these. We are revising the shooting script. To make it as accurate as possible to what happened here."

"Sure. Okay."

"Great." And Charlie is gone.

Jankowski, not yet ready to follow her, notices a map spread on the table by the stove.

"Do you need some information on the area? What sort of travel are you planning?"

Simon cannot explain his goal: to find a secret place in a landscape he does not know based on a hand-drawn map made seventy years before, which Ania photographed and printed for him. The best he can do is to say that he wants to explore the river.

"Our Wkra?"

"Yes. What's the best way?"

"Well, certainly, by canoe. We have a kind of canoe here we call the *kanadyjka*. The Canadian. Here." He places a hand, fingers spread, on Mike's map on the table. "Sit. Do you mind?" With a pencil in his hand, Jankowski is ready to provide guidance by way of markings on the map. "Are you a veteran?"

At first Simon takes the word for its conventional meaning.

"A *veteran*. Have you canoed a good deal?"

"Well, with my father. It was something we did together. We have a place in Vancouver, a waterway right in the centre of the city called False Creek. It opens into a bay. People sail there. We canoed."

Jankowski, wielding the pencil like a knife, marks arrows at a beginning and an end along this route, and highlights points of interest using tiny perfect asterisks.

"If you are tough"—he balls up a fist and hits Simon hard on the bicep—"start here. Działdowo. The riverway is called Nida. It feeds the upper course of the Wkra river valley. I am friends with a guy who has a good boat rental." Jankowski writes the name of the business in the margin of the map. "The Wkra proper begins at Żuromin. Here. Once there," he looks up, "you encounter lovely flowered meadows. If you are lucky you will see otters. Beaver. Like back in your country. Simply follow the river from there. You can stop at Radzanów, but these places. Here. I will write them. Bieżuń. This is on the map. You also have Mazyn. Królew. You will cheat yourself if you don't see the Wkra Valley. *Dolina Wkry*. Here. And the gorge at *Lasy Pomiechowskie*. Very beautiful. I would suggest, at Pomiechowo, come up to the land. There is an old mill weir, with a bridge. This is thirty, no, maybe twenty-five kilometres from your starting place. Can you manage?"

"Oh sure. Tomorrow. Can you call your guy to let him know?"

The answer is yes. They shake, a firm gentlemanly handshake, and Jankowski is out the door.

Simon has a plan. Through his front door he sees the film set taking shape for the day. He sits on his stoop like a local. The air is piney and crisp The Secret Place hovers somewhere in the faraway woods beyond the village.

Dolina Wkry

Simon drives out of Radzanów the next day. He prays the car will make it to his destination, not more than fifty kilometres north of town. It is doing something strange, backfiring, trembling like it might come apart when he hits third gear. But it's fun, taking in the landscape through the great wide lightly cracked windshield. It provides a wonderful Soviet-imagined frame of central Poland as it flashes by. His canoe rental is arranged, and thanks to Charlie, a driver from the film shoot will pick him up at the end of the day and return him to his car. He has certain hopes and expectations, which include, after Żuromin, an investigation of the riverway near to Radzanów. This is his true goal. He imagines scouring both sides of the river, on the lookout for teardrop islands, especially those he can find near to a bridge and a mill. He knows that the mills, and even the bridges, of the late 1930s could be gone after war and so many years. And the riverside itself could change. He'll take what he can find. He has his camera, a notebook, a knapsack to carry things in. And he will follow the full route suggested by Jankowski, all the way to the gorge at Pomiechowo. If Jankowski is right, the route will leave him time in the afternoon to see the sixteenth-century church before the driver collects him in front of it. Never in his life has he taken a trip that was so well-planned.

The weather is perfect. The morning sky is clear and light, almost white. He rolls through Żuromin, with its blocks of Soviet style apartments, and then the last stretch into Działdowo, where he stumbles, almost without thinking, upon the boat rental shop owned by Jankowski's friend. The owner is young and trim, wearing a Los Angeles Lakers cap. He speaks no English at all, but Jankowski has set things up with care. Together they slide a bright red canoe off its rack. It has a matching red paddle. Simon accepts the offer of a GPS. This would usually be of no use to him, but on this trip, how else could he gauge the distance he's travelled, to know with any confidence when he has reached Radzanów? He has seen things from dry land and has no idea what it will look like from the water. The rental shop is a few hundred metres from the river. They carry the canoe to the bank, where the water ripples dark and soft as velvet.

Off he goes, feeling like the only man on Earth. The river is shallow, sometimes so much so that reeds and lilies grow a good distance into the current. They wave in the breeze. He sails into what might have once been a mill pond. On the bank stands a substantial brick ruin, and then he paddles into the cool under a nearby bridge. He checks the GPS. He is still some kilometres from Radzanów. It's not likely that the Secret Place served the town from this far away. The riverbanks are grassy hills topped by oak and maple trees. In fall, their colour would give them away. Now they vary in emerald and darker greens, their crowns round and full. The morning passes like this, in soft discovery.

He is surprised to find men in rubber waders out in the river, their fishing lines arcing away from them into the water. Simon canoes around their bobbin lines and works himself back upstream to ask one what he is catching. This man speaks no English. But by pointing questioningly at the water Simon gets answers that sound like *shupak* and *sandatch*. He is a nuisance here, disrupting whatever the fish might be doing. But the fishermen are a nuisance to him. He'd hoped to make his slow way up the river to see whatever nooks and crannies he could find, without having to duck around the arcs of their fishing lines.

But as he carries on, another hundred metres at the most, a little byway shows up, not more than fifteen feet wide, separating the riverbank from an overgrown island. From where his canoe is, he cannot tell what shape the island is—whether it is tear-shaped or not. He pulls the canoe up to its grassiest stretch, where the overgrowth of trees has been held back, he guesses, by the damp shoreline. He steps into the water and pulls the canoe up on the edge of a meadow. There is a pull in his gut as he makes his way into the trees. What could he possibly find here? But the obvious answer to this is offered as he rambles around in the scrub and trees. It's a largely untouched little place, birds on the branches, the water wearing away at the edges of the land, the wind in the leaves, but so lightly it can hardly be heard. There is no sound at all of the rest of the world.

What would a Secret Place contain? Herbs. Bark. Flowers to be dried and ground. He has not thought properly about this. It's not something he can ask the locals about. Any appreciation of the landscape has to come by stealth, or, as he is doing now, by what he thinks might be called an archive of the feet. Walking and gathering. He sets his little knapsack down and opens it. Inside: a notebook the size of a paperback novel. Carefully, he gathers as many different plants as he can find, paying attention to leaf and stock, scent and bloom. He uses a small flat stone to scrape lichen from the trees—there are oak and maple and others he can't name. He places each distinct plant, root, leaf, bloom on its own page in his notebook, using a bit of Scotch tape to fasten them. With a rubber band, he fastens the book of collected specimens shut, and slips it into his bag. He settles on a patch of grass, which is not quite a clearing, but which offers a full view of the sky. Without meaning to he falls asleep, one hand under his head as a pillow.

When he wakes everything is as he found it. But of course, nothing is familiar.

The rest of the canoe ride passes as a kind of blur. His mind is set on returning to Radzanów to find out what he has collected. What the wealth of the shoreline provides. He might be a medieval village magician-in-training who has been sent out to learn his trade. When the GPS confirms that the white spire in the near distance belongs to the church at Pomiechowo he pulls the canoe to the riverside. Here the river valley is wide and flat, with forested plains off to the east and west. The bank is sandy. A series of hydro wire supports, some fifty feet high, skirts the bend in the waterway. He has left the lonely discoveries of the river behind in an instant. He must get the canoe over to the church, across a rough field with no obvious path. He cuts through high grass then joins ruts whose parallel lines aim more or less at the church. But almost immediately he is met by a group of horses coming from that direction. They are big, chestnut-coloured, with flaxen manes. Simon places the canoe face down and watches as they mosey by, heads low, sampling the grassy way. It takes the animals a long time to pass. He waves at the teenager who guides them at the rear.

Clutching the canoe, he heads for the church. His pickup—Charlie told him to look out for a black Skoda—is not there, so he puts the canoe by the building's wall where the rental guy will see it. He peers inside the church's big front doors. The pews are full of grey-haired parishioners. Something special is taking place. There is a calendar of events in the vestibule, but Simon cannot read anything on it beyond numbers, dates, times of day. It's remarkably bright inside, walls painted the colour of pumpkin, and a pair of brilliant chandeliers hanging from the vaulted ceiling.

Their light reflects off the gold- and white-painted altar.

Back outside, the sky has begun to cloud over and the evening is turning indigo, violet at the horizon above the trees. The Skoda rolls up. The driver gets out to open the door for him, offering a wordless nod in greeting. Simon sets his bag with his specimens beside him on the seat and they head home. He cannot stand the idea of a silent ride, the guy up front like a servant and himself in back like royalty, so he asks the only thing he can think of that the two of them might have to talk about: "How is the film shoot going?"

The driver makes eye contact for the first time via the rearview mirror. He shrugs, eyebrows raised. "I can't complain. Good driving weather."

"What about the shoot?"

"Too many actors dressed as Nazis. You know. To hell with them. These guys, it's like they think the dogs are theirs."

Simon thinks about this. He's been distracted, he realizes, by all the film paraphernalia, trucks and vintage motorcycles with their clattering sidecars. The antiquarian in him had been drawn to these.

"Tomorrow, you can see a big scene in the square. I'm bringing the director out for it."

Well, a show for them all tomorrow.

A Night Jew

Ania's mother stands at her window watching the film crew set up for what is supposed to be the last day of shooting in the old square. Ania said so, and she hopes it is true. It would mean one less thing for the girl to do in town, but enough was enough with Poles dressed as Germans. It turned her stomach. Sometimes it gave her a headache at the very front of her skull.

What it brought to mind, too, was her younger self, in the square at night, in wartime, greeting her own Night Jew. She was barefoot. She could not remember why. The moon lit a street empty of life. The Night Jew's name was Ahronovitch, but she knew him as Aronek. He was no figment. He was the real thing. Aronek was his nickname and that's what he was called by her friend, the cousin of Aronek, who was now long gone, to America. First the boy left. Then his immediate family was taken away by the Germans. Aronek kept their house for them. He somehow avoided deportation. But eventually he vanished and the *Reichsdeutsche* moved in. And then even he was gone. Arrested or reassigned. Maybe up to Działdowo, where the Germans had set up a concentration camp that they called Soldau. These names. Their brutality. She did not know where these people disappeared to.

But she felt a strong responsibility for the house when it was left empty. When Aronek and the German had both been gone for a month, she worried that the neighbours would break in and take what was left of her friend's family's possessions—Jewish things, which were both talismanic and taboo. She went barefoot—now she remembered—to be as silent as possible, like a cat. She would see if the house was locked up tight, if she could see inside and if anything needed protecting. Then she would figure out what to do next. Whatever it was a girl her age could do.

The moon was almost full and she saw the outline of the town—rooftops and barnyards and the curve in the roadway—in a new way. The pinprick stars in their crazy whirls and bursts reminded her of embroidery that the shops on the market sold before the war. Now there was nothing.

The empty house beckoned. But before she was halfway across the square she saw a figure. A hand waving from the space between two houses. She knew at once. It was Aronek. The cousin of her friend. He was calling to her quietly in Polish, by the name used by people who knew her well. *Ewunia*. She was not frightened, but hesitated. She was anxious to perform her duty—reconnaissance of the house on the square, and then a safe return to her bed.

She sidled over to the Night Jew.

He said, in his steady, serious voice, "Ewunia. We are starving in the forest. In my cousin's house, you know the one?"

She did.

Hidden there, and then he began to explain where to look, but she grew hot as she listened. She did not think she could pull off what Aronek was suggesting. It meant, he said, another nighttime meeting. He told her: See if you can find, somewhere in the house, sheets of postage stamps in different colours, ochre and orange and robin's egg blue. Of the kind you needed scissors to separate one from the other.

Would she go now? To the house? Just then a noise in one of the nearby homes broke the quiet. A shutter blowing open? Or something more threatening? All of a sudden, her Night Jew disappeared from the place where he'd stood. She remembered still the very thought she was about to express, that she would return tomorrow at the same time.

Now, as she gazes out her window at the costumed Germans in the square, her fear—or was it simply adrenalin, excitement, the notion that she could do some good in response to the surrounding disaster?—returns and she feels as she did on her barefoot run back home. So many things were wrong with the way the film showed the wartime. She wishes that Ania had nothing to do with it, but she knows that it is helpful to the town's economy. And certainly, when the shoot is finished, she will see less of Ania.

Another daydream. It is sometime in the eighties. She cannot remember those years as succinctly, as clearly as she does the war years of her childhood. This is a memory about Ania, and of how the world, the system, can beat you down. In those years it seemed like it would go on forever, even though the last decade of the dark Communist story had begun. You could not get anything you needed. Even the things they grew and made in the area around Mława and Radzanów were packed off for the Russians. Or sent further afield, to Cuba or southern Africa. Anyway, the things their fake subsidized economy produced—shoes, televisions, and whatever else—her family could not afford. Ania was a great lover of books, which were as inaccessible in their countryside as cheap shoes or affordable television sets. Even the Polish standbys, Tuwim's *Lokomotiv* and other children's books with a government stamp of approval, had to be brought from Warsaw. One non-European book that made it into their little place was the writing of the Canadian, Lucy Maud Montgomery, with its portrait of Anne of Green Gables. For a time, the girl with hair turned green by a wandering Jewish peddler was Ania's favourite. This was before she was tall enough or curious enough to discover her mother's backroom collection of American novels in Polish. Radzanów had a lending library, at the time set up in the derelict synagogue, but Ania had read everything in its collection that suited her age. She was so bursting with the pleasure of them that she dreamed her favourites. She woke in the morning and said, *Mummy, I dreamed the whole book last night, you know, the one about* . . .

So she'd sought out a friend who'd moved to Warsaw, who traveled sometimes by train, on the way to business in Bydgoszcz and Plock. Ewa would stand out on the train platform—she went to Mława to do this, because back then a train still came through town—and wait until her friend's train was due. When the engine clattered to a stop, one or two riders got on, a few off. Her friend would appear, keeping one foot on the metal stair they put out for people to step down on. She would hand off a package, neatly wrapped in brown packing paper. Books. Then her friend would get back on and off she went toward Plock. They did this a number of times over the course of a year. In passing the books, they exchanged a few words: How are you? What's doing back home? Until a railway man must have reported them. She was called in to the local police office. What, they demanded, were you exchanging at the railway siding?

But she knew the boys who were behind the desks. They were the sons of men who had not done great things during the war. She mentioned this to them. Did they know that there were things about their fathers' wartime behavior that their superiors might like to know? Maybe even over at the party office they would be interested in hearing. She had a very good memory, a perfect memory, really, and what kind of memory did the person have who had told them she was exchanging things at the railway platform? Maybe that person was a person worth forgetting about. The two men nodded in unison. *Proszę, Pani!* They showed her the way out and goodbye, all smiles. It was one of the first occasions when she realized that things she knew, things she'd done and hadn't done, things she'd seen others do doing the war, could come in useful in their tight little village. But she stopped the book hand-offs and missed them greatly. She missed her friend, but even more she missed the gifts for her daughter.

*

Ewa is daydreaming about her young-mother self when she hears the key in the lock. It is Ania, back from the mayor's office, with a handful of contracts, promises of support in kind, permissions from locals allowing the film crew onto their land. As the liaison between the town government and the film commission in Warsaw, Ania oversees contracts and invoicing, then carries it all back to the city. The film commission office is just down from her, near the Grzybowski Square. Without her, what a tangled bureaucratic fiasco it could all be.

Ania stands beside her mother at the window. "Let's watch. This is the last of it. What it takes to make things work on film is worth seeing."

Together they watch the shoot unfold. If weather is what makes an outdoor shoot succeed, the director and his cinematographer are experiencing a lucky streak. There is not one cloud in the sky. Not even a hint of a breeze. The tech people busy themselves with a camera that rolls on a pair of silver rails. The director of photography sits atop a chair on the rolling contraption, his eye to the camera's viewfinder. Two young men move him along the rails to track the shot. Filmmaking is slow business. Reflectors are rigged beside house fronts to cast away shadow. Overhead, a boom mike, with its fuzzy jacket, is lowered into place above the actors. These include at least eight, maybe ten men dressed in green Wehrmacht greatcoats. They will roast in these on this lovely day. Then come the Jews. They are Poles, young men gathered by a casting call in Warsaw, but they are dressed as Jews. For some reason their costumes look less convincing, more makeshift than the Wehrmacht stuff. Their beards look pasted on. The black gabardine on the older men looks distinctly costumey—not like clothes so much as something you'd pull out of a drama-school closet. Ania asks her mother if this is how the scene strikes her, and the answer is a firm yes. It's as if, Ania says, they took the look of the Jews from the tourist art you see around Krakow, aimed at Americans. Jews from outer space. Her mother nods, arms crossed tightly over her chest. She continues to nod her head, ever so slightly.

They are ready to roll. An antique truck roars into the market square with Wehrmacht guys in the back. It shivers to a halt. The army men break from the truck and prowl the roadway. They march over to one of the low red-brick houses, chosen for its pre-war authenticity, or maybe for the rich ochre shade of its brick front. Out of one of the houses they drag a family of dressed-up Jews. The grey-bearded elder in the group stumbles into the road, and then come girls, women, teenagers who are all pushed toward the back of the idling truck. Up the captives go and the truck gate is secured with a length of rope. Women with kerchiefs on their heads are visible as the truck careens back the way it came. From inside the house, Ania and her mother hear someone yell, "Cut!" Everyone on the set falls into a leisurely stance as they revert to casual waiting. Some walk toward the craft service trailer by the church. Ania and her mother agree that they do not want to watch this scene being reshot, if that's what's coming next.

A Polish Movie

Charlie drops by to invite Simon to view the rushes. They sit on the step in front of his house, which allows her a view of the set, and a chance to roll an unlit cigarette around in the palm of her hand.

"We're nearly finished shooting," she says. "It'll be quiet when we're gone. You'll miss us."

He's not sure if this inevitable change will be an enticement to stick around, or if it will feel like driving off a cliff, the absence of the world, to be surrounded by the real small-town life, its smoky night-smells and half-awake doings in daytime. Ania's mother's apple and poppy seed cakes.

"Will you come to see the rushes?" Charlie asks. "It's movie time in Radzanów! The first and last time to see what a good cinematographer can do with this place. Like the extinction of the dinosaurs. It only happens once."

He wants to come. Yes. Sure.

"Great. So, today, around four. At the building over that way." She points at the white two-storey structure with the city crest by the door.

"We've got one last problem to solve. But we won't, I think, hang around. If it comes together, we'll bring a small crew back for a day or two. Maybe try some interiors then too."

"What's the problem?"

"Do you mind?" Charlie holds the cigarette out for him to consider.

He shakes his head. She lights it, using a wooden match from a box marked with the Polish word—*zapałki*—in red.

"It's a music problem. The script calls for two Jewish kids on violin. To sit there." She points at the red-brick house where the filming took place earlier in the day. "We worked that out. One teaches the other a little run on the instrument. It's kind of nice. Kind of fake, I think, but kind of nice. We brought these two little prodigies from a music school in Krakow. But then there's music from the Polish side of the story. The idea is to show things from before the war that Jews and Poles shared. So the script calls for a *kapela*. A little band, with a drum. A squeezebox. A fiddle. A cimbalom. That would be the standard makeup. You still find them around here. Old guys at a country fair. But it hasn't worked out. We've not found the right fit. So I suggested, maybe the other kind of dulcimer."

"The Joni Mitchell dulcimer."

Charlie shifts on her haunches and squints hard at him over her cigarette. "You read my mind."

Simon shrugs.

"That was it. You know. Enough with the whole *cymbały* obsession. Go fresh."

"So what did he say?"

"He said yah! But can I find, in this country, an Appalachian dulcimerist of note, who can swing with the old *kapela* guys? I cannot." She smokes, shakes her head. Charlie is not used to a challenge she can't meet.

Simon catches a breath of Charlie's smoke. It's sharp and invigorating, along the lines of the lignite coal smoke that wafts from the local houses at evening.

"I know someone."

"What?"

"A dulcimer player. A girl I know back home."

"Really?"

"Yes."

"Well, can I get an email for her?"

Simon nods. He goes inside for a paper and pen and notes down the name, Nadia Baltzan, with an email address.

"Great! So, see you at the rushes? A production manager's work is never done." Charlie hesitates before adding, "What about your house?"

"Oh, I'm getting used to it. Maybe it'll fall on top of me one of these nights."

"No. Remember. Interiors. We still need interiors. I went back to the accountant. He said I could up the offer to $500 US a day. We'd use it for maybe two days. One day to set up. We would put you up wherever you want. Warsaw if you need a change. I stayed in a neat place in the Old Town when I was there last. You'd like it. Little churches everywhere. Good restaurants. It's kind of mysterious. I found a restaurant I go back to whenever I'm there. I'll give you the address. On the *Rynek Nowego Miasta*. Freta Street."

Simon wouldn't mind helping out, but he doesn't think he wants any Germans in his house. Costumed or otherwise. After all Ania's mother's care, it would leave a stain. A willed catastrophe when none was called for. As before he agrees to think about it.

"Okay." Charlie sounds pleased. "Let me know. I'll book the hotel for you."

The film crew gathers late in the afternoon to watch what they've accomplished in a makeshift screening room down the road from

Ania's mother's villa. The building is some sort of community hall the crew has rented. The town is doing well on the shoot. The little stores sell out of ham sandwiches and bottled water every day.

Well. He sits. At the back, arms spread behind his neighbours, sits the cinematographer who rode the camera track in the square.

Charlie steps to the front of the room. "Dariusz?" She beckons, not to the cinematographer but to another figure, dark-haired, who sets himself up in front of the screen, both hands in his pants pockets. This must be the director. The man's words are a blur of Polish. Then the room goes dark.

A lot of what he watches is awful. Not filmically, but existentially. Jews being pulled from the red-brick houses. The actors, suited up as Germans and the Polish Blue Police, parading, stone-faced. The losers in their ragged wartime clothes, a little too round-faced—even Simon can recognize this, because he's read the usual complaints about more famous film projects, *Sophie's Choice* or the *Holocaust* TV show. But what were they going to do, starve the actors for a year for the sake of historical accuracy? The attention to detail in some areas was impressive, such as the hulking open-back trucks, which, for all he knew, came from the motorization graveyard where he bought the Moskvitch. But he is distracted by the continuity mistakes. The power wires. How could they miss these? Would they edit them out?

But then something different catches his eye. A kind of running motif. It appears in a set of scenes that the director had redone, slightly differently each time. Next to the others, with their effort at brute, bludgeoning historical realism, these short scenes are darkly fanciful. Watching them, he doesn't feel that the director is saying: *This is how it happened*. Rather, the scenes telegraph something personal, narrower. *This is how I imagine it to have happened*. The scenes use a filter or a colourization technique that has given them the tone of an old hand-tinted photograph. It has a powerful effect. *Here is the colour of the pre-war Polish-Jewish world,* it seemed to say. *I've discovered it and I have used it to cover this scene in something unusual, even beautiful.* Simon knows a little about the history of film, the use of colour in early photography. He taught film studies for a time, when his department's specialist in the field took a maternity leave. He'd started out knowing almost nothing, but at course's end he was willing and able to do it again with less of his characteristic diffidence. He could get behind film studies if they paid him to.

What filled the screen? The hundred-year-old red-brick house that had been the backdrop for the scene he'd watched the crew shoot. On the stoop of one sat two little boys in knee pants and caps, each holding a little violin under his chin. One listens to the other play. The listener then shows his mate how to improve on the little motif he plays. Then the learner tries again, sounding better than before. Little boys doing a grown-up thing; one teaching his mate the way an adult might. There are figures in the background, but in this scene, the roadway, even the whole town, belongs to these two. The eye moves from them to the upper half of the screen, filled with an oddly coloured sky—grey and peach and violet, the heavy shades of an oncoming evening storm.

Well done, Simon thinks as he watches. *I could watch that again.*

And this is where the shot list ends. The screen goes white. Someone turns on the lights. Simon blinks at the suddenness of this. He glances around the room, but cannot see Charlie. He decides to slip out and manages to disappear as the crew embarks on a discussion of their work. On the street he is struck by the mundane light. The down-at-the-heels mix of new and antique buildings. The teenagers scooting by aimlessly on their dirt bikes. The town, he thinks, needs a filter. Or colourization. Something. He makes his way across the square and along the curving road that runs by Ania's mother's villa. Over his shoulder he checks her big front window. The curtains are drawn. He cuts across the square and down a side road. He walks with his hands in his back pockets. He feels bad and uplifted at the same time. The revelation of film. Its made-up-ness, and its surprises. Its ability, when done well, to transport you. In the case of what he'd just seen, back to wartime, and even before the war, when his father was still in the town, still in love with Ania's mother, riding skiffs with cats on the Wkra.

Simon holds onto the image of the two boys, the sky, the red-brick backdrop, as he meanders along a road that is, with each property he passes, more rural. He comes upon a woodlot. Chickens. Great rust-coloured featherballs. One with an elaborate black headdress over its eyes. Cords of neatly piled firewood. Beyond this a field. In the near distance, there are three things. First, a cow, which seems to look up as Simon approaches. Then, a gnarled tree, which might be dead, its branches pointed and irregular, more like a made thing than something alive. A tree manufactured for a theatre set. Then, a figure, from behind, bent at the waist picking things from the scrub grass. From further off, another slimmer figure appears. It is Ania and her mother.

Simon makes his way over and tries an awkward *dzień dobry*, but the old woman waves this off.

"English," she says, as she gathers a basket she was filling, "is alright."

Ania smiles. "Mama."

Simon is eager to apologize for his lack of language, his crooked *dzień dobry*s. These are all he has to offer the local shop owners.

"What are you collecting?"

"Herbs."

"Which kind?"

"*Ziola zydowskie.* Jewish herbs."

"How are they Jewish?"

"This was the cemetery." Ania waves an arm beyond the tree, the cow, the rolling field. "My mother is generally, almost to a rule, a realist. But when it comes to this she will entertain a bit of magic."

He gazes at the ground where Ania's mother has been harvesting things. Might his father remember who was buried there?

"*Katastrofa.*" Ania's mother puts her fists on her hips and spins a long narrative connected with the place where they stand.

"She watched the Germans bring the ark from inside the synagogue to this place and burn it. And she knows that some Poles helped. But Poles and Jews alike believed in the power of things grown in the cemetery. Very old beliefs."

"What grows here, besides grass? That, I guess, is what the cow comes for."

"You never know. It could be looking for special things. Just as mother is."

"What is she looking for?"

"Mama? *Kozlak lekarski*? I'm not always sure of the right English word."

Ania's mother runs a hand around in her basket of goodies.

"I think from some she just makes potpourri. And some might be for sleep."

"Or if you're depressed."

"Yes. Sure. For depression. Although my mother wouldn't use that word."

"And the tree." Ania points at the art tree.

"Is it alive?"

This draws a look of surprise from the old lady.

"Alive, yes, according to my mother. And very powerful. Here. Come over." They march through the high grass to the tree, the basket tipped on Ania's mother's hip. She lays a palm on the tree trunk, then spreads her hand against the main bough at the height of his shoulder.

"These," Simon tells them, "we have at home. Lots of them."

"Sure. Lovely trees. I believe it's the bark my mother's interested in. *Kora wierzby*. You'll see that they grow like weeds along the Wkra. Willow bark is big business in Poland. But we must compete with the Chinese. And they are like the Germans in war. The Chinese in business. If they can bury you, they do it quickly. Clean up. Off they go."

"I was on the river," he tells them. "Your river. I collected some things. I wonder if your mother would look at them, to tell me what I have."

Ania suggests this and her mother nods, absently. Simon can't tell for sure if she's agreed to his request or dismissed it.

The day has grown warm. A summer day out of a fairy tale. Windless. Flies buzz by. The grass around their feet like a wild carpet. Ania's mother draws a breath, then a long intake from the nose, and she smiles, telling Ania something.

"This is odd. Mother says that you smell the way your father did. Now that it's hot.

It reminds her of when they went together to the field collecting things."

"What did she think when he left in, what was it, 1937? That he would return?"

Ania asks about this, and her mother hesitates before answering.

"No one was returning. But my mother says they did have an agreement. When it was possible. If it was possible. She would come to America."

"Canada."

"Well, first it was America. He had New York plans. But once he made it up to Canada. To your city. She knew. Whatever he was doing, it did not concern his Polish girl. They exchanged letters. She has them still. He sent her a postcard from Quebec when he went there on a business trip. Then it stopped. But she kept his presence alive here with the house. And she read. When the American writers were available in Polish. She would seek them out. Even Salinger. Their onetime pal. A real American, in the ham business, who went on to true fame in the larger world. It was this reading that finally drove my father crazy. We'd abandoned him for America, he said. *In our minds.*

"She accepted her loss for what it was. So many others lost everything. Her family was alive. They had their old home and continued to farm land they owned before the war. She had lost friends. And Radzanów was not the same. Nobody has really taken the measure of this. How it felt to grow up in a Polish town like ours after the war. But on the surface, her life was whole."

"It was a lot for my father to forget."

Ania looks at him and then at her mother, but he is not sure if she's caught his point. It was such a shitload of forgetting that it had landed him here, in a field of willow and valerian.

Ania's mother smiles.

"Well," Ania asks, "do you want to show us your collection from the riverbank?"

Back they go, quietly. The old lady carries her basket. He with his hands in his pockets. They enter the town from behind the church. People gather on its steps, holding great bunches of cut flowers. "Another funeral," Ania explains. "A few of my mother's friends. They're eagerly awaiting hers. They are counting on surprises, revelations, on her death bed."

From across the square, he takes in how beat-up his house is. The weird way the cement sidewalk kisses the bottom of the wood frame front. The old shutters—like the kind you see on either side of a window—that frame the doorway. The tattered lace by the window frames. Simon opens the door and they step inside.

"Let's see what you have. Mama?" Ania stands with a hand on the old table, her mother beside her.

Simon gets his notebook with the specimens and sets it out. They flip through the pages. A few days have passed since he picked the leaves and stems, which are wilted, but green. Ania's mother handles each one lightly, running a fingertip over them. In a few cases she brings a leaf up to her nose and smells deeply. The effect as she does this, even on Simon as he watches, is remarkable. He moves a little closer in order to smell what she holds. She turns the pages back to the first specimen.

"Just as my mother has in her basket," Ania explains. "*Kozlak lekarski*. But this bark she has not seen for a long time. She'd be interested to know where you got it. And this is for the heart."

Ania's mother thumps her fist on her left breast. "*Naparstnica*." She takes a chair out from the table and settles down on it a little roughly. It's the first time Simon has seen her look anything less than composed. She speaks at length to Ania, who listens and then translates her mother's words.

"She felt for a moment as if she were a girl again. The last time she was inside this house for longer than a few minutes was in wartime. Because of the *Reichsdeutsche*. He had a scheme he wanted her help with. Everyone back then wanted help. She walked across the field and someone would pop up, begging."

Simon nods. He does not know what to say.

"He had postcards. The *Reichsdeutsche*. What he had in mind was too complicated for a girl to understand. Friends of his back home had made them. Handwritten. Anti-Hitler. They had slogans written on them. The war was against the worker. The worker! Back then they put you against a wall and shot you if you were caught with such things. If they found a child with them, up against the wall. What was the *Reichsdeutsche* doing with them, you're wondering? Well, mostly, he was hiding them. Here." Following her mother's outstretched arm Ania makes her way to the chimney by the stove. She runs a hand over the bricks and finds the loose one, removing it. With her other hand she reaches inside.

"There's nothing there now." She replaces the brick and returns to the tale of the plea her mother received from the *Reichsdeutsche*. This is the name Ania's mother calls him by. She might have known the man's name, but either she cannot remember it or she cannot bring herself to say it.

"The postcard people became a little famous. They were both executed. A German novelist wrote about them. It's a summation of wartime, really, of the kind of experiences one witnessed and also the Germans' nature, their brutality. They teach kids about the war all over the world. In Germany. In North America and Europe. They should tell them stories like this one. It's less distracting than Auschwitz. Bergen-Belsen. Even near here there was a concentration camp. The Germans called it Soldau. Działdowo is the name of the town. It's where they brought the handicapped from the German borderlands. But you try to explain this to young people. That they were bringing the handicapped, the disabled, the helpless to Działdowo, where the Wkra valley begins to really be beautiful, to kill them. Who's going to stand up in front of a classroom and tell this story? My mother's story is one you could tell. The *Reichsdeutsche* had the postcards here, in the chimney. From the Ciechanów Gestapo office a sheaf of sheets of postage stamps. These had been confiscated further east and were meant to be sent back to Germany. To be destroyed. Somehow he got them. Would she, he wondered, if he were to put the stamps on the cards, take them to a certain contact who would mail them? She could not remember who the contact was. Maybe he wanted to send them to Gestapo offices in Polish towns, like the outpost at Ciechanów. They might think there was a network of resisters about to rise up in the occupied lands. In Germany, his friends had caused this fear with the delivery of their cards in apartment lobbies. What a crazy scheme."

"Did you do this for him?"

She shakes her head.

"I was in the house once more. After he was gone. I took things. And it was dark for years after that."

PART THREE

West Cordova Noir

He felt he'd hit bottom. Was this the price you paid for doing what he'd done? Some murderers sailed off into the sunset. Others opened dry cleaning stores. Raised a family. Cut the lawn. But not Little Tommy Eden. Sometimes he caught sight of his reflection in a shop window—what was left of his hair sticking up, the back of his jacket trailing its lining—and he knew he'd sunk as low as you can go. What had he accomplished in his life? He'd come full circle, back to the old neighbourhood, after all the other lousy places he'd hid out. Like a homing pigeon, or a cat seeking the owners who'd abandoned it. He'd changed his name, the way they do in the movies. Now he was John Jenkins. The little moustache he'd worn in the old days to distinguish himself from the other layabouts was gone. Clean-shaven and clean-living. That was the private credo of self-protection he relied on.

He had been the little guy in the team. But he was the one most likely to blow his stack. When the pawn guy told them to get out of his shop, Tommy lost it. He and Zane had planned the whole thing for minimum trouble. They'd gone in after lunch when the place was quiet. They'd brought no weapon. Their target was known as a soft touch. The Gentle Jew was what they called him on the street, so what was he doing going off the way he did? It all could have been over in a couple of minutes. But he'd panicked when the guy didn't do as he was told. That's when he'd grabbed the bottle. There were a thousand weapons in the place. Fireplace pokers. Hatchets. Tools for scaling island timber. Carpenters' awls. Sledgehammers. It was a weapon store. What came to hand was the 7 Up bottle. It was half full, and when he raised it, the leftover pop poured down his sleeve. Then the pawn guy was on his knees, still fighting. He thought maybe the bottle had broken, but a quick look told him it was intact. So he kept at it. They had the shop to themselves, unless one of the regulars wandered in with a watch to pawn or to beg for a loan so he could go up the road to get himself a pint at the Hildon.

It all blazed up before him. The pawn guy fighting back, and his own response, which was to keep swinging, even as the two of them retreated like backwards crabs to the rear of the shop. It wasn't until years later that he became curious about the life he'd snuffed out. He felt that if he was going to get away with murder, the least he could do was find out who the guy was. They were linked, he and his victim, in some sort of embrace.

But first it had been necessary to get as far away from the scene of the crime as he could. So he'd headed east. First to Banff, where he ran an elevator at the Banff Springs Hotel, talking to German and Japanese tourists and kids who likely thought the world was a perfectly benign place. After two years of this, he started to worry he was going to blow his stack if someone in the elevator asked him, once more, if he'd ever seen such a lovely morning. So he hopped a bus to Calgary and made his way—where do you think?—to the streets that more or less replicated the east side of Vancouver he'd been forced to flee. In Calgary there was no real skid row, no logging or shipping or mining, the type of work that drew itinerant single men. There was one street corner everyone knew about—was it on Tenth Avenue?—where men hung around and guys came by in trucks to pick them up and take them off for a day's work. You had rummies and dead-broke native guys on Eighth Avenue. Not far east you had pawn shops. Just like in Vancouver, many of them owned by Jews. The first time he walked down there, east of Centre Street, he pretty near had a heart attack, because standing out front of Centre City Loan and Pawn was the ghost of the guy he'd mauled with the 7 Up bottle, or it was his double or maybe his brother. The sight caused his heart to leap into his mouth, even though it became clear as he walked by the store that this was no ghost and not even the dead man's double. It was just another short, balding, bespectacled, benign-looking middle-aged guy, who ran a place on Calgary's Seventh Avenue like the one that had become a murder scene on Cordova. He went on past, looking once over his shoulder, toward the Stampede Grounds, where he found work as a stable hand. A shoveller of goat shit and a raker of straw and a painter of fences, which kept him going, in a marginal sort of way, for five or six years. He didn't remember exactly when that ran its course, because by the time it did he was drinking so much after work at the King Eddy that his brain had softened up and his sense of time had shrunk down to two focal points: the day it was, that is, *today;* and the day on which he'd sealed his fate with the pop bottle. He became a two-day machine. Today and *that day*. And so he remained to this day.

Murder Monday, as he came to think of it, bloomed in his imagination. It haunted him, no matter how he tried to blot it out with Canadian Club and jugs of watery Pilsner. On an average day, he'd wake up, whether to a remembered dream or his own antic thoughts, reliving the nonsensical plan he and Zane had concocted, the reason they chose Reliable Loan as their target. He recalled the nervous stomach that nearly felled him hours before they planned to go in, leading him to spend the morning on the crapper before they headed up Cordova. He rehashed his decision not to follow Zane up to Osoyoos, where Zane hid out with his aunt. As soon as the Army and Navy put up a reward—first $2,000 and then, with community contributions, it hit $4,000—Zane's goose was cooked. His aunt hardly knew him but she knew for certain that $4,000 would make the coming winter a lot warmer. So she set her nephew up, John Dillinger style, and the cops corralled him in his aunt's trailer. They ineptly, or possibly intentionally, cut him in half in a hail of bullets, as if they'd been watching too many Edward G. Robinson films and figured their watch-stealer, their pawnshop bottle-wielder was a real danger to society, a power to reckon with, when what he was was six feet and a couple hundred pounds of ignorant, whiskey-reeking weakness, not a monster who, ironically, had not even wielded the bottle. The whole fiasco, a regular manhunt, was on the radio and in the papers, and it became clear, as Tommy read about it, or, holed up in a beer hall in Banff, listened to the far-away news crackle across the mountains, that with Zane dead the trail to Tommy Eden went a good deal colder.

So: Banff, then Calgary, a stretch in Toronto. Ultimately, Vancouver drew him back. He could not help himself. He was a product of the old downtown, of the streets around Cordova and East Hastings, which had in many ways become so much worse than they'd been when he'd preyed on a shop-owner's easygoing reputation. The mayor had come down after the fact to talk to the shopkeepers and look around. The newspapers had a front page photo of him as he stepped out of his chauffeur-driven Lincoln. A lush sitting on an overturned milk box was said to have asked, "What are ya, the head cop?" The aftermath of the murder had a small-town feel.

He'd made his way back to the city in '92. He lay low at first, stayed away from Cordova, kept out of any kind of trouble, found a place way out east in a tumbledown house owned by a landlord whose mailing address was in Hong Kong. When he went into the city, he did not jaywalk or loaf on park benches. His greatest fear was that he'd be picked up on some random police check for looking nervous as a cop sat in his car by the curb, eyeing the passing parade. The cop would turn out to be the one guy on the force who remembered what happened on Cordova in April of 1962. Could there be such a cop? He would have to be the keeper of the cop archive, because no one his own age could still be on the job. All the incompetent clowns of the mid-century force were in old folks' homes or buried in Ladner, in Surrey—underground, like his crime itself. But there it was, the possibility that the cold case of cold cases might be solved. And a cop would lay a hand on his shoulder and say, without a hint of irony, *Look who we have here. Little Tommy Eden.*

He visited the old public library on Robson, wearing his one neat jacket, his hair slicked back. The second-floor reference area was never busy, and he had a favourite corner by a window where he read the newspaper. He started with the morning paper, but eventually he worked his way back to the archive, because whenever he read about something that happened in the city yesterday, he ended up thinking about the way the morning had gone fifty years before. They had the old newspapers, some of them on rolls of fiche. To request these, you needed a library card, which he didn't have and didn't plan on getting. By then he was living off Hastings, near Dunleavy, where he came to know his share of deadbeats, guys who'd open your coat and look to see what was in every pocket if they found you passed out or dead in an alley.

That's where Ace came in. Ace Bailey. A more or less sane guy who had risen to the top of the Hastings hierarchy. He lived in a perfectly fresh, subsidized apartment in the Patricia Hotel and fancied himself a prince of the neighbourhood, a kind of street philosopher. Ace had spent about fifteen minutes in the Canadian Army, driving a truck in the Korean War. So there were benefits for that. He had a library card, which he kept in an old tin cake box on the shelf above his fridge. Tommy put in an hour, listening to the guy's wisdom regarding the books that everyone should read before he died—Dostoyevsky and Dos Passos and Tolstoy—and he received the library card, on loan, and went off with it in his breast pocket. Sometimes Ace had a fine that needed paying, and Tommy did that, counting it out for the library staffer in dimes and nickels.

Reading it so many years later, the obituary scared the shit out of him. They described a life distinctly worthwhile, in relation to his own wholly worthless existence. The guy did community work, had a family and a business. A real immigrant story. His old-world European father was a Torah scholar somewhere in Poland, not that Tommy knew what that meant. But it had to be an accomplishment. Mordecai Batzanoff. The son abandoned everything and arrived in a new country with nothing but a beat-up brown leather suitcase. No English. How, he wondered, did guys pull off such turnarounds?

He'd take the *Sun* and the *Province*, when they had the originals, always happy to avoid the fiche and the contraption you used to view it, to a chair by the window that overlooked Burrard. Below, the city flew by. Above the apartment buildings of the West End the sky was always blue. So beautiful it was wounding, a thing not yourself, so perfect and real. He was surrounded by the usual regulars, retirees doing crossword puzzles and students reading up on Leonardo da Vinci, Albert Einstein, Hitler, and Joe Stalin. The more he read, the less easy it was for him to dismiss the man he'd killed as *the Jew, the pawn guy, the pop-bottle man*. Israel Batzanoff—the Gentle Jew. He'd lend a guy a buck without lecturing him about drinking it.

The papers luxuriated in the story. It wasn't the only murder in the headlines that season. Murder was going around like the flu. He read and reread the coverage of these others, alongside the reports on what he'd perpetrated. John Robb. Sixty years old. Five guys in a room in the West End drinking wine. Robb made the mistake of boasting about some big payday, then: strangled with his own necktie.

There was a shooting at the Bayshore Hotel. And a sex crime. A boy was kidnapped and driven across the American border into Washington State. There, kidnapping turned to murder.

Escalation. It accounted for a lot of crimes. They started small then exploded. In every one of these murder cases the reporters looked for a story. By banging Batzanoff over the head on an April morning, Little Tommy Eden had increased circulation. Ad business revved up. The byline that was most often attached to his murder story was F. Lewis-Smith. Someone told him that this was a lady journalist on the downtown beat who specialized in painting the scene on Cordova, and she'd stayed with the pawnshop murder story until everyone lost interest. In the *Sun*, he found a two-part feature by her, depicting the final morning that Israel Batzanoff drove downtown. She wrote it up in a style that reminded him of the voiceover in old movies, so the events leading up to his act took shape in a way that he could never have envisioned on his own. He'd borrowed that edition, dated April 18, 1962, more than once, but tried to keep this urge under control. It was his life but someone else was writing it up. Making it so much clearer. What if repeated borrowings tipped some wary reference librarian to the fact that the subject had a life of its own on the second floor? Increasingly, it was all he wanted to look at. Like an itch that needed scratching.

The headline was "Community Leader's Final Hours":

Israel Batzanoff rolls out of the outer ring of Shaughnessy in his grey Morris Minor, and appreciates the car's leather-smelling seats and burled walnut dash. The car is proof of his up-and-coming status in the local business community. He shifts down Granville and heads east, along the last western block of Cordova before Carrall, where he rents space for his shop from the family that owns the Army and Navy. He parks on Carrall.

What does he see as he walks toward Reliable Loan? Men in shirtsleeves, hats low on their heads, out front of the Rainier Grocery and Hotel. Beside the grocery is one of his competitors. "Buy—Sell—Trade" is all the sign outside says, with a bigger front window than his, six doors up at Reliable Loan. He stops in front of his competitor. The contrast with his shop is obvious. Here, it's work-related stuff on show, the stock in the window pressed close to the glass. Embossed leather belts, jackets on dummy torsos, singles of cowboy boots, lace-ups and loafers at the window ledge. On the cement outside, shovels, axes, sledges, tied with a rope hooked to the wooden storefront.

Batzanoff steps up to his window at Reliable Loan to appreciate how much more impressively his place is organized. On the top shelf: mechanicals—barometers, radios, cameras, drills, binoculars, clocks, telescopes. On the shelf below: fishing reels, pocket and wristwatches, desk clocks, precision tools in neat wooden boxes, scissors and Bowie knives. Below that, smaller stuff: military medals, magnifiers, tool and die and key-lock mechanisms. On the lowest shelf, carpenters' awls, wrenches, clamps, compass points and measuring rules.

The precedence of his shop over the others in the neighbourhood is proven by the fact of the boy out front.

The boy is often there when he arrives. He wears the same buttoned-up checked work shirt and brown corduroys. He is William, nine years old. Today the sidewalk needs a good sweep.

Batzanoff unlocks the shop, brings out a broom and tells the boy to "Go to it."

Inside, Batzanoff turns on the lights. He unlocks the cash box and sets it behind the front desk. He hangs his suit coat on a hook, loosens his tie and settles on a stool with the morning paper. Outside his window, Cordova Street in April is in trouble. Woodward's is still the main draw, for tea sets, mattresses, and cake flour. But seediness has taken hold. A storefront across the street has been empty for months. Its dark, half-curtained display window shows an open New Testament. Men have dollar haircuts on their minds. The Chinese cafés advertise grilled-cheese sandwiches and watery coffee in steel urns. Over in Chinatown things are less depressed. But the steady decline on Cordova doesn't bother him. He has his uptown life, his synagogue work, his young family.

That was how the first installment ended. After a number of weeks, the coverage petered out. Zane, sold out by his aunt, was cut down in the mobile home in Osoyoos. The little guy who'd wielded the bottle was eyeing the world through a half-open elevator door in Banff. Interest in skid row evaporated, and people forgot about the old blocks downtown that had been targeted for wholesale disappearance. If you never went over there, who cared? The decline on Cordova and Hastings and Powell settled in like a vicious, gradual disease. Batzanoff's storefront disappeared into the long red-brick block of Army-and-Navy display windows, but was never revived as a retail space. Loading docks were added in the seventies, and the access from the front of the building was sealed up behind wood and chain link. The alley out back became a shooting gallery. Sometimes he viewed the facade of 36 Cordova as he marched by on the far side of the street. Recently, to his surprise, they'd removed the loading docks and a business appeared—some sort of restaurant or café. The city had a slow and unpredictable way of repairing itself.

Dunleavy

The Patricia Hotel on East Hastings: a great white hope of some kind. A regular place in the midst of all the wreckage downtown. But on the way over, Jesus—it was like a bomb went off, and they never managed to clean up afterward. How, Tommy wondered, could they pinpoint ground zero? Was it right at the corner of Main and Hastings, or somewhere a little off to the east? Cordova was getting a cleanup, so it wasn't there. But everywhere there were cop cars rolling slowly along the curbside, as if the cars were designed to do just that. Roll slow. Those assholes. What was it exactly they were being paid to do?

He takes the elevator up to Ace's floor. Ace. The King of the Bums on flophouse row. He knocks on the door and it swings open in slow motion. And there's Ace, wearing one of his weird hats. Who does he think he is? Zero Mostel? Ace tells him to come in, and that's when he sees the girl. He pretty near trips on the carpet when he sees that Ace is not alone. How in the hell did Ace get a woman to come up to his room? Ace did not have guests. And he wasn't the type to bring one of the street's prostitutes up. But this one wasn't dressed right anyway. Everything about her was normal. Normal face and hair and clothes and a brand new pair of what looked like expensive running shoes. They were white as a newly painted wall. He heard Ace introducing him, and he thought, in slow motion, *thank God he knows me as Jenkins*. Old Johnny. J.J. He was a regular comedy routine with the names. Only now, as Ace tells it to the woman, it sounds like a fake name. Whoever she is, she's gonna know it's fake. She'll smell it.

"Ace," he says, not looking at the woman at all. "Can I borrow the library card?"

"The library card?"

"Yes, the library card." That was the only card he came by for. Tommy stands there as Ace heads off to get it. Now the woman is asking him questions.

"How long have you lived down here?"

He tries to knock her off track, asking his own questions instead of answering hers.

"What's in the case?"

"Oh. That's my dulcimer. I sometimes play near here. Or I just go for the show. Tonight, open mic was cancelled."

"You know Ace from there?" Tommy knows this is nonsense. Ace sits only on park benches and in his armchair at home.

"I don't know him." This brings her around to her first question, and she asks it again. How long has he lived in the neighbourhood.

"You mean near Hastings?"

"Yes."

He feels he should lie, even in this casual conversation. He tells her ten years, when the truth is more than twenty.

"What's it like living down here?"

"Well, it's a great big sunbaked shithole on a hot summer day. But it's home."

She starts to tell him why she's down on East Hastings. And that's when he realizes he really should make a break for it. Where the hell is Ace? Is he baking his library card into a cake? Jesus.

Pawn shop. He hears that. And murdered. But with a pop bottle. He feels like his heart might pop. She wants, she says, to find out as much as she can.

Tommy can't remember if there is a working fire escape outside Ace's kitchen window? This girl and her possibilities. They are the last indignity, after every other ridiculous thing that has happened in his life.

Ace holds the card out in his wavering hand. Tommy drops it. Bends to get it off the rug. Then he's out in the hall. Forget the elevator. He takes the stairs, clattering down the metal from floor to floor. He bursts out the emergency door into the alley. This sets off a fire alarm, which sounds like crows drunk on apples up high in a tree. He breaks into a vicious, gut-splitting run, hoping to hell he doesn't slip on the silver pavement. What does he look like from behind? A scuttling bug, legs flying, his worn-out jacket shining in the grim east side sun.

★

It is a week before he allows himself to even walk in the direction of Dunleavy. But he feels compelled to find out what was going on the last time he was there.

The lobby of the Patricia is full of tourists. They look like Muppet characters in their matching white sun hats, backpacks neatly positioned. They hold pamphlets, water bottles, and phones. He is tempted to warn them about what they'll see when they emerge to walk toward the centre of town. But to hell with the Muppeteers. He's on a mission. His first such in many years. Self-preservation. He has honed his skills at this. A forgotten fugitive. But safe as a baby.

He takes the elevator to Ace's floor. Knocks lightly. No answer. He tries again, and the door opens. His friend looks a little worse for wear.

"Here," he holds out the library card. "I paid your overdue fines. Eighty-five cents on *The Great Gatsby*. Can I come in?" He settles himself in one of Ace's old armchairs. The light from the street is hot in his face. Ace stays on his feet.

"Is something up?"

"Yah. Can we talk?"

Ace looks a little annoyed but settles opposite in a deeper, darker chair. Usually he talks. That's his role. He talks, and others listen.

"Last time I was here. That girl."

"Who?"

"The girl. In the bright white running shoes."

"Oh." Maybe Ace really is slipping into some new demented stage. "Oh, that one. She asked a lot of questions."

"What was she doing here?"

Ace has to think about this. "You know. They come around. Like I know the answers when it comes to this side of town. Journalists, what have you. Everyone seems to believe there's some unfinished work to be done down here."

"Is she a journalist?"

Ace shakes his head. He doesn't think so. But if she was, she had a photographic memory because she didn't carry a notebook or a recorder. He was tired the day she invited herself up. Maybe the medication they were trying for his blood pressure had made him lightheaded. He recalls the visit as if it were a particularly vivid dream. She said she was following a family story. She expected him to know about it. Something about Cordova in 1962. But on this, he had to correct her. 1962. Spring. He'd been on the road throughout that year. Day in and day out. He drove a truck loaded high with cedar from one end of Vancouver Island to the ferry terminal. It was good-paying work and it kept him, for once, far away from Cordova. How, he wanted to know, had she found him? All she would say was someone had mentioned his name. Then she left. What more could he say? She'd been downtown looking around. They'd agreed, things were a disaster. She'd come via Hastings, past the Empress. She'd peeked into the beer hall there. Dark as a cave. Pints for three bucks. She wondered about the cage over the attendant's cubicle at the Hazelwood. Was that really necessary? And then he remembered.

"Tommy Eden."

"*What?*"

"That's the name she said. I remember now."

They stare at each other across the room. Ace doesn't have a clue. But that makes sense, doesn't it? He knows him as John Jenkins. As Johnny. Old J.J. Ace never listens to anything anyone else says. Other people, Hastings denizens in worse shape than he is, are supposed to listen to him. He doesn't have a clue that he has just uttered the name of the man who sits before him, who, on a lovely early April morning, raised a pop bottle above Izzy Batzanoff's skull and nearly got the street razed.

So he's safe. As long as he can keep clear of the girl in bright white shoes. That's how he'll know her next time. Running shoes.

The Dulcimer Girl

The offer arrives by email. Life-changing surprises come this way The note is signed, *Charlie Wiespolska,* under the address Lewandowska Pictures. Warsaw, Sienna 42/46. It reads:

Dear Nadia Baltzan,

We have had word of your lovely way with the dulcimer. We are at a loss here. The whole of Poland will not cough up a player who can make your instrument do what we need it to do. Our mutual friend Simon Hanover directed me to a YouTube film of you. You are playing Mary Hopkin. As they say in poems: my heart is broken. I am not sure you are aware that you were filmed. There is no attribution and your involvement in the post is not noted. But thankfully, you are not viral. You are our own little secret. The Dulcimer Girl. Please let us know if you accept from Lewandowska Pictures:
1. first class airfare Vancouver-Frankfurt-Warsaw return
2. driver to Radzanów for a one-day shoot, return

3. downtown Warsaw recording location with recording engineer Jacek Uchman, who has worked with Tomasz Stanko
4. accomm. Warsaw Old Town, Hotel Regina
5. payment $500 US per day including travel days

I have brought us in under budget so far, so we can splurge on you. The film we are at work on appears on our company website if you want to see details. It is historical, and your scene is set in a small village called Radzanów.

If you are willing, I will forward dates and flights, which are booked and await your confirmation. I have informed the airline that your dulcimer must not be taken from you. They will likely inspect it in weird secure backrooms (I experienced this when another project required a costume from an Italian museum, which had been worn by a compatriot of Marie Antoinette!). I await your hopefully agreeable response.

Yours from Poland,
Charlie Wiespolska,

The offer seems unreal. Like the fake emails that arrive offering an escrow account of £45 million. *The Emir of Zuru informs you that you are his long-lost descendant, sole heir to his castles, his gold mines, and his priceless stock of Scottish malt liquor.*

But Simon's name gives the note an element of reliability. She replies, "Sure. I'll be your Dulcimer Girl."

Then she goes back to the job at hand. Nadia prints the pictures from the website attached to Magdalena's project. The objects in the photos are painted wonderful shades. A dark green cowboy hat; girlish shoes with a single strap and button painted orange; work boots in mustard yellow, their laces as carefully coloured as the shoes themselves; a deck of cards, redesigned like a psychedelic fan; a hardcover book sealed in glossy black paint.

She sets her bouncy walking shoes on the kitchen table. Her first thought is to reuse the box Jess sent the bottle in. But she cannot bring herself to take it in her hands and make something new out of it. The box, its contents, what is she going to do with them? One possibility is to simply repack everything as it came to her. Remove her name. Try her best not to leave any of her own fingerprints on it. Was that possible or a fantasy? Put it in the mail to the fortress of a police building on Main not far from the site of the original crime. So that's it. Off it will go, and her other package to Łódź, capital of outlandish design projects.

She must go downstairs to find Mr. Marini to see if he has a box he might let her have. She's heard him busying himself in his garden garage where he keeps his tools, glass jars, garden pots and gloves, cedar shakes and, of course, boxes.

When she finds him he is eager to talk. Mr. Marini. Her secret sharer. Her one and only fan. What is going well for her of late? He always wants to hear. Surely it was best to indulge him, the man who kept her rent low and fixed her stove when it went stone cold.

"You look like you could use an espresso," he tells her. But she insists, she's in a hurry. Does he have a box this big by this?

Up he goes on the little kitchen chair-cum-stepladder inside the garage. On a shelf just above head level, there is a museum of boxes.

He hands her one. She lifts its flaps to peer inside. It is pristine. They say so long, and she heads up to her apartment. She places her shoes in the box. The best way to identify them is to include her response to the questionnaire. As she returns to the computer to print what she wrote an answer from Charlie pops up on the screen. It includes flight times, booking number, a contact who will pick her up at Warsaw's Chopin Airport. The address of a hotel on Kościelna. A booking reference there.

Once the box is sealed with Magdalena's address on its top in thick black marker, she bends into her closet and chooses a pair of black army boots, the only thing, beyond the dulcimer, which she saved from her time with Rosemarie downtown. They are not so different from the pair she saw in Crazy Janie's West End shrine. She pulls the boots on and marches around the room. Wearing them, she is someone else entirely.

Warsaw Old Town

Nadia thinks of the ruins back home in Vancouver. She holds them in her mind's eye as her plane crosses the Atlantic: Hotel Balmoral, with its blind clock; the Hotel Empress, its windows frosted with tinfoil; the Regent Hotel—once among the street's more substantial buildings. A hundred years before, the Fishermen's Union ran its business office out of the Regent. The Hazelwood Hotel, woe to the sad Hazelwood, with its stained brick front and haphazardly repaired door. Wasn't it at—she tests her visual memory, based on walk-by after walk-by—342 East Hastings? Or was it 344?

Across the road, the Patricia, with its refurbished red-and-white neon hanging over the sidewalk, theatre-style. At night, if you left your curtains open, the neon would colour a darkened room cinematic blood-red. There she found Ace Bailey, who'd known nothing, less than nothing, about the murder on Cordova in the spring of '62, and who, rather ironically, considering his surprising personal library of "great works"—Dickens, Dostoyevsky, and Tolstoy—could not remember what he'd been up to the previous week. Things that happened decades before were somewhat clearer.

These were her ruins and she loved them in her way. Included among them was the weirdly razor-wired gate across the gaping space where her father's older brother had tendered loans to the wild and ruined men of Hastings and Cordova. This is where he received, for his efforts, a head-bashing, a fight on his knees for his life. She felt pleased and a little proud that she'd stood inside that ruin too. Even if it had been repurposed as Simon's shop, for carrot cake and open mic. Thinking about these things makes her need her music, so she slips on her headphones and reaches into her bag to start the song she's been playing over and over, to appreciate every drum tap, each slide of the guitarist's fingers on the strings, and the singer's whispery voice, telling how she's been waiting for Jimmy in the alley, waiting for him to come home.

Charlie Wiespolska has done her job flawlessly. Nadia gazes at an unfamiliar ruin, Warsaw's lovely Old Town, which was purposefully reconstructed in the 1950s. She knows nothing about European architecture, so she cannot appreciate which era each stuccoed villa is meant to imitate. Her guidebook makes it clear: everything here was turned to rubble by the Germans during the Warsaw Uprising.

This morning, beginning at dawn, she walked from a hill overlooking the Vistula back toward the *Rynek Nowego Miasta*, the square near her hotel, then on to the Barbican, what remains of the city's old fortress gate. In the distance, she glimpsed the spires of a gigantic church, then further along, a glittering sports stadium. Both of these were across the river in the Praga district. She'd used her guidebook to consider how long it might take to walk to these sights, but there wasn't time. So she headed back along Kościelna, to Freta, taking in each roof dormer, every variation in the cobblestone detail, the delicate glass-and-iron fixtures announcing street number and name. Few people were out. She could stare without fearing that she looked like a tourist.

In the *Rynek Nowego Miasta* she is alone. Umbrellas, shut tight over café tables, await the day's customers. Pigeons congregate on granite steps. She'd done well to get up early, to see what she could before the driver was due to take her to the film shoot north of the city. No one had said anything about what to wear, so she is in her usual outfit, jeans and a T-shirt, along with her extremist boots, her default footwear after mailing her joggers to Łódź. She is surprised by how comfortable they are, how they invite and promote walking. *Keep on going*, they seem to say. *We're not done yet.*

The one thing she needs is the dulcimer, which she left under the bed in her room. She felt foolish doing this, but she worried that someone might peek inside the case and mistake it for some kind of Stradivarius, a rare old instrument worth stealing.

Through the glass doorway of what looks like a Renaissance church, she watches a nun rearrange pamphlets on a tabletop. Their eyes meet and Nadia thinks, I must get back.

The Hotel Regina is fronted by a series of arcades, just off the sidewalk. White tablecloths flap in the breeze. She listens for a moment to a bird call—an owl? In an email, the driver had insisted he would find her inside the lobby. Nadia takes the stairs up to her room to collect her dulcimer. She returns and settles onto one of the gigantic white sofas that dominate the lobby. Opposite her sits a man with closely trimmed grey hair. Something about him makes her think he is a traveller on his way over to the royal castle to see the Rembrandts. With the instrument case between her knees, she awaits her pickup.

The man looks at the case and nods in greeting. He says, "Please."

Nadia shrugs. What does he mean?

"*Proszę.* Play your *cymbał.*" He crosses his arms.

Nadia opens the case, takes her instrument out and begins to play. The acoustics are fine. Her audience of one smiles and closes his eyes. She can hear him breathing softly, in a kind of meditative response to the music. Nadia plays one of the Polish-Jewish pieces she suggested to Charlie Wiespolska when she agreed to come. She practiced it so many times before she left home, she plays it with ease and thinks as she does about adding little Polish touches. The riffs and details she hopes will please the film people.

It will be a new experience to play for money. This has never been her modus operandi. She received her university scholarship to study music. She appeared on little rickety Vancouver stages for open mic nights because these were entirely anonymous surroundings. She thinks of what she's read about the Polish fiddle, the *suka*, which gains its timbre by the player stopping its strings with her fingernails. She cannot play like this on her dulcimer, but she aspires to such playing, an old-time *kapela* feeling. She hopes that this will be expressed in her song.

A dark-suited man comes through the lobby door. He wears sunglasses and one of those Bluetooth pieces in his ear. The driver. She lets the song run its course and puts her instrument back in its case. The grey-haired man opposite, her listener, gets up off the sofa. He holds his hands out and takes her hand in his.

"I have not heard anything like this in a long time," he says. "The real Polish music." His response confirms that she will give the filmmakers what they want.

The driver holds the lobby door for her and then opens the rear door of a long black car. She falls into the back seat with the dulcimer beside her. Once the driver has taken his seat, he looks over his shoulder and says, "Radzanów. One hour." They are off to the countryside.

Nadia cannot read the landscape. It is well-tended, punctuated by distant forest. The driver does not address her, as if she is a visiting dignitary and *must not be bothered*. This makes her smile. She is the only person in the world who can play Polish-Jewish music in a way that pleases the director of a wartime drama.

They approach the village on a road that curves through trees. They pass an old wooden church. Or is it another rebuilt replica? The village appears around a bend in the road and takes shape upon a central square. On one side, a large white church with its wedding-cake steeple. Decrepit wooden buildings. Newish two-storey stucco homes and much older brick houses. The sky above is the lightest blue. The driver turns his head as they roll to a stop and says, "Radzanów. Market square." Nadia gets out to stretch, and there, in a doorway, is Simon. Framed by the weathered wood, he looks, as she catches sight of him, more or less like he belongs. He is a picture in a frame. He has on a pair of pants patched at the knee and a white jersey. When he sees her, he leaps off the stoop and jogs along the sidewalk toward where they have parked. The driver reacts as if this might be some sort of attack—a village mugging!—but he relaxes once they've taken each other's hands, laughing at the strangeness of meeting here in the middle of who-knew-where. Nadia's driver reassumes his professional distance, talking quietly into his earpiece. But before much can be said the little film crew appears. A group of five young people moves in a tight huddle toward them. Out front is a woman. She reaches for Nadia's hand to pull her close.

"Hi. I'm Charlie? You're right on time. Witold is always reliable behind the wheel of the Skoda."

The rest of the group keeps its distance. One studies a clipboard. Another talks into a cell phone. It is Charlie's job to welcome her, to make sure the expensive visiting musician from Canada does her job well and is sent on to Warsaw.

Simon hesitates as the business of why Nadia is there takes over. He backs himself up and settles on his stoop, arms around his knees, to watch as the film crew takes her in hand.

"We have one scene to do with you," Charlie explains. "It takes place in a nearby meadow with no one in sight but you. The rest of what we need you for takes place in the studio tomorrow. Is that okay?"

Nadia nods. For what they are paying her this is entirely okay.

"Great." Charlie nudges her toward the others. "We have a short walk. It's easier than roaring up in a vehicle." They take a dirt road through what looks like a farmer's back property. The village falls away behind them as the flat land, the church spire, and a low brick building become the only things in view.

They cross fields and a meadow. Soft humps and gullies are marked by fence posts hewn from tree boughs. In the distance, a scattering of trees. Behind these, an escarpment that is a rough blue shoulder against the sky.

"So. Here." Charlie motions at a coat rack where a black jacket and a pair of pants hang.

"There's a belt too, if they're too big. Over here." Charlie leads her to what looks like an oversized outhouse but turns out to be a makeshift changing room. Nadia pulls the door shut behind her. It's hot and dry inside like a sauna. She takes off her boots and pants and puts on the black clothes. The belt is looped into the costume pants. It is long and narrow enough for her to tie in a knot, so she does. She sits on a tiny stool in the corner to tie up her boots. A pair of shoes sits along the wall for her to try, but this idea repels her. Her boots match the rest of what's been left out. Tramp stuff. On a hook on the back of the door hangs a dark felt fedora with a shiny copper-coloured band and a little blue feather. She tucks her hair inside its crown and pulls the hat low over her brow. Who, she wonders, is she dressed as now? Estragon from

Waiting for Godot? A Polish circus clown? She takes the dulcimer from its case and steps out into the midday sun.

"Okay?" Charlie points to a chair that sits on a rise in the meadow some twenty metres off. "You sit there. We'll film from the back, and with that"—she points at a raised platform—"from above as well. The chair is miked. In Warsaw, we'll have you play the same piece in case we need a fill."

"What is this field?" Nadia wonders aloud as the camera people jostle with their equipment.

Charlie glances at her a little shyly. "We needed something, you know, unpeopled. With a good view into the distance." She waves at the trees, the escarpment, the cloudless sky. They walk toward the chair. Nadia settles herself on it.

"We need you," Charlie says, "to sit still when you play."

Nadia puts her boots firmly on the grass and gets her instrument in place, mid-thigh, to feel the right looseness. She gives the strings a strum.

Charlie hovers nearby and then is gone.

Gazing into the distance Nadia wonders if she will ever again play music in so strange a setting.

"So?" Charlie is back. "Are you ready?"

Nadia nods. Her song is titled "*Rumanische Fantasien*." Of the recordings she sent as possibilities, it's the one that fit the filmmaker's idea of a Jewish-Polish song. Or a Polish-Jewish song, depending on who she corresponded with. Charlie had written to say the director thought Nadia played like "an old Polish bluesman." "BURN THIS AFTER READING," she wrote. "CAN YOU BELIEVE HE SAID THAT?"

Charlie lays a light hand on Nadia's shoulder and speaks quietly. "When I've backed away, count fifty. Then play. You won't be aware of us at all. The camera guy will be able to shift his depth of field, so we'll bring you in close. Okay?"

Nadia nods. Once Charlie is out of view she counts from fifty to ten, nine, eight, seven, six, five, slowing herself at four, three, two, one... and into the slow repetition of the song's first chords. A bird calls and she takes this as her cue to shift into the quicker pace at the centre of the song, a whirl of rhythm, four times as fast as the rest, which might have once given dancers at a wedding what they needed to propel the bride up on a rickety chair, like the one she sits on. Ecstatic music. Then back to the slow, stately march in order for the song to close in on itself and return to where it started. It's a song that could, effectively, go on forever, in and out of its fast and slow sections.

Nadia listens to the way the dulcimer sounds in the meadow. As she nears the song's final movement, a crazy thing happens. In the near distance, by a line of fence posts, a figure appears, bent over at first, then upright, carrying something under her arm. The figure comes closer and Nadia sees that it is a woman. Old and stout. She carries a basket under one arm. Her hair is white against the greens and browns of the countryside. The woman stops to listen. This is a distraction, but Nadia winds the song up without a hitch. She sits still, hands on the dulcimer's strings. The crew begins to grumble and call in Polish.

"That was great!" Charlie rushes by, heading toward the woman on the field. Nadia watches as they talk. Then the old woman walks off toward town. Charlie makes her way back. "That was beautiful. The crew loved it. That," she points at the old woman heading down the road, "we didn't expect. But we're going with it. A little local flavour. Okay?"

Nadia nods.

"Listen. Our driver has to leave at five. He's got another passenger for Warsaw. Is that alright? You'll be back early and you can grab a good dinner at the hotel. You'll be rested and ready for the studio tomorrow."

Nadia hesitates, since this will make it nearly impossible to see Simon, but he can come to Warsaw if he wants to see her.

She reenters the makeshift dressing room, hangs the jacket, pants, and hat on the hook on the back of the plywood door. By the time she is outside, dressed as herself again, the crew is almost packed up. With Charlie, she makes her way toward the village.

"Are you hungry?" Charlie rummages around in a white plastic bag. "Craft services left us these. Sandwiches. A salad. I have coffee."

The idea of the back seat of the chauffeured car on an empty stomach makes Nadia feel sick. They eye a stump, a couple feet wide, off the rutted road, and sit. Charlie sets out what she has on the stump and they gaze across the sandy ground at the church in the distance. Its wedding-cake tiers sparkle in the sunlight. Nadia is happy for the break. The coffee tastes almost fresh.

"This is a peaceful spot."

Charlie leans back, pulling a cigarette from a shirt pocket. "Sure. It is."

"How long have you been filming here?"

"Oh, we took over for a few weeks. The planning took longer. I'm a Radzanów expert. The only one in the world, it seems, under sixty-five."

"Where does my scene fit?"

"Well. You're the music. When we record tomorrow, you'll put down a lot of what we'll use on the soundtrack."

"No. I mean the scene you just shot. The old woman who wandered into it. What was she doing?"

"She said collecting."

"Collecting what?"

"Jewish herbs. *Żydowskie zioła*." Charlie hesitates. "Before the war that meadow was a graveyard." She sighs, for the first time less than forthcoming. "It's a long story. You know? I could get you a copy of the script."

Nadia feels uneasy at the thought of her name appearing in the film's credits, forever linked with a scene she cannot comprehend. The meadow, its backdrop, the apparition of the woman walking into the scene. It all seems unlikely to her now as they picnic by a farmer's cast-offs—a spare tractor grille and tires in a neat stack.

She looks toward the town.

Charlie brushes herself off.

As they point themselves toward the village Nadia wonders, but not out loud, about the distant mountains, the trees, and the meadow where a bird signaled where she was in her song.

Kot / Ketzele / Cat

Piłsudski Square is lively but not with film work. The last cube van is at an odd angle to the road. Simon leans against it with one hand, while beside him is the woman who walked toward Nadia as she played. She holds her apron with two hands, as if she is performing a square dance.

As Nadia comes closer, she sees that the woman is weeping over what she holds in the folds of her apron. She is begging. Polish words, but clearly begging the young blonde woman who stands beside her to do something.

"*Proszę. Proszę.*" The old woman pleads, gazing at Simon. She says the word again and again, but Nadia understands nothing beyond the misery in her voice.

Simon sees Nadia coming. He manages a wave and a look of dismay.

The blonde places a hand on the shoulder of the weeping woman. "*Mama,*" she says. "*Proszę.*" But the older woman will not be calmed.

As Nadia comes closer she sees what fills the apron: a cat. Tortoiseshell, with a touch of gold on the tip of its tail. The younger woman smiles at Nadia. "You're the dulcimer girl." She offers a hand to shake. "It's my mother's cat, from a very long time. We don't even know how old it is. Or was. The film truck backed up—she says she saw it from the window. Maybe they were rushing to get out of here now that they're done. She is begging Simon to bury it. She says it's a Jewish cat. It must be done the right away. No waiting. I think she won't let him be until he agrees."

Simon raises his palms skyward. What can he do? It's a job he can't shirk. The old woman takes this as a yes, the upturned hands and contrite shrug. She tells her daughter something and the younger woman nods, heading off. Simon follows her. Nadia and the woman holding the cat stay put by the killer van. The old woman has calmed down. They wait.

Simon reappears carrying a shovel with a shiny metal point over his shoulder.

Then the younger woman. A black bag on a strap over her shoulder. She is followed by a boy, maybe seven years old. He has one shoe untied. From her bag, the younger woman takes a box, at little bigger than a shoebox. The boy takes it from her and holds it before him. They form a line. The old woman leads. Simon is at the back. As the little parade marches off, Simon calls, "Nadia. Wait at my place. The door's not locked. It's the old one, without pain and a tin roof. I'll see you when this is done."

She watches the procession disappear behind the church, in the direction of her morning shoot. The four of them—tall and short, young and old—look serious in the sun. Simon rests the end of the wooden handle of his shovel in the palm of his hand, as if to impersonate an honour guard. When they have passed out of sight, far into the farmland in the distant flats, Nadia is alone in the square. The van has pulled away. How strange to be here like this. Who here even speaks her language, let alone knows why she is standing by the unlocked door of Simon's bedraggled house? She stands this way for some time. She is, on this afternoon, the town's central question: Who has arrived here from far away?

Nadia opens the door and steps inside. She sets her case down and sits on another rickety chair, pulled from under the table by the stove. Every now and again she checks her watch. But she feels at ease letting the time pass. It moves around her like a slow river, deep in its bed. The sun angles in through the front window. Soon the driver will appear to take her to Warsaw.

The Good Ground

They come across the meadow in the bright afternoon light, the Grabowska, Ania, Simon, and the boy. At the head of their parade is the cat in the old woman's upturned apron. She leads them to a corner of the field that is protected by a roll in the earth, a kind of furrow. If they chose to, they might all sit on its rise and look into the place chosen as the cat's burial ground.

Ania's mother separates herself from the others. She stands before them, lowering her apron to show the animal. Simon gets his first good look at it. He saw it the night he ate dinner at the old woman's house, but he had not paid any attention to it then. Its eyes are closed. The tip of its tongue shows ever so slightly between its teeth, and its coat shines in the light. It was a beautiful animal.

Ania's mother kneels in the fold of ground and the animal tumbles onto the grass. She removes a rock where she wants Simon to dig. The cat lies in the grass as if asleep. At first Simon thinks his job will take no time at all, but the ground is full of stones. Each time he moves to stop, Ania's mother signals that the hole must be deeper. When the shovel's point strikes a stone, sparks flash. He must carve dirt away from stones bigger than his fist to pry them out of the hole. A little cairn takes shape beside the hole, but Simon is not sure if this is a suitable marker. While he works the others stand nearby or turn in circles, pacing. The boy crouches by a fence post, his box between his feet.

Ania's mother comes close and taps Simon on the shoulder. She nods. He has done his job well. She waves the boy over. He places the box beside the grave. Ania's mother moves to pick up the cat, but she backs away. So Ania does it, bends down low and scoops the animal up so it lies across her hands, head and tail hanging. She hands it to Simon who lowers it into the hole. Out of her black bag, Ania draws a candle in a glass container, a box of matches, and a book. The candle is placed in the cairn of rocks and Ania's mother lights it. The flame gutters in the breeze. To Simon's surprise the book is handed to him. The old woman whispers, "Please." Then she backs up, head lowered.

It is a Hebrew prayer book. Where has it come from? He tells them that he cannot read it.

The old woman is crestfallen. He'd come all this way, seeking his father's past, and is unable to speak any language associated with it? She contemplates this new disaster and gazes into Simon's eyes as she speaks.

Ania translates. "It is a Jewish cat."

She brings the boy over to open his box. He does this with care, lifting from it the old studio photograph of the skiff, the bridge, the children. Ania's mother holds the photo and points to where Simon should look. Her finger moves on the picture's shiny surface.

In the skiff, his father. On the bridge, herself. Her fingernail directs him to the skiff's gunnel where he knows, because he saw it in Brooklyn, a cat's face peers out.

"This one"—Ania motions at the dead animal—"comes from the one in the picture. How many times removed she forgets. This one," she points again to the photo, "was *Ketzel*. So my mother called hers *Ketzele*. She hoped, since you are here, that hers could be buried in the right way."

Simon has no idea what to say. He gets down close to the hole, his knees pressed together, hands curled under his chin, eyes closed. The others do the same, except the boy. He returns the photo to the box, and with one foot haphazardly hanging into the hole, lowers the box in. Simon sees him lay a hand on the box and then a soft touch on the cat's furry side before bringing himself up level with the rest of them.

Ania's mother points to the dirt dug from the hole and shows with both hands that he must put it back. Which he does, tenderly at first and then with more haste. Ania leads the boy off, back toward the village. When the grave is finally full, Simon is filthy, his shoes full of dirt. It's in his hair and in the corners of his eyes. They stand for a moment. They've been out in the meadow for quite some time. He wants to catch Nadia back in town, but the Grabowska stands with such a solemn look of regret that he cannot make a move.

An Unreadable Map

Ania and the Dembrowski boy come across the meadow. They reach the fringes of Radzanów, with its old wooden houses, its two-storey red-brick buildings. At the church, bouquets of carnations are being unloaded from the back of a van. The priest, in black robes, his white hair like cake icing, oversees the job.

The boy turns to run but Ania takes him by the shoulder. "We agreed. If we buried the cat. Please. Let me have the map."

At first, the boy makes no move.

"It belongs to the visitor. I've thought about this. Would you like to take it over to him? He will appreciate it. You can put it through the mail slot."

Something about this catches the boy's interest. An overture to the visitor from far away is an adventure. He makes his way up to Simon's house, stands out front, and knocks. But it is Nadia who answers. Ania watches them talk, the way that two people do who don't share a language. He holds out the map and looks back at Ania as he hands it over.

He had been anxious to bury his box. The Archive of the Jews, as his parents dubbed it. They told him he must put it back. So he came to her, saying, "*Pani* Ania, Father says we must put the Jewish box back in the ground. It is bad luck to have kept it."

When the handoff is finished the boy turns and runs off as fast as he can, his big adventure in gravedigging complete.

Before Nadia can turn back inside the black Skoda rolls up. The car idles by Simon's window. Nadia sets the boy's rolled paper on the kitchen table. She steps outside and with her instrument over her shoulder pulls the front door of the house shut. The driver holds the car door open and she folds herself into the leather back seat. From the other side comes, Ania, who offers her hand. Before they can manage a word to each other the driver, in his businesslike tone, says, "Warsaw. Exactly one hour."

As they roll out of the village toward the highway, the driver turns up the music he is listening to, just enough for them to hear it in the back seat. It is Van Morrison, a love letter to poets of the English countryside. "Ah," the song pronounces, "my treasury in the sunset." Nadia and Ania listen together, leaving the mystery of Simon and the village behind as the song insists: "It ain't why. It ain't why. *It ain't why, why, why*. It just is."

Nadia is happy to sit in silence and watch the countryside pass. She thinks of the burial procession. Herself in the meadow with a hat on her head, the dulcimer flat out before her. The bird that called to her to *pick it up. Pick it up, girl*. She edges up on her hip to gaze out the back window. Once, when she was a child, she did this as her family departed a magical seaside hotel on the California coast. How old had she been? Ten? It was the year, she thought, that her father left them in his mind, and in his heart, to become obsessed with work, with walking across the city, with whatever it was that drove him off. She remembered how the hotel and its seaside setting stayed in view as they drove away.

But Ania prefers to talk.

"How did your scene go?"

Nadia does not know what to say. She manages a nod and then looks back out at the passing countryside.

"How do you and Simon know each other?"

This, too, is a bit of a puzzle. Not easy to say, really. She is awfully tired. The car is making her feel sick. Couldn't they ride in stately silence?

"Has he told you?"

Nadia has no idea what this is about. It may be that Ania mistakes her sleepy-headed response for a nod.

"I am a bit surprised myself. It's only because of Simon's arrival in Radzanów that I came to fully understand my mother's attachment to the house. I told her, she must tell him. If it were your place, and you'd come all this way, wouldn't you want to understand? But she insisted that I swear. Not to tell him." Ania looks at Nadia. "If I tell you, then I've not broken my word to her."

It is Alice-in-Wonderland stuff, what Ania has to tell. Something about a Night Jew. And *Reichsdeutsche*. Forest partisans. Postage stamps. Nadia listens but she feels as she does in class, when the meandering nature of what the professor is saying renders it incomprehensible, like a dream. Maybe it is the music playing in the car's plush interior, the landscape rushing by, the lightness of the lunch she was offered by Charlie on the farmer's back property, the early evening light over the plain, the farmhouses, leading to the outskirts of Warsaw. Poplars. Gas stations. Villas here and there that stand as mementoes of the pre-war countryside. The long straight roadway approaching the airport, surrounded by its little city of dachas, *grobkes*, leftover Soviet-era country huts and cottages where families come to pick fruit, cook over an open fire, sit contemplatively with pipe and plum brandy while they watch the sun set over Mazowia.

The Typewriter Girl

Ania settles into the chair behind her immaculate desk. On it: the old-fashioned telephone she will not let the IT people exchange, and a lamp, which she switches on. The first fall rains have begun. They rattle and rake the big office window. Two pigeons try to stay dry on the outside ledge, shifting their grey behinds along it.

Then the noise starts. It begins with one calamitous crash, then a moment of calm, then a return to a crashing, tumbling racket.

Ania places both hands on the desktop and gets up to see what is going on. The pigeons have gone. The sky beyond the glass is a pile of wildly moving grey thunderheads. The noise, she thinks, is coming from the back of the building where the old tenement courtyard has been transformed into something modeled on a chic Parisian inner court, with cobblestones and stunted trees in wrought-iron boxes. She takes the service elevator to the back shipping area where the clerks sit on wooden crates, eating their sandwiches. They are oblivious to the racket pouring with the rain into a pair of green dumpsters set up against the building's back wall. Two yellow chutes hang from windows at the eighth floor, where much of her own research staff works.

Typewriters. She is sure that's what is making the noise. She knows well the windows to which the chutes are attached. For more than two years she used the view from them to consider the changes in the cityscape, the office towers and hotels. Now she thinks she might be able to distinguish the sound of each individual machine as it plummets and hits the dumpster at the bottom. The bigger cast iron ones, and the newer desk machines from the fifties and sixties, then the lightweight portables. Each one tumbles down a chute and collides with its compatriots in the past work of the country's outmoded *nomenklatura*.

It's strange that she has not been told that this was planned. This may signal a change of her status in the ministry; the obsolescence of her expertise, which was so crucial when her boss convinced her to take on the job of examining government files for their accuracy and completeness as a record of the country's Communist dark age.

The rain is cold on her neck. She is Ania Grabowska once more, the strange, yearningly sophisticated girl, walking to the bus stop with her Salinger, her Hemingway, her mother's contraband American treasures slipped inside her mathematics textbook. She would simply stop being the Typewriter Girl. It was that easy.

Final Movement

First the countryside. Down Puławska toward the airport.

Then Nadia flies over Germany, the Atlantic, and all of Canada to her city on the Pacific Rim. She takes the train from the airport. With her little bag and her instrument, it is a breeze getting back to town. The train car is full of Richmond kids—contemporary versions of herself at fifteen—heading downtown. They chatter and stare at their phones. She enjoys watching them so much—the awkward boys and gangly girls—that she does not get off at the Broadway station when she should, to get the bus that heads to her place. Instead she gets off with the crowd at Granville Street and comes up onto the pedestrian avenue. She takes Georgia for a few blocks but the traffic begins to drive her crazy. Is this what the city sounds like now? Over on Robson, things are calmer: tourists and kids shopping and strolling, which takes her back to the good old days when she was a punk on Broughton Street, with Rosemarie hung over in the morning and the West End hookers hobbling up the back alley on their heels at dawn, tired, with cash in their bags.

Oh. How it broke her down, what she sees before her, how it took her out of what she had been doing in Poland, threw her back against the pavement of her real life. She was no dulcimer girl. She was Nadia Baltzan, and she stood alone in Nelson Park at almost-dusk, in view of the huge wilted sunflower, the crowning growth of the neighbourhood garden. She gazed up at Simon's window, or at least the one she takes for his. Its glass is dark. She sits on the bench in the centre of the park, which is surrounded by a cloud of lavender and broom. The scent of it somehow takes her back inside Simon's broken little house on the village square. Her patient hour on his wooden kitchen chair. The black Skoda driven by a man of few words. Warsaw. One hour.

And Ania, telling her what Simon needed to know. A history lesson. A child's nightmare. But it was, she understood, Simon's story. He lived now inside it, slept in its bed, lit fires under it and ate it with his soup and dark bread at dinnertime.

It went like this.

When the war ended in the neighbourhood of Radzanów, Russian contingents arrived in columns of vehicles and tanks, dirty, smiling recruits atop them, to which the local people ran with vodka, cigarettes, clean underwear. They came running, shouting, their underwear offerings streaming like flags. Later, the Jews would be accused of celebrating the liberators' Bolshevik ideology, but everyone, everyone except for the partisans who remained in their hideouts in the woods, came running. Women, children, and old men.

Jews appeared from their hiding places. Hutches. Holes. Attics. It was at dusk when the one surviving member of Simon Hanover's family came up the Mławer Road, a Soviet blanket over his shoulders, tears in his eyes. He was a cousin of Simon's father. Roughly the same age. Aronek. The two were said to have resembled each other—the high forehead and the puckered, full Russian lips. Aronek had fled east and survived, following the Soviet armies back to Poland, always a mile or two behind the fighting and chaos, but picking up things necessary for survival along the way: the blanket, a dropped potato, scraps of bread the army left by the side of the road once the local villagers had met them with something better.

For most who returned in this way, things were impossible. In cities, Jewish neighbourhoods were destroyed. Rubble. People walked down roadways with nothing on either side of them. In Radzanów, everything, down to the market cobbles, survived. But everything was tainted by the war, by Germans laws and minds, their genius for pornography, plunder, spectacles of public murder.

In Radzanów, the Jewish houses had been occupied first by the *Reichsdeutsche*. But then by peasants who'd found it impossible to survive on the land during the war, or who simply understood that after an *aktion*, and then again after the German retreat, houses stood empty. Shops and workshops once stolen were again up for grabs.

But not the Hanover house. This was not Aronek's last name, because he was a cousin on Simon's father's mother's side. This made it impossible for him to reclaim the house. The Polish Communist authorities set up restitution laws, but not altruistic ones. Only immediate heirs—children, parents, grandparents, siblings, spouses—could reclaim property. But Ania's mother had done her job well. Her girlhood responsibilities during wartime had made a hardened woman of her. Thanks to the headman and the German marks she'd fed him from the stash she'd found hidden in the house, no one had moved into the house on the square.

So, Aronek comes up the Mławer Road at dusk. He stands in the square as the first stars appear in the sky. He sees that around the market all the houses, shops, workshops—those of his family's compatriots, as well as his father's glazier's shop—have been taken. Lamps burn in windows. Laundry dries on lines in backyards. Horses shake their tails to chase away flies.

But his cousin's house opposite the old red-brick synagogue appears to be uninhabited. As he approaches he sees a girl. Familiar. The Grabowska. She is running to him. Her hair is loose. She throws herself at him. He is so light, just bones in a sack of skin, and she nearly knocks him off his feet. She calls his name. *Aronek. Aronek!* She is loud enough that others appear. They are together an object of shock and fascination. Aronek hears someone say, "Christ. Mary. Another Night Jew."

And so he knows himself. He is a Night Jew.

Ewa takes him by the hand. She opens the house to him. She sits him by the stove and makes a fire. She takes from a cupboard the things she has on hand to prepare a meal. But she needs to go back to her own house, and this she does, to get onions, barley, whatever else she has for the soup she prepares on the iron stovetop.

Violence surrounds them. War is over. But the land is upside-down. The Soviet Army and Polish partisans rape and steal. They throw people off trains. News comes of violent outbreaks in Lublin, Przemyśl, Rzeszów. These are far away, but even in nearby Mława, where the Jews are gathering at the Hotel Polski, the partisans shoot out the windows at night. A sympathetic Russian soldier—Ginsburg, Yiddish-speaking from Leningrad—seeks out the bandits and imprisons them.

"But tell me," Aronek asks one night, as Ewa mixes the ingredients for a honey cake, prepares a chicken for him, "what will happen when Ginsburg goes back to his girlfriend in Leningrad?"

Word gets out that the restitution law will not cover distant relatives. Aronek makes contact through a refugee organization with a friend in a DP camp in Germany. The idea of going there appalls him. Stay, Ewa begs him. I am keeping you safe here. I kept the house for you.

But Aronek loses heart. He is alone. Ewa's love and work are one thing. But they don't provide a life for him on the devastated Polish plain. One day, he leaves. Ewa finds the house empty. She never learns where he went.

He arrived like other Jewish ghosts, and then, in the same way, he was gone.

★

Nadia sits on her bench in the warm night air. The story is her gift for Simon. But he is caught somewhere between this park at Comox and Bute and his house on the village square. She will try to hold on to it for him.

She rises to walk all the way home, feeling the distance of it under her sturdy black boots.

When it is almost dark on Piłsudski Square, Simon returns. He has been out on the country roads, taking backwoods routes, all the way down to the marshy bank of the Wkra, watching the pines waver in the low light. He walks up to the door of his house. At the window he is not surprised to find Nadia gone. He feels a twinge in his chest.

Everything inside is as he left it, except for a rolled piece of paper on the wooden table. He places a hand on each of its curled edges and recognizes the map that marks his tour of the local riverways. The Yiddish commentary alongside it requires translation. Maybe this could provide an overture to his father. He could be invited to lead an afternoon's exploration of the countryside. What might come of that?

Simon busies himself in the kitchen. He puts a meal out for himself. Bread and dried fish and a fizzy drink called *3 cytryny*. By the time it is all gone, he sees, out his front window, the dark skies, the characteristic ribbons of orange and violet in the west.

When the first stars appear, he steps out onto the square. Everything, every sign of the past days' events, is gone. He feels alone on the face of the earth. Lights turn on in the old houses, the newer villas, in upper bedrooms and front parlours. Simon recognizes for the first time who he is—who the people inside, looking out, will see. A returnee, haunting the place, certain to disappear and return once more.